> ## "When it happens, you'll know."

It's a feeling, warm as mulled cider on a winter's night, or like the sudden shock of a cork bursting from a bottle of champagne.

It's instant recognition, the fabled "love at first sight," or the quiet, still moment of clarity that alters the course of a friendship.

It happens in broad daylight, on a crowded city street, or at midnight, in the intimate darkness of a car humming along a country lane.

He's the man you like to argue with, the man you bring your troubles to, the man who shares your sense of humor, the man who dreams your dreams, the man who understands you better than you understand yourself.

And in a moment isolated from time, clearer than thought, deeper than instinct, something tells you . . . he's the one.

When it happens, you'll know.

ABOUT THE AUTHOR

Spring is here and all thoughts turn to love . . . and marriage. So it is for Anne McAllister, who in *I Thee Wed* introduces us to a lovestruck Diane Bauer and Nick Granatelli. Be sure to read the follow-up to Nick and Diane's rocky courtship. This month, look for *With This Ring,* the story of four couples who attend the Bauer-Granatelli wedding and find their own thoughts straying to matrimony. Anne McAllister is one of the four talented authors of this collection of short stories. There, she reprises Diane's best friend Annie D'Angelo, who, as a bridesmaid, finds herself paired with none other than the man from her past—steamy Irishman Jared Flynn. Anne McAllister invites you to join her once again, in *With This Ring,* available wherever Harlequin books are sold.

Books by Anne McAllister
HARLEQUIN AMERICAN ROMANCE

Don't miss any of our special offers. Write to us at the following address for information on our newest releases.

Harlequin Reader Service
P.O. Box 1397, Buffalo, NY 14240
Canadian address: P.O. Box 603,
Fort Erie, Ont. L2A 5X3

ANNE McALLISTER

I THEE WED

Harlequin Books

TORONTO • NEW YORK • LONDON
AMSTERDAM • PARIS • SYDNEY • HAMBURG
STOCKHOLM • ATHENS • TOKYO • MILAN

To Ethel, Philip and Diane,
for sharing St. Louis with me

Published April 1991

ISBN 0-373-16387-8

I THEE WED

Chapter One

"No, Ma. *No.* Ma, I just can't...I have things to do, that's why."

Diane watched, amused, as her roommate rolled her eyes and strangled the phone receiver with her hands.

"Besides, the North End's miles from here," Annie went on. "Miles."

The Arctic Circle at least, Diane thought, silently applauding her roommate's theatrical ability. Annie had theatrical ability in spades, but she was never in better form than when she was arguing with her mother. Diane watched as expressions of first agony and then weariness crossed Annie's face.

She gave up for the moment on the obscurities of Hegel, lay the book beside her on the bed, stretched her full five feet six inches, wiggled her toes and grinned. Her own life was so deadly predictable, so completely boring. It was one of the reasons she enjoyed living with Annie. There was so much opportunity for vicarious angst.

"Yes, I know you called on daytime rates, but I don't want to meet him. No! Ma...Ma... Really..."

Poor Annie. Diane stuffed the pillow back under her head and propped Hegel up again on her stomach. But her mind drifted from the conflict between theses and antitheses to Lucia D'Angelo's conflict with her daughter.

Diane knew she should be ashamed of her unabashed eavesdropping. It wasn't the thing, her very proper grandmother would have told her in no uncertain terms. And even her less assertive mother would have doubtless made an effort to pretend that Hegel fascinated her.

But she could hardly help it, really. A 15-foot x 30-foot studio apartment didn't offer much opportunity for privacy.

Lucia and Annie's running battle over the men that Lucia wanted her daughter to meet and marry and that Annie had no intention of meeting, much less marrying, had been a constant in Diane's life since she had met Annie as a freshman at Harvard four years before.

"Besides how gorgeous he is," she heard Annie say. "Besides how smart he is. Besides whose nephew he is. I don't care whose nephew he is! Remember Guido Farantino? Remember him? He was your cousin Maria's nephew and he was a dork!"

Another furious volley from Lucia.

"Ma, I don't care if he goes to Harvard Business School. Just because a guy goes to Harvard Business School does not mean he is not a dork! On the contrary..."

Diane grinned and picked up her book.

"What do you mean I have to?" Ominous silence.

A storm gathering, Diane could tell.

"What did she promise him?" There was a deadly note in Annie's tone now.

Diane's brows lifted. She raised her head and peered over the top of Hegel to watch.

Annie was standing ramrod straight now, glaring out the window across their two-inch-wide view of the Charles as if it were Lucia D'Angelo and not a fleet of sailboats she had in her sights. "Mother..."

Diane waited, watching. When Ma became Mother it was only a matter of time. There was another long silence. Then Annie expelled a long, pent-up breath. Her shoulders slumped. She bent her head.

"What time?" A pause. "All right."

And before Lucia could say another word, Annie dropped the receiver back onto the phone with a thud.

"Let me guess." Diane said into the silence. "His name is Luigi Capoletti. His family are wine growers from Piedmont, and he's been sent to Harvard Business School to learn how to best earn the family more and more millions."

"His name," Annie said, turning around and fixing Diane with a hopeless look, "is Dominic Granatelli. His family is in the restaurant business in St. Louis. And he's at Harvard Business School because he is fulfilling the American dream." She tore at her long, dark hair with both hands. "God, where on earth does she find them?"

"I thought he was somebody's nephew."

"He is. Her godmother's best friend's sister's...or some damned thing. How should I know?" Annie made a face and sank down onto her bed.

"And is he gorgeous?"

Annie gave her a baleful look. "Are any of them gorgeous?"

Point taken.

"Why do I let her talk me into these things? I need to go rehearse tonight. I have a paper due in Greeley's class tomorrow. If Wallace calls, I'm supposed to go in to work." She slapped her hands down on the bed in exasperation.

Diane gave her a sympathetic smile. "Who knows?" she said lightly. "Someday she might actually find the right man for you."

Annie glowered at her. "I thought you knew better than that. There is no right man for me. I don't have time for a man, right or otherwise. I have ambitions of my own, and a man would only get in the way."

Annie was going to be the next Sarah Bernhardt or Dame Edith Evans. She was consumed with a passion and a fire for her actor's vocation that at times made Diane's head swim. It always left her out of breath. She couldn't have matched it if she lived to be a hundred.

She never wanted to. She was content for life to come to her. She wasn't going to go out and wrestle life. "So are you going to go or not?"

Annie grimaced. "What do you think? But only briefly. *Very* briefly. And only because Ma promised her godmother I'd be there and *she* already told Granatelli. He's 'expecting' me. And if I don't go now, he'll probably end up here, worried that I'm lost or have been abducted or something. And if he comes here, God knows how I'll get rid of him."

"He might be nice," Diane felt obliged to point out.

Annie shrugged. "They're all nice, but that doesn't mean I want to marry them. You want to marry them? You come with me." She brightened at once. "Yeah! You come with me. It's not an exclusive party, just Patty Lombardi's engagement."

Diane shook her head quickly. "I can't. I have Hegel."

"You have a week to finish Hegel."

"I also have my Paul Valéry paper to work on. Plus a test tomorrow in Italian."

Annie laughed and grabbed her hand. "Gotcha. You can practice your Italian on him."

"I don't want—"

"Of course you do. You're always blathering on about people needing to expose themselves to other cultures. 'We must open our minds and hearts to those different than ourselves,'" she quoted one of Diane's international relations papers with a pomposity belied only by the twinkle in her eye. "Isn't that the garbage you're always spouting?"

"It's not garbage," Diane denied.

Annie spread her hands. "Well, what could be more different for a blue blood like you than an Italian engagement party in the North End?"

"It's not—"

"It is. So if you believe all your blather, come with me. Open your mind and heart to an Italian from St. Louis. Cripes, you're from St. Louis, too. It probably won't be different at all. You probably have more in common with him than I do."

"Annie, I—"

Annie pulled Diane to her feet. "Please. Come. Come on, Di." She was imploring now, putting every bit of the vast D'Angelo theatrical potential to work. "Please. For moral support. You know I don't want to do this. You know I hate it."

Diane looked at Annie pouting, pleading. She looked at Hegel, gray and dog-eared. There was no contest.

"All right," she said. "But only for an hour or so, mind you."

Annie threw her arms around her. "I knew you'd be a sport."

"But," Diane added with a sternness born of experience, "I'm not going to meet him instead of you. You're not going to try any of those tricks this time. You promised to meet him. You're going to meet him."

"Of course," Annie said equably.

But Diane had heard that tone of voice before. She didn't trust it. Not a bit.

"WOULD YOU BE TELLING ME again why I'm doing this?" Jared Flynn's soft Irish accent broke into the Feinemann Plastics case study that Nick was analyzing in his head as they walked.

"You're my friend," Nick said frankly, "and I bullied you into it."

Jared gave him a slow grin. "That I know. But why? An engagement party doesn't sound so very threatening, un-less—" the grin broadened "—you're the one getting en-gaged."

"No fear." Nick shook his head adamantly. "I need a little protection, that's all. I promised Aunt Lucy I'd do this. Her cousin set it up." He grimaced. "And appar-ently she owes her cousin. So I have to meet the girl."

"And I?"

"Have to sweep her off her feet."

Jared rolled his eyes. "There's optimism. She won't be looking twice at me with a handsome devil like yourself standing alongside."

Nick laughed. "You haven't noticed the girls dropping like ten pins when they see you behind the counter at Fiorello's?"

He was scarcely exaggerating. The girls who came in to eat at the funky Mass Ave restaurant used to stare at him as he dashed in and out of the kitchen bearing plates of spaghetti and linguine. But since out-of-work actor Jared Flynn had come to work there, Nick scarcely got a glance. His thick, blond-streaked brown hair and reasonably good looks had paled in comparison to Jared's tousled dark hair and craggy handsomeness.

He was hoping that, whoever Anna D'Angelo was, she would prove equally susceptible. He wanted nothing to do with her himself.

It wasn't that he wasn't interested in women.

At other times, in other places, he was very interested indeed.

But he was far too busy to be bothered this year. The first year at Harvard Business School didn't leave a man time to breathe much less to look at women. He couldn't remember the last time he'd had a date.

Yes. Yes, he could. It was at Christmas, when he'd gone home to St. Louis and his sister Sophia had invited him to a party at her house and had told him to bring Virginia Perpetti.

Ginny Perpetti was maybe twenty-three. A year or so older than his sister Frankie. She was pretty, soft and smiling. As dark as he was fair. Sicilian where he was Lombard. A couple of generations back that would have mattered. Now the fact that she was Italian was enough.

He suspected Sophia's motives, but he didn't demur. He'd called for Ginny, took her to the party, and afterward, on the way home, they'd walked around the neighborhood.

Ginny had pointed out the classroom at St. Ambrose's where she taught second grade. Then she had shown Nick the new house her brother Eddie and his wife had bought right behind it.

It had started to snow by then and the flakes caught on her lashes. They sparkled, tempting him, and before he knew it, he had bent his head to kiss them away.

Ginny had laughed, embarrassed, and batted at him, ducking her head shyly when he'd tried again.

Ginny.

"That Ginny Perpetti, she'll make a good wife," his mother had said the next morning.

It was no secret where his family's thoughts lay.

Right now she seemed light years away.

She might as well be. Sophia had mentioned in the letter he'd got yesterday that Ginny was busy cutting out cherry trees for Washington's birthday.

Cutting out cherry trees with a bunch of second graders at St. Ambrose's was a million mental miles from Harvard Business School. Maybe more.

But, he thought—and sighed as he thought it—her counterpart, Anna D'Angelo, was right here.

Another shy Italian girl on the lookout for a husband. The daughter of somebody who was related to somebody who was related to him.

He understood how it worked.

He didn't think it was necessarily the best way to meet someone—and certainly not tonight.

But someday—who knew?

In a couple of years he'd be in the market himself. And if Ginny Perpetti weren't available, he might need to know someone who knew someone who had a daughter.

In the meantime, he would, as always, play his part.

Never let it be said that Nick Granatelli didn't pay his dues.

So, in half an hour or less, he was going to have to smile at her, make small talk with her and, hopefully, throw Jared at her and make his escape.

He glanced at his watch. It was seven. He still had another fifty pages of the Feinemann Plastics case to read and take notes on. His study group would be meeting by eight. He was going to be late; that was a given. But he didn't want to be very late.

"Come on," he said to Jared, beginning to sprint. "Let's get this over with."

IT WAS, in fact, a cultural experience. Diane Bauer had, in the course of her twenty-two years, participated in her share of sweet-sixteen parties and debutante balls back home in St. Louis. During her junior year at Harvard, which she'd spent abroad, she'd partied at university get-togethers at bierstuben in Munich and heurigen in Vienna. And wherever she'd been, as long as she could remember, she'd danced and dined her way through plenty of black-tie affairs.

But she'd never seen a celebration that equaled the engagement party of Patty Lombardi and Greg Delvecchio.

For one thing, it was a crush. She'd read about such things in regency novels. She had no idea they still existed in Boston's North End.

But there was no other word to describe the pulsing throng of humanity that had crowded into the small private club.

The smoke, the laughter, the jovial press of people surging this way and that as they congratulated the happy couple and moved on in to talk to each other and get something to eat overpowered her.

She stuck close to Annie, trailing in her wake.

Annie, for her part, was muttering under her breath, craning her neck, peering first one way and then the other, obviously trying to ferret out Dominic Granatelli.

"How are you going to know which one he is?"

"I told my mother to tell him to stick a carnation in his ear."

"You didn't."

Annie rolled her eyes. "No, I didn't. He's supposed to be wearing a blue T-shirt that says something Italian on it.

Campanella's or some such. The name of a restaurant. That ought to narrow things down.''

Diane, who'd been scanning the crowd for the short dark type of guy Annie's mother seemed generally to come up with, found her eye caught suddenly by a tall, muscular man in a blue shirt with *Fiorello's* scrawled across it. She stared. ''Him?''

Annie followed her nod and did a double take.

Diane understood why immediately. If ever any man was destined to make a woman forget her resolve to remain celibate in pursuit of a higher ideal—be it acting or the Church—this man was it.

He was, perhaps, a shade over six feet, with sun-streaked brown hair and lively blue eyes. His shoulders were broad, his arms muscular.

For the first time in her life Diane began to think there might be some redeeming social value to be found in wet T-shirt contests, providing this man was wearing one.

He wore a pair of faded jeans and ratty-looking tennis shoes and, on the whole, looked about as unlikely a member of Harvard Business School's class of '88 as she could imagine. There was undoubtedly some mistake.

But Annie apparently didn't think so. She threaded her way through the throng and strode right up to him and stuck out her hand.

Diane followed, pushing past several already tipsy revelers, in time to see the man nod and to hear him say, ''Nick. Everybody calls me Nick.''

Heavens above! *This was actually the man Annie didn't want to meet?*

Diane took a close look at her now, trying to see how being confronted with such a hunk of masculinity was affecting her resolve.

But Annie was saying quite bluntly, "Sorry you got roped into this. It wasn't my idea."

Nick laughed. Diane felt her heart kick over at the sight of his grin. She wondered why her mother never thought to send her men like this. Cynthia Bauer had a disgustingly hands-off policy where her daughter's love life was concerned.

What love life? a tiny voice inside her chided.

And that was true, of course. But Diane refused to do more than acknowledge it at the moment. She was far too interested in Annie's new man.

He had turned and was hauling another man forward now. A man not quite as tall as he was, but with dark, tousled hair and reasonably good looks.

"I'd like you to meet my friend. This is Jared Flynn. Annie D'Angelo."

Annie spared the friend a brief glance, said, "How do you do?" then reached behind her with the ease of long practice and latched on to Diane, tugging her forward. "And this is my friend Diane Bauer."

All sound, all movement stopped.

It was, Diane thought later, as if the heavens had opened and a voice had said, "Well, kiddo, here he is."

It was, Diane thought later, the moment she'd been waiting for since the age of four when she'd decided to be like Mommy and have a husband, too.

At the time she didn't know where she'd get him. Like everything else in her life, he would, she'd always expected, simply show up when the time came.

But she hadn't expected the time to come now!

She was amazed, startled, distracted.

And what a man, too, she thought.

Annie's.

Annie's man. The man Lucia D'Angelo had sent to meet her daughter. *Remember that,* Diane told herself and abruptly tore her eyes away from the dark blue ones fixed on her own.

She took a deep breath. "I'm pleased to meet you," she said with all the facility of years of polite upbringing. "And you," she added almost as an afterthought to his friend.

"Likewise," Jared said.

His gaze, unlike Nick Granatelli's, flickered from Annie to her, then back to Annie. Nick's never wavered. He never spoke, either. Just looked. At her.

For the first time in her social life, Diane felt flustered.

"Can't stay long," Annie bellowed at Nick over the pounding of the music. "I'm rehearsing."

He blinked, then focused for a second on Annie, before his eyes turned once again to Diane. "You're searching?" he said to Annie, not looking at her.

"Re-hears-ing," Annie said, breaking it into syllables. But she spoke with more forbearance than Diane imagined possible. "I'm an actress."

"Right," Nick mumbled. He licked his lips, swallowed, then seemed almost physically to pull himself together.

"Does he speak English?" Annie asked Jared.

Jared shot his friend a sidelong glance, then grinned. "After a fashion."

Annie looked doubtful. "I wondered," she said darkly.

"Sorry," Nick said. There was a hint of red beneath his tan. He raked his fingers through his hair. "I—I have a study group tonight. And I haven't finished my case study. I—" The music suddenly evolved into something recognizable as a slow dance tune. He held out his hand to Annie. "Want to dance?"

"I suppose," she said with bad grace.

Diane looked to see how Nick was taking this stunning lack of enthusiasm.

The smile she got in return was in danger of melting her right where she stood.

She stood, bereft, and watched Nick take Annie into his arms and dance away.

"Shall we?" Jared Flynn asked her, and she turned back to see him hold out a hand to her.

Diane pasted on her best smile. "Thank you. I'd like that."

She did her very best to listen when Jared talked, to make sane and sensible responses to his questions, to be the perfect partner she'd been taught to be.

Annie told her later that Jared was an actor, that he was Irish, that he was waiting tables at Fiorello's and working on a construction crew while he auditioned for acting parts.

For all Diane knew he could have been a Syrian taxi driver from the Bronx.

She smiled and nodded and made all the small talk she could think of. Her eyes and her mind were following Nick Granatelli around the room.

"How will I know him?" she'd asked her mother when she was five.

And Cynthia had got a faraway look in her eyes for just a moment. Then she'd pulled herself together and patted her daughter's hand. "Don't worry, lovely. It will happen. And when it does, you'll know."

"Did you know?"

For a long time Cynthia hadn't answered. She'd sat staring into the mirror at her dressing table. But then her gaze caught that of her daughter's reflected behind it, and she'd smiled. "Yes, darling. I knew."

Later, when it became clearer to Diane that her mother had been married twice, that Matthew whom she'd always known and loved as her father, actually wasn't, that there had been another man who'd once, briefly, been Cynthia's husband, she'd wondered. Which of the two had Cynthia known at once was the man for her?

She'd never asked. She almost never talked to her mother about the man named Russell Shaw. There were topics too painful even for a mother and daughter as close as Cynthia and Diane to share.

When the music ended, Diane found herself standing next to the punch bowl. Jared got her a cup of punch. Nonalcoholic. She didn't need any other mind-muddlers tonight. Nick Granatelli was quite enough.

He and Annie had finished dancing on the far side of the room, and she wondered if it might be possible to sort of wander over that way, if there was any nonchalant way of threading her way through fifty or sixty people and looking available the next time the music began to play.

But she had barely formulated the thought when the music started up again.

And at the first strains of the clarinet solo of "Stranger on the Shore," Nick materialized in front of her, holding out his hand.

Diane had a punch cup in hers. Wordlessly he took it, handed it to Jared, drew her into his arms and danced her away.

Afterward she could remember every second. Every sensation seemed imprinted on her memory forever—the firm strength of the arms that held her, the soft cotton of his T-shirt, the rough calluses on his hands. They weren't Business School hands, Nick Granatelli's. But they were capable hands, strong, yet gentle hands.

She would have trusted her life to them, and she'd known him all of fifteen minutes.

She remembered what they talked about, too.

"Annie said you're from St. Louis," he began.

She nodded. "Frontenac."

Nick grinned. "A little ways from The Hill."

"Is that where you're from?"

The Hill, Diane knew, was a largely Italian neighborhood first substantially settled in the last years of the nineteenth century. Italians first from northern Italy, then later from Sicily, settled there to work in the clay mines and the foundry. A strong, insular, largely working-class neighborhood, it was not the St. Louis she knew well.

Nick seemed to think the same. "Yes, it is," he said and there was a flash of defiance in his blue eyes.

Diane met it, looked right at him and asked, softly, "Does that make a difference?"

For a moment he looked taken aback. Then he shook his head quickly and firmly. "No. Of course not. No."

She found that she'd been holding her breath. And at his reassurance, she let it out, and her breasts brushed the front of his shirt. The contact seemed to startle him as much as it did her. He drew an unsteady breath, bit down on his lower lip and pulled her more closely against him.

It was like coming home.

She couldn't help it; she nestled in, laying her cheek against his shoulder, letting her hand slip a little farther around his waist. She felt his cheek brush against her hair. She sighed and felt Nick smile.

Together they moved as if they were one, and the music wrapped them in a world all their own.

IT WAS PITCH-DARK and three o'clock in the morning. Diane's eyelids wouldn't close. She lay in her bed, all her nerve endings, all her muscles, all her emotions at attention—exactly the way they'd been since she'd come home an hour ago.

She'd tried tiptoeing and discovered promptly where she'd left Hegel, abandoned on the floor. Her muffled curse had prompted an equally muffled "mmph," from Annie's bed.

Diane hadn't seen her since she'd left for rehearsal at eight, taking Nick's friend with her.

Over her shoulder Annie had tossed a casual "Nice to have met you. Have a good time" at Nick. But that didn't necessarily mean she condoned Diane's stealing the man meant for her.

"You awake?" Diane whispered. Quietly. Guiltily.

"Mmmph."

"Annie!"

"Mmmph!"

Diane sighed. They'd have to talk about it in the morning, she supposed. She wouldn't feel right about it, until they did.

She'd stripped off her clothes and tossed them onto the desk, then padded into the bathroom and brushed her teeth and washed her face in the dark. Then she crawled into bed and willed herself to fall asleep.

No such luck.

An hour later she had tossed and turned so much that she had a nest of tangled bedclothes, but she was still no closer to dreamland. Her mind, her heart, her very being seemed entirely consumed by Nick.

She flipped over again and banged her elbow on the bookcase. Her grandmother would have been shocked at her response.

It apparently jolted Annie, too. She sat up straight. "Wha'?"

"Sorry. Nothing. I just banged my elbow."

"Oh." Annie still sat there, so quietly and for so long that Diane thought she'd gone to sleep sitting up. Then she turned her head slowly so that she was facing Diane. "Wha' time'd you get back?"

Diane hesitated a moment, then opted for the truth. "Two."

"In the morning?" Annie sounded aghast. She squinted at the clock, then lay back down. "I wanted you to distract him. You didn't have to stay out all night with him."

"I didn't," Diane said indignantly. Then spoiled it by adding, "But I'd like to."

Annie jerked upright again. "What!"

Diane glared defensively. "I would," she said firmly. "I'd marry him, if I could."

"Marry?" Annie choked. "It must've been a hell of an evening."

"It was," Diane said simply.

Annie stared, then shook her head. "Better you than me."

"You...don't mind?"

"Me?"

"Well, he was yours."

Annie rolled over onto her side, obviously fully awake now. She propped her head up on an elbow. "Are you drunk?"

"No!"

There was a moment's silence. Then, "He must've done something."

"He's a nice guy," Diane said firmly. "Very nice."

"Better than the usual from my mother," Annie admitted, then added, "But that doesn't mean you have to marry him."

"I know that."

"Then why'd you say...?" Annie couldn't even bring herself to repeat it.

"Because I meant it," Diane said with all the earnestness she was capable of. "There's something about him. We're on the same wavelength or something. We connected. We—"

"You didn't!"

"Didn't what?"

"Connect," Annie said. She reached over and flipped on her study lamp, bathing the room in a garish green glow while she fixed Diane with a basilisk stare. "You didn't sleep with him?" She sounded horrified.

"Of course not!"

Annie heaved a sigh of relief. "Thank God. That's all right, then. I mean, I would've felt terrible. I know you take your duties as a friend seriously. And I know I told you I had to get to rehearsal. But, believe me, I would never want you to go to that length just to distract him. Really, I—"

"Annie." Diane was laughing. "Don't worry. I won't sleep with anyone just to keep them from disturbing your rehearsal schedule. I honestly like Nick Granatelli."

Annie looked doubtful. "Enough to marry him?"

Diane gave her roommate a stunning smile. "On the basis of gut instinct, yes."

Chapter Two

If some classes at Harvard Business School, Nick told Jared the following morning, could be likened to aerial dog-fights, his 8:30 course in management techniques the day following his meeting with Diane Bauer was the one during which he went down in flames.

He sat in the kitchen at Fiorello's, watching Jared get ready for the noontime rush, nursing a cup of black coffee, and tried to forget the mess he'd made of the Feinemann Plastics case study that morning.

It wasn't as hard as he'd expected; his mind was full of Diane Bauer. Still.

His verbal fumblings and mumblings and the well-aimed chip shots that had reduced him to incoherence all seemed to fade in comparison to his memories of Diane.

He couldn't ever remember being so taken with a girl. There was something about her smile, about her warm brown eyes, about the welcoming way she'd looked at him, that—the moment he saw her—made him forget everything else.

He'd certainly forgotten his study group. He'd taken one look at Diane Bauer and Feinemann Plastics had gone right out of his mind.

He'd done exactly as he'd intended, foisting Annie D'Angelo off onto Jared. But instead of heading back to campus to a night of work, he'd found himself spiriting Diane off to a little coffee house in the North End and, later, to an all night café on Mass Ave, not far from her apartment, where they'd sat and talked for another two hours.

It was crazy and he knew it. Aberrant. Foolish. He had no business getting mixed up with anyone now—especially someone like Diane Bauer. It was the wrong time, the wrong place, and she was, without question, the wrong girl.

She was beautiful, charming and, he could well imagine, loving, given the right circumstances. But the circumstances were far from right.

And even if they had been right, there was too much difference in their backgrounds. Ginny Perpetti might make a terrific wife for the man who ran Granatelli's Restaurant on The Hill. But, even if eventually he also ran a whole series of Granatelli's restaurants across the country, Diane Bauer was out of his league.

Forget it, he told himself. *Forget her.*

So when Jared stopped long enough to ask, "Will you be seeing her again?" Nick shook his head. "No."

Jared's eyes widened. "And why not?"

"No future in it."

Jared's mouth quirked. "There's got to be a future?"

But there would be a future with a girl like Diane Bauer. There was always a future with girls like her. Nick sighed again. "Yep."

Jared still looked skeptical, but finally he shrugged. "Whatever you say."

Nick pushed back his chair. "I say I've gotta go," he said, getting to his feet and stretching. "I need to see if I can salvage something out of the day."

Jared grinned. "And the best o' Irish luck."

Nick flashed him a brief smile. "I'll need it."

"I HAD THE STRANGEST DREAM last night." Annie stood brushing out her long dark hair, but her gaze was on the Diane she could see in the mirror.

"Mmm?" Diane, sitting cross-legged on her bed, had all her Valéry notes spread out around her and was wishing whoever the patron saint of term papers was, he would bring it all together; she certainly didn't seem able to.

She hadn't got a thing done all day. She'd slept through her linguistics course, and while she'd managed to make it to Recent European History, what went on at Gallipoli was likely to remain shrouded in mystery forever, unless she read it in a book. She'd skipped lunch, knowing Valéry was waiting.

And Valéry was still waiting and it was almost three o'clock.

She didn't need Annie's contribution to her scattered state of mind. But Annie was her friend, and regardless of how pressed Diane was, she never ignored her friends.

"Dream?" she mumbled, her gaze flickering up to meet Annie's.

"Mmm-hmm. I don't remember what I was doing, but all of a sudden you were with me, and you told me you were going to marry Nick Granatelli."

"I did."

Annie blinked. She stopped brushing her hair. "You said you're going to marry Nick Granatelli? I didn't dream it?"

"You didn't dream it. But whether I'm going to or not—" she shrugged and gave her friend a little smile "—that remains to be seen."

In the clear light of day her pronouncement should háve seemed outrageous, but somehow, oddly, it didn't. She still felt that certainty, that sense of inevitability, that she'd felt the night before.

"Good grief," Annie said, eyes wide. "What did you two *do* last night?"

"Talked."

"About getting married?" Annie was aghast.

"No." But about nearly everything else. Life. Death. Eternity. Childhood memories. Family squabbles. Favorite poets. Beloved tunes. You name it, Diane thought, she and Nick had probably touched on it.

"We talked in Italian," Diane said with a grin. "He says I do pretty well."

"He speaks it?" Annie didn't. Or not much anyway. But then, she was three generations removed from Rienzo, whereas Nick's parents had only emigrated right before his birth.

"He speaks it," Diane affirmed. "He learned it at home, of course. But he also spent two years in Italy after he graduated from college. He worked for his uncle at a restaurant in Milan. That's why he's going to Harvard."

"So he can run his uncle's restaurant in Milan?" Annie's eyes bugged.

Diane made a face at her. "No, so he can expand the business. He's definitely got the American dream. The whole family does. His dad runs a restaurant in St. Louis. When he mentioned it, I remembered where I'd heard his name before. It's quite well-known, but Nick wants it better known. He wants a Granatelli's in every city of over one hundred thousand people."

"More power to him," Annie said.

Diane nodded. That was one of the things she'd picked up on right away with Nick—the sense of destiny, the determination. Very much like Annie, actually.

Not in the least like herself. Diane knew she was a background person. She always had been. But, she told herself, the world didn't need only leaders. It needed people who came along and mopped up as well. She didn't think she'd mind as long as she could mop up after Nick.

"And you're going to marry him?"

Even though the baldness of the statement when someone else said it made Diane give a nervous little giggle, she still didn't deny it. "I know it sounds crazy, but I really felt some very strong vibes the minute I saw him."

"It's called sexual chemistry," Annie said dryly. "Or lust, if you prefer."

"There is that," Diane admitted. "But it's more than that, too. I don't quite know how to explain it. It's like we communicate on some deeper level."

"Oh, brother." Annie rolled her eyes.

Diane threw a paperback copy of Valéry's poems at her friend. "Cynic. Wait till you meet someone."

"I'm never—"

"What about that friend of Nick's? Jeremy somebody?"

"Jared." Annie shrugged. "He's okay. He went to rehearsal with me. He's an actor looking for a break." She sighed. "Aren't we all?" She began brushing her hair again. "Anyway, he's waiting tables and working construction right now, haunting the casting calls and waiting for a chance to do what he really wants. Another dreamer—straight off the boat from County Cork."

"Is he any good?"

Annie shrugged. "Who knows? He was interested, though. Hung around until the end and walked me home."

"Maybe it wasn't the play he was interested in," Diane teased.

Annie shook her head. "It was the play. Otherwise he wouldn't have spent the entire walk explaining how, when he played Hamlet, the Ophelia in the cast had taken an entirely different approach than mine."

"He played Hamlet?"

"So he says."

"He must be good, then."

Annie shrugged.

"I'll ask Nick."

"When are you seeing him again?"

"I don't know." They hadn't set a date. But he knew where she lived. She had given him her phone number. He would call. She didn't know when, but she knew he would.

HE DIDN'T.

Days went by, then weeks. February in Boston was unrelievedly soggy and gray. Not unusual, Diane knew after having lived there four years. But this February seemed soggier and grayer than any she'd yet experienced.

It was, she admitted at last, because she never heard from Nick.

"He knows where you live?" Annie asked as they tossed a Frisbee back and forth in front of Widener Library. Today for the first time this winter, the sun was shining and the temperature seemed almost balmy. It looked like spring was coming—everywhere except in Diane Bauer's life.

She nodded. He did indeed know where she lived. He'd walked with her all the way to the front door before heading toward his own place.

"He has your number?" Annie persisted.

"Uh-huh."

"And it was really as wonderful as you thought?"

Was it? Diane was beginning to wonder.

As a teenager she'd read magazine articles about what to do when "he didn't call." They had been interesting, she supposed, but only academically. It had never happened to her.

For her the phone had rung off the hook. Tom Switzer, Cal Grable, Andrew Daly, Stephen Peterson, Mike Cambridge, Jeff Steinmetz, Hank Forrester. The list went on and on.

There was another list of names equally long of the men who had called her since she'd come east to college four years before.

No one said, "I'll be in touch," and left her flat. No one but Nick.

She wasn't so much angry as she was puzzled. She was usually a good judge of character. She sized people up easily in a matter of moments. She didn't think she'd been wrong about Nick Granatelli's interest in her.

So why hadn't he called?

"Call him," Annie said and flung the Frisbee so high that, leaping for it, Diane practically impaled herself on a tree branch.

"I couldn't!"

"Why not?"

"Women don't call men. It isn't done."

Annie shrugged. "I do it all the time. Just yesterday I called Jeff Grissom and told him he'd damned well better return my tennis racket if he wanted to live to graduate."

"Not the same thing," Diane said gently, tossing the Frisbee back.

Another shrug as Annie caught it. "Same principle. You want to talk to him, call him up."

Diane shook her head. She couldn't. She wouldn't.

Annie sighed. "You and your antiquated scruples. Run into him, then."

That bore some consideration. "How?"

"Like Freddy in *My Fair Lady*. On the street where he lives."

"I never go over there."

"So go."

"I . . ."

"Listen, do you want to marry this guy or not?"

Now, almost a month after their first meeting with no further contact, her expectations sounded idiotic. Marry a man who never even called her back. Come on, Diane, get real, she chided herself and knew her blush told Annie exactly what she was feeling. But, oddly, Annie didn't tease.

"Maybe he's shy," she said. "Bowled over by his feelings and fearing you don't reciprocate."

Diane doubted it. Annie was flinging the Frisbee with great abandon now, and Diane felt like an Irish setter fetching for its mistress as she bounded after it.

"Maybe," she panted. "Or maybe I was wrong about him in the first place."

Annie stopped and looked at her. "Do you really think so?"

Diane held the Frisbee against her chest, thinking back on the night, on the man, on the wonder of them both. "No," she said slowly. "I don't."

"Then you have to see him again. I'll go with you. Don't know why I didn't think of it before. I'll stop over and tell Jared about the casting at Hayward. They're doing *Elephant Man*. Come on."

"Now?" Diane felt her stomach knot.

"Why not? No time like the present. Unless you want to sit around fretting about it all day. Do you?"

Diane gave a rueful grimace. That was the trouble with Annie—she knew her roommate far too well. She knew that, given a choice, Diane would much prefer to have things over with, finished, settled. Sitting around worrying drove her crazy. And she would definitely sit around worrying about what she would say if, when they went, she did happen to run into Nick.

Happen to? she mocked herself. Did she really think for one minute that Annie would leave anything to chance? She girded herself mentally, emotionally.

"All right," she sighed, resigned. "Let's go."

Harvard Business School, on the other side of the Charles River from the main campus, was a world unto itself. Used to the occasionally seedy, sometimes pompous air of Harvard itself, Diane thought the neo-Georgian red brick buildings of the Business School simply exuded purpose. They were made for the men and women who were destined to lead, not for thinkers but for doers, and certainly not for contented followers like herself.

Nick and Jared, she knew, shared an attic apartment not far from the campus. Diane wasn't too familiar with the area. She'd have been quite lost, but Annie knew exactly where she was going.

"I've been here before," Annie said when Diane expressed amazement as she practically trotted after her friend who marched purposefully down the street.

"You have?"

"Mmm-hmm." Steps quickened.

"To see . . . Jared?"

"Mmm-hmm." Annie rounded a corner at breakneck speed.

Diane's mind was working furiously. "Are you ... you and Jared ... ?"

Annie stopped dead, and Diane barely avoided crashing into her. "No, we are not!"

"I didn't mean—"

"Yes, you did. You always do. But just forget it, will you? I am not interested in Jared Flynn! He is a friend. A fellow actor. And I have no desire to marry him!"

"I know you don't."

Nothing made Annie angrier than the suggestion that she might find something—or someone—who might interfere with her accomplishing her professional goals.

"All right, then." Annie began once more to walk. "So long as you don't get any stupid ideas."

"No, of course not." Diane caught up with her friend. "Have you—I mean, did you—I mean, was Nick—" She stopped, floundering.

Annie grinned. "If you're going to marry him, you have a right to ask."

Diane felt her cheeks burn. "Forget I ever said that. It was insanity speaking."

Annie shrugged. "Whatever. Anyway, I haven't been keeping anything from you. Jared and I were reading some plays together, working out scenes. He is good," she admitted. "But Nick was never around. He lives in the library, I think."

"Oh." It was on the tip of Diane's tongue to say that maybe they should lurk around the library then. But once Annie had made a decision, there was little chance of changing it.

Besides, Diane didn't really want to lurk around the library. It would be all too obvious what she was lurking about for. Accompanying Annie wasn't nearly as obvious. She hoped.

The three-story red brick building in which Nick and Jared lived was even seedier than the one she and Annie shared. Diane liked it as much as she liked her own.

She remembered how it had horrified her grandmother, but her mother had said she thought it was fine. Diane wasn't sure even her mother would accept Nick and Jared's building. She stopped, swallowing hard, reconsidering.

"I don't know, Annie. Don't you think..." she began, but Annie went straight up the steps and rang the bell.

Moments later she heard a window rattle open above and Jared's dark head poked out.

He grinned when he saw Annie. "Oh, it's you. Come on up, then."

Diane still hesitated, but Annie took her arm and hauled her through the door.

The stairway was narrow and dark, winding its way upward, ever upward. When they reached the top Jared had already opened the door and stood waiting, a welcoming grin on his handsome face.

Nervously, Diane found herself trying to see behind him, to catch a glimpse of whoever else might be in the room.

"Got to leave in a hour," Jared said, ushering them in. "I traded lunch for dinner today. I heard there was a casting."

"At the Hayward." Annie flopped on the lumpy sofa, making herself at home. Diane lingered just inside the door.

"Ah." Jared nodded. "You going?"

Annie shook her head. "Not me. I've got enough work on campus. But I thought I'd tell you."

"Yesterday in the restaurant I heard talk of it, but I didn't want to ask. It's less than thrilled Fiorello gets if you do more than wipe tables and set out the plates. So I thought I'd check a few of the theaters this afternoon. Now I don't have to. Thanks.''

His gaze shifted from Annie and for the first time he seemed to notice Diane still standing just inside the door. There was a knowing look in his eyes that made her want to slip right out beneath the door. She half expected him to say, ''Come for Nick, have you?''

But he didn't. He smiled and pointed to the sofa where Annie was sitting. ''It isn't comfortable, but it's all we have. Want a beer? A soda? Tea?''

''Tea,'' Annie said, surprising Diane. Her friend noticed her lifted brows and shrugged. ''He makes a good cup of tea.''

Taking a seat next to Annie, Diane smiled. ''Then I'll have one, too.''

She perched on the edge of the sofa—or rather, tried to. But the sofa had long ago given up the last of its springs, and the stuffing seemed intent on swallowing her. Finally the effort of remaining on the edge was too much for her and she settled back, finding that as she watched Jared puttering around in the end of the room that served as a kitchen, she was actually able to relax a little.

Perhaps it was the fact Jared didn't question her presence, or the fact that Nick was nowhere to be seen. Or maybe it was the very everydayness of Jared's movements and the casual conversation between him and Annie that she let simply flow over her. But by the time Jared handed her a cup—with milk, no sugar, just the way she liked it— she felt much, much better.

She sat and sipped, feeling more relaxed by the minute, chipping in now and then when the conversation veered away from plays and toward a subject she knew something about. Outside Jared's neighbors tromped up and down the stairs, laughing and chatting, banging against the walls as they went.

Diane stopped fretting about meeting up with Nick who was, Jared mentioned in passing, studying somewhere and not expected back for hours.

Annie looked as if she were going to take this as an excuse for leaving, but Diane cut in quickly, "We're not really in a hurry, are we? What part of Ireland are you from, Jared?"

His answer, followed by another question, effectively settled Annie in again.

Ireland was a subject Diane knew little about. But years of exercising her social graces had taught her how to make conversation with the best of them. It was no strain to talk to Jared Flynn.

They were discussing Irish poets, in particular Yeats, when there came more thundering up the stairs. The door flew open and Nick appeared.

He stopped dead at the sight of her.

On the way over, the worst scenario she had imagined was that he wouldn't remember who she was. The reality, she discovered, was far worse.

He remembered her well. And the memory—whatever it was—was clearly not what she had hoped.

He turned white, then red, then swallowed hard and dredged up a caricature of a smile from somewhere south of his toes. He looked as if he wished he were anywhere else but here.

Diane wished a rabbit hole might appear down which she could bolt. Not surprisingly, none did.

She managed a nod. Anything else would have to wait until she unstuck her tongue from the roof of her mouth.

"You're back early," Jared said brightly into the silence. "Have a cup of tea, why don't you?"

Nick looked at him, stunned. Diane was sure Jared was normally nowhere near that solicitous of his roommate.

"Come on, join us," Jared went on with the aplomb of the perfect host. "We're having a go at Yeats."

Nick shook his head quickly. "Can't stay. I forgot my Porter and Cain."

He strode into the room, stepping across Annie's and Diane's feet. Annie left hers outstretched, Diane retracted like a turtle into a shell. There was a brief shuffling of piles of paper, then Nick snatched a book off the desk, gave a small triumphant wave of it and headed back for the door.

Doorknob in hand he turned, his eyes scanning the room before lighting on Diane. Aeons passed. Or maybe it was only seconds. His eyes spoke volumes, but Diane couldn't read a word they said. She could only look back at him, baffled and oddly hurt.

He pressed his lips together for a moment, then opened his mouth as if he were going to speak. He didn't. Finally he gave a tiny shrug and a faint apprehensive smile flickered across his face.

"I gotta go," he said. Diane thought his voice sounded rusty.

SHE HADN'T FORGOTTEN HIM.

You thought maybe she had? Nick berated himself. He leaned back against the glass phone booth and stared unseeing out across the rush of traffic going past. No, he hadn't ever thought that. He'd simply *hoped* she had.

It would have made life so much simpler.

But when had life ever been simple? he asked himself.

It certainly wasn't now. Harvard Business School was not designed to make your life simple. It was, he thought, designed to streamline your priorities.

School was number one on that list. Also numbers two through nine. A distant, fast-vanishing ten, was Fiorello's. As it was, he barely had time to breathe. A woman like Diane Bauer was the last thing he needed.

He'd thought it would take a few short days to forget the effect she'd had on him.

He was wrong.

She'd been there, lurking, in the back of his mind throughout his days. And nights.

Sometimes half a day would go by without him having time to think of her. But then, all at once, he would hear a laugh that sounded like the soft feminine chuckle he had managed to elicit during that one evening they'd shared. Or another time he would overhear a comment that brought to mind one that she had made, one that had made him smile, or think, or nod his head in agreement.

It was odd how strong an effect she'd had on him in the space of those few hours.

It was, he'd told himself at the time, because he had been otherwise deprived of female companionship. She was the first and last woman he'd gone out with this year—if you didn't count Annie D'Angelo, of course.

He didn't. He found Annie perfectly nice—albeit a bit intense—and a far cry better than the usual women his family or friends dredged up for him. But she held nowhere near the attraction to him that Diane did.

Seeing her again, however, would have been crazy.

What point was there? he asked himself. It would only make things more complicated than they already were.

Besides, chances were, the feelings were all on his side. A girl like Diane Bauer probably had her pick of men. Pretty, smiling, wealthy blondes usually did.

If he were to call, she wouldn't even remember him, he'd told himself. So he turned back to his work and tried to put her out of his mind.

Sometimes, lately, he thought he was getting better at it. Whole afternoons would go by in which he managed to get lots of work done. Like yesterday afternoon.

He was steaming away on his case study, remembered something in the Porter and Cain that he wanted to look up, hurried back to the apartment for it, and—there she was.

Smiling, wide-eyed. Tempting. Vulnerable. And hurt.

He could see it in her eyes. The bewilderment. The sense of rejection. The wondering. She hadn't forgotten.

And for the rest of the day, neither had he. So much for his powers of concentration. So much for all the work he'd been planning to get done.

Instead he'd spent the rest of the afternoon staring into space. He couldn't even remember what he'd wanted to look up in Porter and Cain when he held it in his hand.

Finally at six, when he was sure she'd be gone, he went back to the apartment, irritated, ready to snap at Jared for having invited her there. Jared wasn't there.

When he did come in, Jared had stared at him like he'd lost his mind.

"Annie came to tell me about a casting, and Diane was with her. What's the matter?" He gave Nick a conspiratorial wink. "Guilty conscience?"

That was part of it, yes. But it wasn't only guilt. It was also desire. She touched some chord deep within him that he didn't ever remember having been touched before.

He was an idiot, and he knew it, but the desire to feel that resonance again hadn't left him in the month he'd tried to forget her.

So, what was he going to do now?

Call her.

Two words. Surely not difficult. You simply picked up the phone and punched out the number.

He still had her number; he'd been carrying it in his wallet for weeks. He didn't want to think about the number of times he'd slid his fingers into the pocket of his billfold and pulled out that much-folded piece of paper. He didn't want to remember all the times he'd been almost to the phone when he'd thought better of it and pulled back.

No longer.

He couldn't get her bewildered expression out of his mind. He couldn't rest until he'd explained why he'd done what he'd done. He certainly hadn't meant to hurt her.

He dropped coins in the phone box, took a breath and dialed.

It was Annie who answered.

"I—" He cleared his throat. "Is . . . Diane there?"

There was a pause. "Who is this?"

He hesitated. "Nick," he said. "Granatelli."

Another pause. A slight scuffling sound in the background. The receiver being handed over. Then another voice, softer, also hesitant. "Hello?"

"Hi. It's Nick."

"Oh."

It was amazing how many emotions he heard in that one word. They sounded as tangled as his own. "I'm . . . sorry I had to cut out the other day when you were at the apartment."

"I wasn't expecting—"

"I would've liked to have stayed. I had a report to finish."

"I never—"

"But I got it done this afternoon, and I was wondering…was wondering if…if you'd like to…come out for a cup of coffee?"

She didn't speak for an eternity. So he'd botched it, had he? He was cursing his ineptitude, when he suddenly heard her ask, "Now?"

"If…if you don't have a class or something. If you do, I understand. It was just a thought. I realize you weren't expecting—"

"I'll come." Her reply cut right across his objections. "Shall…shall I meet you somewhere?"

"How about Fredo's? Do you know it?" It was a relatively new place, about halfway between his place and hers.

"Yes. All right. When?"

"Half an hour?"

She hesitated. "I have to be back to do some tutoring at five."

"No problem." In fact, he thought, all the better. It meant they would only have at most an hour together. Surely that would be enough time to make explanations, to see her, to tell if the whole thing was a fluke, the case of an overworked male with temporarily undersatisfied hormones.

And if it was, he'd know. He could drink a cup of coffee with her and then get on with his life.

And if it wasn't?

He wasn't going to think about that.

Chapter Three

Fredo's was supposed to be noteworthy for its fifties' ambience, its chrome-and-Formica counter, its neon advertising behind the bar, and its horrible coffee. As Nick drew her into the diner, Diane didn't notice anything except the warm pressure of his fingers wrapped around hers.

Witlessly she followed him to one of the booths at the back, sitting down and watching as he sat down opposite her.

He hadn't had a haircut in the month since she'd met him. His sun-streaked hair was rumpled and brushed the collar of his shirt. He wore a navy chamois cloth shirt and jeans and looked to Diane as if he should be outdoors chopping wood, not cooped up in graduate school.

The waitress appeared, smiled and batted her eyes at Nick. "What'll you have?"

Nick looked at Diane, his smile all for her. "Coffee," she said recklessly.

"Two coffees," Nick said without shifting his gaze.

The waitress looked disappointed, shrugged and left. Diane felt once more as if she and Nick were the only two people in the world.

Don't, she tried to tell herself. *Don't hope.*

But she couldn't help it.

"I should have called you." Nick raked a hand through his hair, rumpling it further. His smile was rueful now. "I . . . wanted to."

Diane, not knowing what to say to that, didn't say anything, just looked at him and savored the moment.

He shrugged awkwardly. "I've had so much to do. I thought I'd better concentrate on it. On school."

"I understand," she said, giving him a smile she hoped was reassuring.

He looked minutely reassured. His smile became a grimace, then he sighed. "Yeah, well, I'm sorry. When I saw you yesterday, I knew I'd made a mistake." He traced on the Formica with his fingertip, finally venturing a glance at her from beneath his lashes. "I had a great time that night."

Diane breathed again. She smiled. "I did, too."

"I'd...like to do it again. If I haven't blown it too bad."

Diane shook her head. "You haven't blown anything."

It wasn't the way one played the game; she knew that. Girls were supposed to be coy, distant, lead men on. And, in the past, to be truthful, she'd done her share of it.

But she couldn't seem to do it with Nick. With Nick she always felt as if she weren't wearing her heart so much on her sleeve as plastered across the front of her shirt.

Nick must have got a good look at it for he said, "Good," and smiled at her.

The waitress slapped the coffee in front of them.

"Thanks," Nick said absently, his gaze remaining on Diane.

He had trouble thinking when she looked at him like that. He'd been having trouble thinking since she'd come around the corner of the diner, her cheeks rosy from the cold, her fair hair flying free behind her, her bright blue scarf knotted casually around her neck. Whatever he felt for her, and whatever it might have to do with underworked hormones, he knew it was also more than that.

She made the day brighter, made the dreary New England spring seem to bask in a golden glow. And the fact that her smile seemed all for him made him stand straighter, breathe deeper, become more the man he wanted to become.

Now he tried to think of something clever to say, something worthy of her note, and could only come up with, "Were you really talking Yeats with Jared?"

She nodded.

"I know from nothing about Yeats." He grimaced again. "About poetry in general. It's all been business with me."

"Well, I don't know much about Yeats, either," Diane admitted. "But I've had plenty of poetry being a French major, so I tried."

"Jared was impressed."

Her brows lifted. "Oh, yes?"

Nick nodded grimly. "He said if I wasn't going to take you out, he was."

Her eyes widened now. She sipped her coffee, her gaze never leaving Nick's face.

"I'd rather not give him the chance."

Diane smiled slightly and cocked her head.

He shrugged and bit down on his lip. "So, I was wondering, what about having dinner with me Friday night? Would you like to?"

Diane nodded. "Yes."

He grinned. "Good."

The hour passed faster than it had any right to. It seemed to Nick like less than five minutes had passed when Diane glanced at her watch, grimaced, and began pulling on her coat.

"I've got to go," she said ruefully. "I have a couple of students to tutor in French this afternoon."

That surprised him. "You tutor?"

She shrugged. "It's a job."

"You need a job?" His skepticism was obvious.

"I like tutoring," she said defensively.

Immediately he regretted his question. "Yeah. Better than slinging hash at least."

"The kids are nice. They're Dr. Edmonds's children. Do you know him?"

"Luther Edmonds?" Nick knew him all right. Luther Edmonds sat somewhere just to the right of the god of the business management pantheon.

"They're going to France this summer," Diane told him as she stood up. "And he wants the kids prepared."

He wanted everyone prepared, all the time, Nick thought. It was in Edmonds's class that the Feinemann Plastics fiasco had occurred. He winced at the memory, then got hastily to his feet.

He should be heading over to the library right now and settling in for a long, hard slough through the pile of material Edmonds had heaped on them just this morning. Above all, he should bear in mind that furthering his acquaintance with Diane Bauer was a pointless exercise, one destined simply to distract him from the task at hand.

Instead he took her arm. "Come on," he said and tossed a couple of bills on the table. "I'll walk you back to your place."

AND, AS SIMPLY as that, it began.

Nick needed a social life. At least that was what he told himself.

A man couldn't live by business courses and care packages of Granatelli's own prosciutto and *biscotti* alone. He needed the occasional walk along the river in congenial company, the rare dinner date with a member of the opposite sex.

After all, he thought, a third of the members of his class were married. *They* had a social life. Why shouldn't he?

So he met Diane for a quick lunch at the Snack Bar in Gallatin on Wednesday. He took her out for another cup of coffee Thursday. And, as he had suggested, they went out for dinner on Friday night.

It was another marathon date. They left her apartment at five-thirty. He didn't bring her home until after two. They talked about life, about hopes and fears, joys and sorrows. She told him about her mother and stepfather, Cynthia and Matthew Bauer. It was a different view of the society swells than Nick had got growing up on The Hill.

He thought he would like her mother. She sounded as generous and loving as his own mother, though in quite a different way. And while Matthew Bauer sounded every bit the staid, responsible businessman he was reputed to be, he didn't sound like a bad father to have. He said so.

Diane tossed her mane of golden hair and smiled. "They are lovely parents," she admitted. "They love me a lot. They want what's best for me. So does my grandmother," she added. "But she isn't as easy to be around."

Privately Nick thought Diane's maternal grandmother Gertrude Hoffmann—the woman who insisted on an hour of piano practice and an hour of flute every day, who thought the Palmer Method couldn't hold a candle to Copperplate and required that Diane learn to write that way as well, who criticized her living quarters, who had always decreed which schools her granddaughter should attend—sounded like a virago.

He hoped devoutly that he never had the displeasure of meeting her. He didn't say that.

"She's a dear, really," Diane said philosophically. "You just have to know how to deal with her."

Nick didn't imagine he would ever know that.

"What were your grandparents like?" Diane asked him.

"Not like yours." He traced a pattern on his plate with the tines of his fork. "I only knew two of them really well. My father's parents stayed in Italy. My mother's lived down the street. And after my grandmother died, my mother's father came and lived with us. He was a fantastic man. The best. He died when I was seventeen."

"You must miss him dreadfully," Diane said, her eyes warm with sympathy.

Nick nodded. Even now, just thinking about his mother's father, Nick felt his throat get tight, his eyes burn. He swallowed hard. "He used to let me watch him work."

"What did he do?"

"When he was young he apprenticed to an instrument maker in Cremona. Violins and cellos and stuff. He loved music, but he loved working with wood more. So he packed up and went off to Cremona to try to combine the two. But he missed home and family, and he went back to get married."

The waiter removed their plates and refilled their coffee cups. Diane didn't speak, just waited for him to continue.

"His wife didn't want to leave, so he stayed there and made furniture instead. He made beautiful furniture," Nick said softly. "The care he lavished on it. The detail." He shook his head. "It was a labor of love. As I got older he taught me how to do it." The memory made him smile.

Diane smiled, too. "He sounds marvelous."

"He was. He saved my life."

Her eyes got big and round. "How?"

"Figuratively, I mean. He gave me breathing space. I was supposed to be in the restaurant working every eve-

ning after school. And most evenings I was. But sometimes I needed a break and *Nonno*—my grandfather—
provided it.''

"I envy you," Diane said, and he could see she meant
it from the look in her eyes.

"I envy me, too," he said, reaching across the table to
take her hand in his. "And never more than right now."

THAT WAS THE WAY it went.

Lots of conversation, sharing. Plenty of smiles. Some
touching. The occasional mind-shattering kiss. But on the
whole they behaved themselves. He might have wanted to
go to bed with her—no, there was no *might have* involved; he *did* want to—but he didn't even try.

It was a miracle.

No, he thought. It wasn't. A guy just naturally behaved
himself around Diane Bauer. She brought out a protec-
tive instinct not a predatory instinct in him.

Not, he realized, because she was defenseless. She had,
she'd informed him with a completely ingenuous smile,
taken two years' worth of lessons in tae kwon do.

No, it wasn't defenselessness that prompted him to
watch over her, but rather her fundamental openness and
generosity of spirit that he didn't want to see compro-
mised or lost.

"It's like she's my little sister," he explained to Jared the
next Saturday afternoon when he was preparing to meet
Diane to go rowing on the Charles.

Jared, who had only met one of Nick's sisters, stared.
"Little sister? Don't be daft, man. Diane has as much in
common with Frankie as a goldfish does with a piranha."

Nick grinned. "Not that little sister. Paula, I meant."

Jared still looked doubtful. Nick didn't blame him. Diane wasn't really like the less fiery, more ethereal Paula, either.

Nor, if he were honest, did he feel about her the way he felt about Paula.

But even though he liked her, even though he wanted to go to bed with her, he wasn't serious about her. Not really.

It would be asinine for Nick Granatelli to get serious about Diane Bauer.

Even though she was the nicest girl he'd ever met, even though his heart beat faster when she smiled and his whole body trembled when she kissed him, he knew better than to think this relationship was going anywhere.

They might be a couple here and now. But here and now was not forever. Forever, for the two of them, would never work. There was far too much distance between them.

He tried to make sure she remembered that, too.

He tried to tell her he was too busy, that he couldn't see her. And she'd nod and say, okay. And then he'd relent and call. But even when he saw her, he brought it up whenever he could.

He said it again the Saturday they went rowing on the Charles. He should have been in the library and wasn't. He should be feeling guilty and, unfortunately, he did.

But he wanted to spend time with her, and even though he half considered phoning her at the last minute and begging off with too much work to do, he couldn't do it. For one thing, she'd understand. She'd say, "Do your work. It's important."

And it was. But it didn't feel, at the moment, as important as Diane.

Unlike any other girl Nick had ever dated, Diane could row and wanted to. It amazed him, and he commented on it.

"No big deal," Diane said, moving the oars efficiently as they skimmed down the river. "I'll row you downstream. You can row back." She gave him an impish grin.

Nick shook his head, grinning, too. "How'd you learn?" he asked her. It didn't seem like the sort of accomplishment a debutante would have.

"Fourteen years at summer camp," Diane informed him. "After that many years, who wouldn't know?"

Nick nodded in agreement. But somehow the camp notion nettled. Visions of little pigtailed blondes in snappy uniforms came to mind. Privileged little pigtailed blondes. Wealthy little pigtailed blondes. "Where was that?"

Diane continued to slice the oars rhythmically through the murky green water. "In the mountains of North Carolina. Pine forests. Lakes. Real log cabins. It was beautiful." She smiled at the memory.

Nick, though still nettled, couldn't help smiling at her. His only experience with camp had been a week-long baseball day camp in a local park when he was ten years old.

All the boys in the neighborhood had come, wearing their holey jeans and too-small T-shirts. But they thought it was the greatest thing on earth, learning the finer points of baseball from their elder brothers, cousins and uncles, some of whom were on a first-name basis with home-grown stars like Joe Garagiola and Yogi Berra.

Still, in comparison to Diane's experience, it seemed a joke. He told her about it, stressing the makeshift quality of the operation. "Not exactly the same quality as yours."

"Sounds like fun to me. I always wanted to play baseball. At camp I did. But the minute I got home, I had to quit. My grandmother didn't think it was proper."

There was very little, Nick thought, that Gertrude Hoffmann seemed to think was proper. He could imagine what she would say if she knew her granddaughter was rowing on the Charles with a guy like him.

"What about you? Where did you learn to row?" Diane asked. The April sun was warm and turned her winter-dulled locks a burnished gold. He fought back an impulse to reach out and touch it. She lifted her face to the sun and closed her eyes for a moment, then opened them again and focused on Nick, waiting for his reply.

He cleared his throat, shifted carefully on the seat trying to ease the tightness in his jeans. "On the Mississippi."

"You had a boat?"

"Hardly. We used to skip school and go down along the riverfront and 'borrow' any boat we could find."

"Sounds a bit daring," she said.

Nick shrugged. "The owners just used 'em on weekends. They never even knew. We were always careful to put 'em back where we found 'em."

"Clever." But she didn't sound censorious.

"Illegal."

"Yes, I can see what a hardened criminal you've turned out to be." Her eyes were laughing at him.

He scowled, irritated that she didn't take his transgressions seriously. She wouldn't have had to joyride in someone else's boat. "It isn't funny."

"No." But she still didn't sound put off.

"I bet you've never done an illegal thing in your life."

Diane stopped rowing, her face growing pensive, her gaze shifting to the middle distance. She pondered, then brightened visibly.

"I have, you know. I am a chronic jaywalker."

"That's not what I meant."

"Well, it's as silly as you're being," Diane countered, beginning to row again. "What am I supposed to say, you were a terrible child? All right, you were a terrible child. Now, are you satisfied?''

He wasn't. He wanted her to back away from him, dislike him, disparage him. He wanted her to see how unsuitable their growing relationship was.

He wanted her to tell him to get lost because he couldn't tell himself. The longer he was around Diane Bauer, the more he wanted to stay around her for the rest of his life.

HE WAS REALLY, Diane thought as she rested the oars in the oarlocks, behaving ridiculously.

Not exactly unusual of late, she had to admit. Every time they were together Nick seemed absolutely intent on pointing out to her how little they had in common.

He was quite wrong.

Diane had met a lot of men in her twenty-two years, and she'd never met a man she had more in common with than Nick Granatelli.

Of course he hadn't had the same monetary advantages she'd had. He hadn't had her vast experience of attending debutante balls and country club soirees. But Diane couldn't see that that had been a particularly enlightening part of her education nor a particularly enviable one. She'd done it because it was expected of her. It meant no more to her than that.

But other things did matter. And it was those things she discovered that she shared with Nick. He loved his family; so did she. He was a Catholic; so was she. He was a Cards fan; she'd been one since birth.

When he went home at Christmas, he, like Diane, went out to root for the St. Louis Blues.

Their schoolday memories were not that different, either. She might've gone to the best of the private Catholic girls' schools in the area, whereas he had divided his time between Shaw Elementary and St. Ambrose Grade School, but they both had plenty of nun stories to tell. And he understood immediately when she talked about literally sweating through thirteen years in St. Louis schools.

"You mean you didn't have air conditioning?" He'd looked at her horrified.

"Never," Diane had assured him. "We were hothouse plants in the very truest sense of the word."

She tried to point out to him all these areas of compatibility. But he just argued with her.

The beauty of it, though, as she told Annie, was that he never left mad, and he always seemed willing to come back and argue some more.

"I don't have time to come around," he'd told her just yesterday. "You better find another guy to go out with."

But Diane had said, "It doesn't matter. I'll wait for you."

He'd tried arguing with her about that, too. But she meant it.

"I'll be here. If you get finished, fine. Come by. If you don't, don't worry about it."

She didn't know whether he'd worried or not, but at least he came.

She wouldn't have blamed him if he hadn't for she did understand the pressures he was under. On the phone just last week she had mentioned to her parents that she was dating a man who went to Harvard Business School.

Cynthia had wanted to know if he was a nice guy. Matthew had asked her how he had the time.

So she was well aware that Nick was pressed. She was grateful for the time they got.

Annie, she was sure, thought she was a sap to wait for the few hours here and there that Nick could give her.

Every time it happened Diane expected her roommate to call her a spineless idiot without a will of her own.

But for once Annie kept her opinions to herself. And if she looked at Diane with worry in her deep brown eyes, Diane didn't want to know.

She even allowed herself to go back to daydreaming about someday marrying Nick.

It wasn't outrageous. No one but her grandmother Hoffmann would think it was. And she was confident that, when the time came, she could talk her grandmother around. When it mattered, she always could.

The biggest problem, so far as she could see, was convincing Nick.

Sometimes she thought he believed their relationship was going nowhere, that they were friends and nothing more. At others she thought his feelings were as deep as hers.

She didn't know. She wasn't sure. But she didn't despair. They had time, she thought. The rest of the school year. The summer.

He was going home to work at the family restaurant for the summer, he told her. And Diane, who had been planning to tour Europe before she started at the Sorbonne in the fall, suddenly changed her mind.

"I'll be in St. Louis, too," she told him one late April afternoon when they were lying on the grass in the Public Garden.

They rarely came into Boston. Their lives seemed contained at their respective schools. But this afternoon Nick had had to observe the workings of a small, but growing corporation and do a critique of it.

He'd asked her if she wanted to meet him afterward and grab a bite to eat. It had been almost two weeks since they'd been rowing. They'd shared coffee on the run three times. They'd sat across from each other in the library one night. And on Tuesday, he had met her at her apartment and they'd walked together to the Laundromat, where Nick had spent two hours reading a case study about something to do with the takeover of a mustard factory while Diane read Maupassant in between loads of his and her laundry.

"You washed his clothes?" Annie stared at her, as if she had just confessed to the most heinous of crimes.

Diane had shrugged. "I did mine, too."

She didn't mind. She didn't even care that Annie rolled her eyes and said, "I suppose you think it's romantic to fold his shirts."

In fact, it was. Being with Nick, in whatever manner, was enough for her. But the opportunity to go on something even remotely resembling a real date was not to be sneezed at, either.

So when he called and suggested she meet him in Boston, she just asked, "Where?"

Then she rearranged her tutoring, prayed that her modern French poetry instructor would come down with a communicable disease so tomorrow's paper wouldn't be due till Monday, and set off to meet Nick by the swan boats at five o'clock.

It was still warm when she got there. Spring had arrived full flower. Blossoms danced on the forsythia. New leaves budded on the trees. New downy ducklings trailed their mothers across the pond. And when Nick suggested they take a ride, Diane was thrilled.

It felt childish and frivolous and wonderful just to be able to lean back against the bench of the giant swan with Nick's arm snug around her, her head on his shoulder while the warm spring breeze teased her hair.

Sometimes she wished they could do more things like this—simple things, gentle things. Things just slightly more sensually rewarding than doing laundry and studying together.

But she knew that as long as Nick was in grad school it couldn't happen. She understood that.

But it would happen. Someday it would. She knew that, too. Just as she knew when she looked into his eyes that he was the most important person in her life and always would be.

And after the ride was over, they walked across the lawn and sat down on the grass. Nick told her about the corporation he'd just visited, about a summer job offer they'd made him and about having to decline. That was when he said he was going back to St. Louis.

And that was when Diane had said she was, too.

"I thought you were going to France?" Nick was sprawled on the grass, looking up at her with heavy-lidded eyes. Diane wanted to reach out and touch him, run her hand along his arm, slide her fingers inside the buttons of his shirt and touch the firm muscles of his chest.

She knotted her fingers together and shook her head. "I'm going home, too," she said, paused, then smiled hopefully at him.

Nick didn't say anything for a moment, but the eagerness she'd hoped for wasn't there. Finally he pressed his lips together in a firm line. "Your St. Louis isn't mine."

She stared at him, disbelieving.

His jaw tightened. He scowled. "It isn't."

"That's the dumbest thing I've ever heard," Diane exploded.

But he just looked at her. "Is it?"

And she heard a real question in his voice.

It struck her forcibly for the first time that he really did worry about the differences in their backgrounds, that he really might fear there was no future for them. She thrust out her chin. It was a replica of her grandmother's, though most people didn't notice.

"Yes," she said firmly, meeting his gaze. "It most certainly is."

Nick didn't say anything. He lay there, propped on one elbow, looking at her, then letting his gaze shift toward the swan boats cruising in the pond. The look on his face reminded Diane of the look he got sometimes when he was wrestling with a case study, weighing the alternatives, trying to see the future.

She had seen the future—and it was theirs, if he would only let it be.

But she didn't speak, only held her breath and waited.

Finally his gaze came back to rest on her face. A slight smile lifted the corners of his mouth. "Yeah," he said.

Yeah.

"ONE FOR YOU, and one for me. And another for me. And another for me." Jared tossed Nick his one letter, then dropped a sheaf of thin blue air mail missives onto his own bed.

Nick looked up from where he lay and scowled. "The Jared Flynn Fan Club at it again?"

"It's jealous you are." Jared grinned and slit open a letter, then sank down onto the edge of his bed to read it.

"Not me," Nick denied, picking up his own letter and studying it for a moment. "Got my own fan," he said with deliberate smugness, waving the perfumed letter in Jared's face.

Jared looked up. "Oh? Who's that?"

Nick ran his finger along the edge of the envelope, ripping it open. "Ginny Perpetti. She teaches school back home." He scanned the letter, barely digesting it, knowing he was only using it to hassle Jared a bit, not because it—or Ginny—really mattered.

Jared, unhassled, laughed. "You're not interested in her."

"What makes you so sure?" Nick countered.

"Diane. Every waking moment you're not buried under the bloody case studies you're with her."

"We're . . . friends."

"Pull the other one while you're at it."

"We are," Nick protested.

"And that's all, then?"

Nick started to say it was and stopped. He thought about Diane, about all the times they'd spent together, about the way she looked at him, the things she said to him, about the way he was growing to feel about her.

"I don't know," he admitted.

"Looks serious," Jared said simply.

Nick sighed, then lay back on his bed, staring up at the ceiling. It felt serious, too.

Ever since their conversation in the Public Garden last week, Nick found that he no longer automatically rejected the notion of a future with Diane Bauer.

For the first time it seemed remotely possible that while he was making the Granatelli name in St. Louis, he might make Granatelli Diane's name as well.

Chapter Four

"So you're not going to Europe?" Annie sounded equal parts aghast and amazed.

Diane shook her head, which was a mistake. She should have known better than to move while she was trying to put on mascara, but she so rarely wore it these days, she tended to forget. She wouldn't be wearing it tonight if it weren't for the play Jared was in.

She and Nick were going. It was going to be a date.

A real one, he promised her; as if that mattered.

Diane had considered all their cups of coffee on the run, all their Saturday afternoons in the Laundromat or Sundays in the little rowboat on the Charles to be dates. As long as they were together, she didn't care in the least.

"So have you told Mama, then? Or, more to the point, Grandmama?"

"I haven't told anyone," Diane said. "But you. And Nick."

"And is Nick pleased?" Annie finished knotting her long dark hair on top of her head and poked the last pin in place.

"Yes." He wasn't jumping for joy. But then, Diane realized, Nick was not the jumping-for-joy type.

Still her commitment to spending the summer in St. Louis seemed to have made him happy. At first he'd looked doubtful, but the last few days he'd seemed less irritable, calmer, more likely to smile.

"He ought to be pleased," Annie said darkly. "I wouldn't give up a summer in Provence with Auntie Flo for anyone. Haven't you told her yet, either?"

Diane started to shake her head again, remembered the mascara, held very still and concentrated on her eye. "I'll write her. She won't care. Aunt Flo never cares what I do."

"How very unBauerlich."

Diane grinned. "Very. It's what makes her such a dear." Her stepfather's older sister, Florence, was the closest thing the Bauers had to a black sheep.

At twenty she'd married a German baron three times her age and moved to New York. Widowed at twenty-two, she remained in the east and never came back to St. Louis unless absolutely unavoidable family obligations required it. The last time she'd been there was in 1966 for her mother's funeral.

The baroness Florence Von Dettmeyer was a dream aunt. She ran an art gallery on Madison Avenue, traveled extensively, sent her only niece outrageous presents and provided her with plenty of opportunities to broaden her midwestern horizons.

Grandmother Hoffmann thought Flo barely to the right of unrespectable and didn't hesitate to say so. She had saved herself from damnation only by having married well. Grandmother Hoffmann forgave many sins of those who had the sense to marry men of whom she approved.

Once, when she'd had a tad too much vodka, Flo had told Diane she thought Grandmother Hoffmann, had she been asked, might have married Baron Von Dettmeyer herself.

Diane, who'd heard tales of the hard-nosed Teuton who'd been her aunt's husband, thought privately that he and Grandmother Hoffmann would have been well matched.

"So what are you going to do instead? Wait tables at Granatelli's?" Annie persisted.

"I doubt it. Not that I wouldn't. But I don't think Nick would approve."

She could imagine the reaction she'd get if she even suggested it. She could hardly believe he was ashamed of her, but on several occasions when he'd talked with his father on the phone in her presence, he hadn't mentioned she was there.

She didn't want to sound pushy, but afterward she couldn't help asking, "Does he know about me?"

She'd been disappointed but not surprised when Nick had said no.

"He has enough on his mind," he said, giving her a hug and a smile. "He's trying out some new wholesalers. Every time you think you've got things settled, they're screwed up again. Supply dries up, the prices skyrocket, the source goes belly-up." He shook his head.

"Sounds difficult," Diane sympathized.

"It is. Besides, Aldo, my brother-in-law, is setting up a new accounting system. And the maître d' just quit. It's all he'd need," Nick grinned, "hearing I'm being distracted by a beautiful woman when I'm supposed to be working my butt off here so I can go home and increase the family fortunes a hundredfold."

Diane knew that that was the plan. Other people used Harvard Business School as a glorified employment agency, getting their degree and expecting, as a reward, a clear entry into a Fortune 500 company. Nick was there to learn all he could and go home to make Granatelli's Restaurant a force to be reckoned with in St. Louis.

"Are you distracted?" Diane asked doubtfully.

He'd pulled her into his arms and given her a resounding kiss. "What do you think?"

Diane didn't know what to think. She could only wait. And hope.

NICK WAS LEARNING to hope, too. Diane was right about one thing—he never would have let her wait tables at Granatelli's. He was having a hard enough time convincing himself that he could make her the owner's son's wife. But he was, for the first time, actually considering it.

He was also considering how he might best introduce her to the family—and the family to her. He would broach the subject carefully once he was home this summer. He'd call Diane sometime and invite her out, drive her through The Hill area, maybe take her past the restaurant.

Then, another time, they'd stop, and he'd take her in, introduce her to his dad. She'd like his father. At least he hoped she would.

As if by some odd chance she didn't, Diane would never let it show. She was far too well-bred to show her feelings.

His father wasn't. Dominic Granatelli never hesitated to show you what he thought about anything.

Nick knew he'd have to do a bit of preparation there.

Even if he did, he still didn't know if his father would like her. Not that there was anything to dislike about Diane Bauer. Nick had never in his life met a woman who was sweeter, kinder, more genuine.

But Dominic Granatelli had his own agenda, made up his own mind.

Nick doubted that the Bauer Brewery and Hoffmann Hardware heiress was exactly what his father'd had in mind as daughter-in-law material. She didn't come with a built-in familial connection to basil growers and olive orchard owners the way Ginny Perpetti did.

Still, Nick felt hopeful. If all went well after she'd met his father, he could ask her to come for a meal. She could meet his mother and Frankie and—

No, not Frankie. His sister's strong personality and unhesitating outspokenness would overpower a gentle girl like Diane.

She could meet Paula, though. Paula, in her last year of high school, was young and sweet. She could meet Carlo, too. His brother was in the seminary in St. Louis. Carlo could be counted on to be polite.

He'd save Frankie and Sophia—surely Ginny's biggest supporter—and his youngest brother Vinnie, who had long hair, an earring and a penchant for drumming on things, for another time.

But he was getting ahead of himself.

"One day at a time, fella," he counseled himself as he bounded up the stairs to Diane's apartment. "One day at a time."

She was ready when he got there, waiting just inside the door, wearing a lightweight spring coat over a demure rose-colored dress, her long honey-colored hair swept up into a barrette at her crown from which it fell in silky, shining splendor over her shoulders. The smile she gave him made him melt, and the last thing he wanted to do tonight was go watch Jared's play.

"All set," she said brightly, holding out her hand to him.

He drew her close, slipping his arm around her shoulders and kissing her. It was not a brief kiss. It simply fed the hunger that grew inside him, making him forget his purpose, his good sense, his intentions.

Someone behind Diane cleared her throat.

Nick jerked back. "Er, hi. *Annie?*" Of course it was Annie. Who else would it be?

But he had never seen her like this—all dressed up, wearing a dramatic black cape over a dress of ivory linen. Nothing demure about her.

"You're coming to the play," Nick said, unable to hide his consternation.

"Not with you," Annie said pointedly. "You don't have to be a French major to know what *de trop* means."

"Really, you're very welcome to come with us," Nick lied.

Annie rolled her eyes. "Get out of here," she said. "I don't like all that mushy stuff. When I go to a play I go to concentrate." She glowered at them both.

"She's right," Nick said. "If we don't hurry, we're going to be late."

He hadn't the slightest interest in *Look Back in Anger* himself. He had agreed to go because it was a good excuse to take Diane out on a real date and because his friend was in it.

If you had asked him he would have assured you that he was always certain Jared had talent, but he'd never seen him act until tonight.

He found out at once how right he was.

It didn't even seem to be Jared up there onstage. The man who left the cap off the toothpaste, who left dirty socks on the coffee table, warbled off-key in the shower and burned toast in the kitchen was nowhere to be found.

The lean, intense, dark-haired man who played Jimmy, Osborn's protagonist, didn't even seem to resemble Jared, except perhaps superficially.

The Irish brogue had vanished. In its place Nick heard an increasingly strident Midlands accent. The droll smile had fled, replaced by sneers and bitterness, then genuine anguish.

Nick had thought the play would give him a chance to do a little bit of petting with Diane. He found that it captured his attention entirely.

So trapped was he in the web of emotions developing onstage, that he forgot Diane. And when it was over, and the curtain came down, he was as exhausted and drained as a man who'd run a marathon.

One look at Diane told him she felt the same way.

It was a shock to see Jared, sweating and grinning as he took his bows, looking once again just like the man who couldn't make a piece of toast.

"He was amazing," Diane said. "I never would've believed it."

"*You* wouldn't have?" Nick laughed, but he still felt shaken.

His roommate had so much potential in him, such incredible talent that he'd never suspected. It had simply taken the right circumstances to bring it out. He helped Diane with her coat, but all the time his mind swirled and he shook his head, still awed.

"He asked us to meet him backstage after," Nick said, steering her up the aisle. "He said we'd go out and grab a bite." He shook his head again. "I wonder he can eat."

"I know." Diane turned and smiled at him. "But I bet he can. Annie's the same way."

"Speaking of whom," Nick said, "where is she?"

They found her already backstage, on the edge of a group of theatergoers surrounding Jared. Everyone else was babbling and chattering, tugging at his arms or poking their faces in his.

Annie simply stood and stared.

She didn't speak, she didn't move. And when Diane and Nick came up to her, she didn't even acknowledge their presence. She just looked at Jared.

Gradually, slowly, his congratulators drifted away, and Jared breathed deeply, stripped off his sweaty shirt and mopped his brow.

"Cripes," he muttered, giving them a grin. "Bit of a mob scene, this is."

"You were wonderful." Diane put her arms around him and gave him a hug. "I couldn't believe it was you."

"Me, either." Nick clapped him on the back.

"Thank you very much." Jared grinned. Then his gaze found Annie and he frowned. "What's wrong?"

She blinked, then shook her head. "Nothing." Her voice was flat, colorless. It made Nick frown, too, and Diane leaned forward, looking concerned.

"It's something," Jared said. His brows came together. "It was that bad, then?"

Annie blinked again, then looked at him, astonished. "Bad? It was marvelous. *You* were marvelous. I just...I just..." She shook her head, dazedly. "I never thought..." she said, her voice trailing off into a whisper.

"Marvelous?" Jared brightened. "You think so?" Again a moment's doubt flickered on his face.

"You were incredible," Annie said with authority, and bestowed on him a smile such as Nick had never seen.

At that Jared smiled, too, and took her arm. "Come and tell me, then," he commanded, hauling her with him toward the dressing room. He glanced over his shoulder. "Be right back," he said to Nick and Diane. "Give me a few minutes to get cleaned up."

Nick grinned. "And have your ego stroked a little."

Jared laughed. "That, too."

"He deserves it," Diane said, watching them go.

Nick nodded, bent his head and kissed her ear. "He does."

IT WAS A NIGHT to remember for all of them.

For Jared, obviously, because it was his first triumph on the American stage. It would not, Diane was certain, be his last.

For Annie, Diane found out later, it was equally memorable because she had finally found someone whose talent she could respect.

"I thought perhaps he was a kindred spirit," she told Diane later that night. "But I didn't know until I saw him onstage. Now I do."

And for Diane and Nick it was a time to be together, to share the present, to hope for the future.

As if the play itself weren't wonderful enough, there was the after-theater supper at Gregoire's, a small cozy French bistro with a string trio playing danceable oldies not far from the theater where they started out as a foursome.

Halfway through the onion soup, Jared and Annie were so far into an analysis of the third scene that Nick had pulled Diane up into his arms and said, "Let's dance."

No one else was, but for once the etiquette of the situation was beyond her. Diane put her arms around his neck and let herself go.

They danced between courses. They kissed, they nibbled, they smiled. Jared and Annie moved on to the fourth scene, their discussion becoming as heated as Diane's blood.

After dinner Jared and Annie left them, still discussing, to go back to the apartment. She and Nick remained behind alone.

The other diners danced now, but they no longer did. Instead they sat close together at the table, talking with their eyes as much as with their mouths, saying things they couldn't yet bring themselves to put into words.

It was on the tip of Diane's tongue to say, "I love you."

She did love him. She knew that beyond a shadow of a doubt. She, like the Biblical Ruth, would drop everything and follow him. He had but to say where.

She didn't speak because it wasn't her place. She had done most of the running; she knew it and was willing to acknowledge it. If she hadn't reappeared in Nick's apartment with Annie that afternoon last March, chances were he'd have never called her again.

But she had. And he had. And things had gone along from there.

Now, set in motion, they would continue, just as she'd always known they would. She and Nick were destined for each other. There was no hurry.

"All things come to she who waits," her grandmother Hoffmann used to say with asperity whenever Diane, a bouncy child, was impatient for something to happen.

So Diane waited. She smiled. She touched her lips to his.

Nick cleared his throat. "I have something to ask you."

Diane smiled, hoping.

He looked uncomfortable all of a sudden. There was a tension in his face that hadn't been there before.

"What is it?" She deliberately made her voice soft, unhurried.

He eased his collar away from his neck, then tugged at the knot of his tie. "I shouldn't even ask you, I guess. It's an imposition, what with it being the end of the school year and all, but . . ."

Diane still waited. Surely he couldn't want to elope now?

He hesitated, tugged at his collar again, then went on, "You know Bennett Hamilton in my study group?"

Diane nodded. She'd met him once in passing. He looked and dressed every bit the third-generation blue blood that Nick did not.

"Yeah, well, his family's putting on an—" he raked his fingers through his hair "—hell, I don't know what you'd call it . . . affair, I guess, to celebrate his brother's passing the New York bar exam. Black tie." He grimaced. "Next Friday down at their place in Newport. The 'cottage' Ben calls it." Another grimace.

"On Bellevue Avenue, no doubt."

"Is that money?"

"Mmm-hmm."

"Then that must be where it is." He tugged at his tie again. "Anyway, he invited me. And a guest. 'Come for the party and stay over,' he said."

Nick made it sound as if he'd been invited to be the recipient of a round at a firing squad.

"So, will you come? Be my 'guest'? Show me which fork to use?" he added with a wry grin.

It wasn't, of course, the question she'd hoped it would be, but she didn't mind. "A man who can run a restaurant knows perfectly well which fork to use."

"You know what I mean." He flexed his shoulders and scowled. "I don't really relish the idea of going at all. It's not my thing."

"So, why go?"

"Ben's my friend. And—" there was a pause "—I'll look like a jerk if I don't."

Diane would have said that it didn't matter what he looked like, that whatever people thought didn't matter, because certainly to her it never would have mattered.

But she realized that to Nick it did. People would have commented if he hadn't gone, they would have recognized his insecurity for what it was. And, recognizing it, never would have accepted him as their equal.

It was idiotic, in Diane's opinion. She also knew her opinion didn't matter. Nick, for all that he would never need to count on these people for his future, still didn't want to appear lacking in their eyes. He needed to show that he could handle their world with aplomb before he went back to his own.

"I'd be delighted to go with you," Diane said and leaned forward to kiss him on the cheek.

Nick turned his head, catching the kiss on his mouth instead, surprising her with the eagerness of his lips and the fervency of his response. He rested his forehead against hers and squeezed her nape gently with his hand. "You're a good sport," he said, his voice rough.

A GOOD SPORT.

As accolades went, it didn't go far. But, Diane supposed as they sat side by side that Friday afternoon on the bus heading toward Newport, coming from Nick, it meant a lot.

Just asking her to go to Bennett Hamilton's affair with him meant a great deal. It was not, as it sometimes seemed to her, Nick against her background; now it was Nick enlisting her support as he took on the society she moved comfortably in.

She slanted a glance at him now. He was slumped against the window, sleeping. He'd been sleeping ever since they'd changed buses in Providence. He'd slept down from Boston before that.

She knew he'd spent the last forty-eight hours in sleepless effort, working up final case-study presentations for two of his classes, going over them with a fine-tooth comb,

sounding them out on his study group, on Jared, on Annie, on her, on anyone who would listen.

And, having delivered them, he'd just had time to take
a last-minute call from his father regarding something
about herb farms and sources of fresh basil, before he
propelled her to the bus terminal, onto the bus, then had
sunk down beside her and given her a tired grin.

There, clasping her hand in his, he had fallen sound
asleep.

But now they were pulling into Newport, people were
rustling about gathering up shopping bags and cases, preparing to get off, and Diane knew she would have to wake
him.

She leaned over and brushed her lips across his cheek.
"Nick?"

Her breath stirred his lashes and he blinked, disoriented. Then he opened his eyes wider and a brief smile
flickered across his face. It vanished a second later when
he realized where they were.

He groaned. "Unfair."

Diane smiled. "What's unfair?"

"Being here with you."

"What's wrong with me?"

He shook his head. "Not you. Here." He scowled
around the bus. "I can think of a million places I'd rather
we were." He paused. "I was dreaming about one of
them."

The look on his face gave her a pretty accurate idea of
the place in his dreams. She blushed.

He laughed, then sighed and stretched mightily. "I'm
embarrassing you." He was still grinning, enjoying her
disconcerted look.

She ducked her head, then lifted it and met his gaze squarely. "You're not, you know," she said bluntly. "I'd like it, too."

She saw Nick swallow. He didn't speak, just looked at her, his blue eyes warm and worried.

Afraid she had said too much, she squeezed his hand and, as the bus slowed to a stop, moved to get up.

Nick held her fast. When she turned to look down at him, his gaze was compelling. "I'm glad," he said gruffly. Then he also got to his feet.

Bennett was waiting, and within moments had shepherded them from the crowded, noisy bus to the air-conditioned comfort of his black Jaguar XJ6 sedan.

"Not mine, actually," he apologized when they got in, Nick beside him in the front, Diane in the back. "My father's."

"It'll do." Nick grinned and put out a hand to Diane in the back seat. She took it in hers.

She'd been to Newport only twice. Once, when her grandmother had visited, they had driven down to visit a college chum of Gertrude's. Once she had come with her father when he had invited her along to crew with him on the sailboat of a man he knew.

Her grandmother's school chum had lived in a lovely old house not far from Hammersmith Farm on Narragansett Bay. But it couldn't compare to the opulence of the Hamilton "cottage" that overlooked First Beach and not the bay.

"What lovely gardens," she exclaimed as they turned into the private driveway and into the gates of the Hamilton estate.

"There's a maze, too," Bennett pointed out as the car purred along the curving driveway. "Tom and I used to play hide-and-seek there as kids."

"We had a small one at my grandparents' place." Diane said eagerly. "Aren't they great fun? I loved it, but my mother used to complain that she always got lost."

"Sounds like my aunt Lolly." Bennett laughed. "You'll meet her tonight. She's a stitch."

He proceeded to tell Aunt Lolly stories as he parked the car and led them up the broad marble stairway and into the palatial entryway of the house.

There a maid offered to show them to their rooms, but Bennett waved her off.

"Never mind. I'll take them up." He headed for the staircase that curved up to a second-floor balcony. "I'll introduce you to everyone else at dinner. Come along," he said blithely over his shoulder. "Scatter bread crumbs if you want, so you won't get lost."

Diane laughed. Nick managed a wan smile. She dropped back and fell into step beside him. "What's wrong?"

He shook his head. "Nothing. Just . . . tired."

He shifted his duffel bag to the other hand and smiled again. It was broader this time, determined, Diane would have said, but it didn't reach his eyes.

She squeezed his hand and pecked his cheek. "Come on. You must be exhausted. You can take a nap before dinner."

HE DIDN'T sleep. He was tired, all right. Exhausted, more like. But there was no point in lying down. He was far too keyed up for that. He might have slept on the way down. But that was before he'd caught sight of Bennett lounging against the fender of his Jag as the bus pulled up. Then he'd awakened in a hurry—to just how far from home he'd come.

This wasn't his scene. He didn't belong here, he told himself over and over as he paced the bedroom Bennett had stuck him in.

A major part of him wanted to cut and run, go home, back to the familiar, the comfortable, before he was discovered for the charlatan he was.

But he couldn't because he'd dragged Diane into this with him. If he vanished now he'd either have to take her with him or abandon her. Neither was an option. So he paced and sweated, glanced at his watch and chewed his lip.

"It doesn't matter," he told himself. But that was a lie; it mattered a hell of a lot.

Oh, not what the Hamiltons thought of him, or what their friends and acquaintances said. No, he didn't care about them in the least. He cared about Diane, about being the proper escort for her, about holding his own, about people not saying behind their hands or, worse, in front of them, "What on earth does she see in him?"

He wished he hadn't asked her. He wished he'd declined the invitation when it had come. Bennett wouldn't have cared, really. He was Nick's friend; he would have understood. Nick could have said he was too busy studying or he could even have told a partial truth, that renting the requisite tux was going to cost him far too much.

His father certainly thought it was a mistake. "What're you going there for?" Dominic had demanded when Nick had told him he'd be gone for the weekend. "You got studies, don't you?"

Nick had agreed he did.

"Then study. That's what you're there for. Next thing you know you'll be getting a swelled head," Dominic grumbled. "Try paying attention to my fresh basil problem if you have free time. We aren't going to have a restaurant if I don't get this solved."

Nick assured his father that he would give it consideration.

But when the invitation came, Diane had just told him she was going to stay in St. Louis. He had considered that, too, had mulled over its possibilities, and had known that he had a more pressing problem than fresh basil. In Diane Bauer he was dealing with more than a semester's fling.

He was dealing with something that might very well be called love.

In fact he had known it for some time, but he hadn't wanted to admit it. He admitted it then, admitted that she was going to come face-to-face with the Granatellis some time this summer. And it suddenly seemed imperative to show her that he could exist on her level of society, too.

Bennett's invitation, therefore, had seemed like a godsend.

Now it seemed like an invitation to doom.

He glanced at his watch again. Bennett had said drinks before dinner. Then dinner. Then port. Then dancing and celebration on the terrace. If he took it a step at a time, he might possibly make it. He'd start with a shower. The colder and more bracing the better.

AT PRECISELY five minutes to seven he presented himself outside Diane's door.

He didn't know if he was supposed to escort her down or not. He thought somewhat grimly that he should have spent less time on Lee Iacocca and more on Emily Post. Maybe they should have made etiquette part of the curriculum for those not to the manner born.

In any case, meeting her here seemed preferable. They'd have a couple of moments alone and Nick needed to see her alone, to reassure himself.

The sight, when she opened the door, was not reassuring.

She was a Diane he'd never met—an elegant, stunning Diane, wearing an off-one-shoulder floor-length peach silk that brought out the honey tones in her hair and in her skin.

She looked at him just as stunned.

His hand went to his tie. "Did I do it wrong?"

She shook her head quickly. "No! Not at all. You . . . you're beautiful."

He flushed, scowled, then shook his head again.

"I feel like an ass. The tie's too tight. I can't lift my arms in this jacket."

"You're not supposed to have to carry the furniture," Diane said, laughing.

He frowned, and eased his collar away from his neck, grimacing as he did so. "I still don't like it. Hell of a price to pay for beauty, strangulation."

Diane grinned. "Smile. Even if you're strangling it will look good on you."

"If you say so," he muttered ungraciously, then remembered his manners. "You're gorgeous," he told her and meant it. "More than gorgeous."

Diane smiled. "You like the dress?"

How could he not? It was the perfect complement to Diane's coloring and a marvel of engineering. Everything hung, literally, from one tiny pearl button at her left shoulder. From there on down everything clung with just the right amount of cling, swirled with just the right amount of swirl.

"It's…impressive," he managed in a gruff tone, which seemed a polite way of saying he'd love to rip the dress off her right then and there.

"Annie says it's supposed to drive you mad with desire," Diane told him.

"Annie's dead right."

Whatever Diane might have replied was lost because Bennett came bounding up the stairs just then. "Oh, good, you're ready. Drinks are being served in the parlor." He offered Diane his arm. "Shall we?"

She held out her other arm to Nick. He hesitated briefly, feeling a sudden stab of panic. Then, when she still waited expectantly, he took her arm.

"Ready," Diane said to Bennett.

"As we'll ever be," Nick muttered under his breath.

Dinner was a family affair, only three forks and a like number of spoons. He had no problems. He didn't actually expect he would—as far as the silverware went anyway. It was something far less tangible that worried him—a sense of belonging or of being out of place.

But dinner at the Hamiltons, even black tie, wasn't as foreign as he'd thought.

Diane laughed and chatted with Bennett's uncle Ralph on her left, and his eccentric aunt Lolly on her right. Periodically she caught Nick's eye and slanted a smile at him across the table.

At first his answering smiles were forced. But as the dinner wore on, he was able to do so more naturally because his fears weren't materializing. Bennett's cousin James, in his last year at Phillips Exeter, seemed somewhat awed by a man who didn't have a Mayflower genealogy and yet was making good anyway. Far from being put off by Nick's declaration of his background, James thought he was heroic.

"You're doing it yourself," James said. "That takes guts."

Nick felt suddenly ashamed of his chip-on-the-shoulder attitude and ducked his head. "I had a lot of encouragement along the way," he said. "I didn't do it on my own. My family helped."

"Well, sure," James said. "Families do," as if it were a given no matter where one lived or what one's circumstances were.

Nick began to feel maybe he wasn't so different after all.

After dinner and before the first of the evening's guests began to arrive, Ben took them on a tour of the estate.

The house was palatial, but not as daunting as Nick had expected. Or perhaps it was because he was more comfortable now. In any case, it didn't unnerve him, and he was able to appreciate it for what it was—welcoming, airy, and, of course, polished to perfection. The grounds were immaculate, the plantings color coordinated, the view incredible.

Diane smiled up at him, her gaze expectant. And this time he took her hand with more assurance, feeling a burgeoning of hope, a tiny bud of promise beginning to develop somewhere in the region of his heart.

By the time they walked back across the lawn the guests had begun to arrive. A string quartet was playing in the ballroom, and waiters were beginning to circulate there and on the terrace, offering trays with glasses of champagne and hors d'oeuvres.

Ben introduced them to one of his father's clients, the president of a stereo components company, apologized with a "Can you manage from here? I have to circulate," and gave them a grateful smile when they assured him they could.

As they stood there, the terrace filled with glittering groups of people, men in evening dress and women in gowns of every color and description. Before long even the cavernous ballroom seemed to be getting crowded.

He moved through the throng with Diane, making small talk with a few of his fellow students, answering the occasional question from one of Bennett's father's colleagues. Diane was in her element, talking and laughing, beautiful and poised in her peach-colored gown.

A starchy old man with a lot of brass on his uniform appeared and claimed her acquaintance. He was, he informed them, General Bachman, a friend of her grandmother's. If Diane had ever met him before, Nick couldn't tell. She greeted him with enthusiasm, asked about his recent tour of duty, which happened to have been in the Far East. This led to a discussion about his interest in ivory, and Diane began to question him about poaching, endangerment of species and the ivory trade.

Nick listened, awed. He was almost certain she had no previous interest in or knowledge of ivory, elephants or game poaching, but he never would have known from her conversation. And when the music started up and the general danced her away, he stood there with his mouth open, slightly dazed.

By the time the music ended she was nowhere to be seen. Nick craned his neck, feeling for the first time since he had got his bearings, incomplete without her. But the crowd was large and he sought her without success until the music began again, and she was danced past him once more.

This time she was in the arms of Peck, who was in his management seminar. Peck nodded to him, smiled at him. Nick scowled. Then they turned and Diane twirled in his direction, saw him and smiled a smile that stilled his fears.

He wanted her now more than he'd ever wanted her. And she disappeared into the throng again.

He didn't see her after that dance, either. Or the next. She was, if not the belle of the ball, certainly one of its foremost lights. While he fidgeted on the sidelines, trying again to catch a glimpse of her, she twirled about the room in the arms of all and sundry. And when he finally did spy her, he was trapped next to a potted palm, captive to three lawyers discussing obscure points of constitutional law.

Nick took a hasty swallow of his still full glass of champagne, slipped out from behind the lawyers and moved in her direction.

He didn't know who her partner was. He was certainly distinguished, clearly handsome, and probably far more eligible than Nick himself. But all evening long his desire for her had been building. It was time to make his move.

He didn't know if Miss Manners or Emily Post or the CEOs in attendance tonight approved of cutting in on dancers. He didn't stop to find out.

He stepped forward and tapped her partner on the shoulder. He turned, his smile fading into puzzlement.

"This dance is mine," Nick said.

"But—"

"Believe me. I'll take good care of her," he promised, then swept her away in his arms.

She smiled up at him, equally starry-eyed and bemused. "I think you shocked Justice Hammond."

"Probably." He didn't care himself, but it occurred to him that Diane might. "Does it matter?" he asked her.

"Not to me. I'm flattered."

"He's more eligible than I am. So's Peck for that matter," Nick said gruffly, wanting to make sure she understood.

"That doesn't matter, either," she said looking straight into his eyes, shrinking the universe until it contained none but the two of them. "No one matters but you."

Chapter Five

Nick was a here-and-now man. A doer.

He'd never been much for fairy tales, and before to-night, even though he'd had hopes, he would have said that that was what this was.

But tonight, with Diane in his arms, with the cellos playing, the trees aglitter, and the rise and fall of cheerful conversation all around him, he finally believed.

Tonight had been the proving ground, the place in which fantasies were tested, and Nick—and his fantasy—had been proved.

He had faced his fears. He had lived through, even enjoyed, an evening in Diane's milieu. He had handled it with aplomb. He knew that whatever future events her society background threw at him, he always could.

Of course he couldn't have her yet. There was one more hurdle to jump. One more year and he would have his degree, the symbol of success that would make him her equal. One more year and he wouldn't feel inferior to Gertrude Hoffmann, to Cynthia Bauer, and to all the St. Louis blue bloods who would wonder at her marrying a man like Nick Granatelli.

He wanted her now. This minute. It had been all he could do this evening to take her up to her door, kiss her with a hunger that ate at his very innards, then leave her to go to his own solitary bed.

But he'd done it because he believed in a future for the two of them.

Even now, still wanting her, still aching for the fulfillment of his love for her, he stayed in bed instead of heading for her room.

He stayed because the future he envisioned with Diane was one he would do everything in his power to make perfect, even if it meant holding off on the fulfillment of his more immediate desires.

He closed his eyes and focused on some nebulous future date in which he stood outside a home just slightly less grand than this one, Diane at his side, smiling up at him, loving him, while a bevy of golden-haired children played at their feet, and a cadre of contented relatives, both his and hers, smiled benevolently in the background.

It didn't make his yearning for her go away, but it did make it bearable.

And, if he allowed himself a few more carnal fantasies before the night was over, well, no one ever said Nick Granatelli was a saint.

THE BRISK TAPPING on the door woke him not long after dawn. Nick groaned, stretched and scowled at the bedside clock. It wasn't even six.

He'd been having a marvelous dream, better—or at least more graphic—than his deliberate fantasies of the night before.

Diane had featured prominently in it. So had the queen-size bed in which he now lay. They had been lying there together, naked, loving, their bodies growing hot and eager for the fulfillment they had so far denied themselves.

The dream was fading rapidly, but the need in his body was not. He hauled himself to a sitting position, waiting for another tap, wondering if he'd imagined it.

And if he hadn't . . .

It came again. Brisk. Impatient. But not loud.

Diane?

Could it possibly be Diane? No, he thought at once. But then a tiny voice inside him asked who else it could possibly be.

He closed his eyes in a moment of thankful prayer, then shifted the sheet to preserve his modesty, leaned back against the pillows, smiled and said, "Come in."

It was a maid he'd never seen before.

"Sorry to disturb you, sir," she said quickly, ducking her head. "You're Mr. Granatelli?"

Nick nodded, frowning.

"There's a phone call for you, sir. A Mr. Flynn."

Flynn? *Jared?* What the hell? Nick started to get up, remembered he was naked, and nodded. "I'll be right there."

"You can take it in Mr. Hamilton's study, sir. To the right at the foot of the stairs." She gave him a quick smile and left, shutting the door behind her.

Nick scrambled out of bed, snagged his jeans off the top of the bureau and pulled them on. Still zipping them he padded toward the door, opened it and headed down the hall.

Gardner Hamilton's study was right at the bottom of the marble staircase. Paneled in cherry, with glove-leather furniture and a thick Oriental rug, it seemed warm and welcoming on a still-chilly May morning. Nick curled his toes into the pile of the carpet and picked up the phone.

"Jared? What's wrong?"

"It's your father."

Nick groaned. "Cripes, what is it this time? More basil?"

"Basil?" Jared sounded doubtful. "I don't think so. He had a heart attack."

"IT'LL BE ALL RIGHT," Diane said. They were speeding back up the highway toward Boston in Bennett's Porsche. "I'm sure he'll be fine."

She wasn't sure at all. She was babbling and she knew it. She'd been babbling ever since Nick had banged on her door almost before it was light.

At first she'd thought Dominic Granatelli had died.

Nick, stunned into incoherence, had just kept saying, "He had a heart attack. My dad had a heart attack." His face had been chalky, his hands cold.

It had taken Diane several minutes to discover that, in fact, the senior Granatelli was still among the living. But just how bad he was, Nick didn't know.

"Do they want you to fly home?" she'd asked, putting her arms around him, holding him.

He had shaken his head. "I don't know."

"What hospital is he in?"

"I don't know that, either!" He pulled away, pacing irritably, slamming his hand down on the fireplace mantel. "I don't know what they want. I don't know what hospital he's in. I don't know how he is. I don't know anything at all, damn it!"

She put her hand on his bare arm. "I'll pack."

She had packed, first her things, then his. At her request the maid had awakened Ben who came hurrying from his own room wanting to know what he could do.

Nick, still pacing, didn't answer. Diane gave Ben a quick, grateful smile. "Just find out the quickest way for us to get back to Boston, will you?"

Nick raked his hand through his hair. "Find out the bus schedule," he snapped.

"Take my car," Ben said when he was told. "I'll have it brought around for you."

"I can't—" Nick began.

But Diane nodded. "Thanks."

Ben left hurriedly. Diane slid Nick's tux into the garment bag and zipped it up. "There. All set. Let's go."

She handed him the bag and his duffel, picked up her own and led the way downstairs. Numbly, Nick followed.

Ben's parents and brother were waiting at the bottom of the steps, all concerned and solicitous.

"If we can help..." Mr. Hamilton said.

"Do let us know." Mrs. Hamilton squeezed Nick's hand.

Tom clapped him on the shoulder. "Drive carefully."

But Nick didn't drive at all. He just stood there, dazed. It was Diane who stuffed the luggage into the back and then slipped behind the wheel of Ben's Porsche.

She looked up into Ben's family's faces. "Thank you all so much. I'll leave your car at your place," she told Ben.

"Don't worry about it. Here's a map in case you need it. Just see that he gets there." Ben's gaze went to Nick.

Diane smiled. "I will. Thanks again."

And without a backward glance, she set off.

Nick sat in silence beside her, his face still pale, a muscle working in his cheek. His hands clenched and unclenched against his thighs.

"Check the map for me, will you?" Diane said. "See if I'm on the right road for getting out of town."

Nick blinked at her. "Huh?"

"The map," Diane said patiently. "I don't know my way around."

Nick fumbled with the map, folded it open, stared at it blankly. "What if he dies?" he blurted.

Diane reached for his hand. "I don't think he's going to die," she said steadily. "He's what? Fifty-three?"

"Four," Nick said dully. "Fifty-four. He turned fifty-four in April, the thirtieth."

"He's a bull, then," Diane said. She gave his hand a squeeze. "A Taurus. They don't give up without a fight."

She wanted Nick to smile. She willed him to smile. But he didn't. He only clenched his jaw and shut his eyes against the world.

She groped her way out of Newport by dint of instinct and the occasional road sign. She couldn't read the map and drive at the same time, and Nick was no help at all.

"Jared said Frankie would call when they knew something," he said, staring blindly out the window as they sped through Fall River heading north. He pressed his palms against his eyes. "I wonder if they know something."

"Do you want to stop and call?"

"No. I'll wait." He gave a despairing laugh. "Who would I call? Where would I call them?"

Diane pressed harder on the accelerator. It was all she could do to help.

The traffic going into the city on Saturday morning was light and they made good time. Still there was no place near Nick's to park so Diane just pulled up at the curb.

"I'll let you off so you can see if they've called. I'll take Ben's car to his place and leave it, then come back. Okay?"

Nick was out of the car and heading up the steps without looking back.

IT WAS UNREAL. It all looked the same—his apartment with its mismatched lumpy and splintery furniture, its cache of unwashed dishes, its scattered books and papers, his final paper in Ethics still in rough form lying beside the computer, Jared's script on top of the refrigerator.

Yet it wasn't the same.

It was a whole new world, Nick thought as he punched out the telephone number on the slip of paper that Jared had handed him.

It was a world in which by now his father might be dead.

Jared hadn't been able to tell him much. When Frankie had called, she'd been gabbling, frantic.

Dominic had awakened in the middle of the night with indigestion, she'd told him. But it became clear quite soon that it was far more than that. When baking soda didn't quell his discomfort, and walking the floor only seemed to make it worse, he'd finally let Teresa call the hospital.

"He got worse before the paramedics got there," Jared had told Nick when he came in. "She said they were using all sorts of stuff to keep him going while they took him to the hospital."

"What hospital?" Nick demanded.

"She called back later to give me this number."

The number Nick was calling now.

It was a direct line to the Intensive Care Unit, but once he got it, Nick could barely form the words.

When he did, there was a pause, a "one moment, please," dead silence, then a nurse saying, "Mr. Granatelli is doing as well as can be expected right now."

Which meant, Nick hoped, that he wasn't dead. At least he didn't think "as well as can be expected" covered that particular eventuality.

"But how is he?" he demanded.

"One moment. I'll let you speak with Mrs. Granatelli. The doctor just talked to her."

Nick waited what seemed an interminable time.

Finally, "It's Frankie. Ma's in with Dad now. They only let you in for a minute or two every half hour."

"What happened?"

Frankie repeated most of what she'd told Jared, the information he already knew. "He had a small heart attack before Mama called the doctor and a major one while they were at the house." She swallowed and Nick heard her voice break. "He was so white, Nick. It was bad. Scary. I've never seen him so..."

She stopped and gulped back a sob. "And Mama...oh, God, Nicky. I've never seen Mama so upset."

Nick could well imagine. Teresa Granatelli's sun rose and set on her husband. He was the center of her world. "What about now? How is he now?"

"Stable, I think. A little better."

"Is he...do they think he's...?" But Nick couldn't even bring himself to ask.

"Going to make it?" Frankie said shakily into the silence. "I think so." She paused, then qualified. "I hope so. Who knows?" she almost wailed after a moment. "The doctors come out and tell you about his enzyme levels and his potassium. They do EKGs and have all these things that go bleep-bleep. But I don't know what it means. I don't know what any of it means! It's scaring the hell out of me!"

"I know." It was scaring the hell out of him, too.

Dominic Granatelli was invincible, unconquerable, the mainstay, the guiding light of his family's life, the rock on which the Granatelli fortress had been built.

Nick couldn't conceive of his father hurt, pained, laid low. He couldn't imagine a world in which Dominic Granatelli wasn't in control.

"What can I do?" he asked. There must be something. Damn it, there had to be!

Frankie didn't answer at once. It wasn't a question he'd ever asked her. It wasn't a question any of them had ever asked. They'd never had to; they'd always been told.

"I don't . . ." she began and her voice faded.

"I mean," Nick said hastily, realizing that she was no more used to making decisions than he was, "do you want me to come home now or what? Shall I catch a plane today?"

"I—I'll ask Mama."

"Then call me, will you? Call me right back."

"I will."

She hung up, but he didn't. He hung on to the receiver as if, even with the connection broken, the phone itself somehow linked him with his family. With his father.

"THANK GOD you're here," Jared said, hauling Diane unceremoniously into the apartment.

She glimpsed Nick across the room with his back to her, his ear to the phone. "What is it?" she demanded. "Is he—"

"He's talking to his sister now." Jared crossed his fingers. "I don't know the latest, but I've gotta run. We have a matinee at one. I was supposed to be there by ten, but I didn't want to leave him alone."

"No." Diane squeezed Jared's arm. "He's not alone now," she said. "I'll stay."

"Right." Jared shot Nick one last worried glance and left.

Diane stayed, watching him, worrying herself.

She wanted to do something, fix something, comfort him, make everything better. And she couldn't. It was out of her hands.

He had stopped talking now. She supposed he was listening. But then, slowly, he put the receiver down and stood motionless staring out the window.

She shifted from one foot to the other and the floor creaked beneath her. The sound seemed to penetrate his awareness. He turned, his face reflecting surprise at seeing her there.

"Where's Jared?"

"He had a performance. He wanted to stay, but—"

Nick raked his fingers through his hair. "I know. I know." He sighed and shut his eyes. "The show must go on." He didn't sound bitter, just dazed.

Diane went to him then, taking his hands in hers and simply holding them. They were still icy, and she chafed them between hers, trying to warm them. "Did you talk to the doctor?"

He shook his head. "My sister." He told her briefly what Frankie had told him, then bit down on his lower lip. "All of which means basically nothing at this point. We don't know a damned thing." There was a frantic note in his voice.

Diane held his hands more tightly. "You know he's hanging in there."

Nick bent his head so his forehead touched hers. Then he took a deep breath, held it, and then, slowly and deliberately, let it out. "Yeah," he said. "We know that."

Diane laid her hand against the nape of his neck, massaging the tense cords, ruffling his hair with her fingers, wishing again that she didn't feel so helpless.

"God," Nick muttered. "I don't believe this. I mean, just last night . . . just this morning I was . . . we were . . ." His voice trailed off, achingly.

"I know," Diane said and pulled him down onto the couch beside her. "I know."

There was nothing to do but wait. There were papers to write, notes to go over, exams to study for, but Nick did none of them, only sat, staring into the distance, his mind, his heart, more than a thousand miles away.

And Diane, whose heart was right here with him in this very room, could sit beside him just so long. Then she got up to move around quietly, make him cups of tea, touch him in passing, and listen to him whenever he muttered. But she didn't leave him even when her own finals, her own papers, her own life beckoned. None of it mattered so much as Nick.

Finally at just past two Frankie called back. Nick talked to her briefly, then to his mother. When he got off the phone he still looked shaken.

"He's hanging in there. They're planning to do a heart catheterization tomorrow if he's still doing all right. Then they'll be able to assess the damage and know what they're going to do."

"What about you?"

"I'm flying out tonight. I have to be there. I have to," he repeated.

And, seeing the tightness in his jaw, the strain in his face and the haunted look in his eyes, Diane knew that he did.

"I'll pack for you," she told him. "You book a ticket, then call your profs."

Having a goal, knowing what he was going to do, seemed to help.

Nick booked a flight, called his ethics prof and arranged to send in his paper, then began gathering together the books and papers he'd need.

Diane finished packing, then made sandwiches which neither of them ate.

"I can't," Nick said after one bite, and got up to pace the room.

"You haven't had anything all day," Diane reminded him. "Who knows when you'll get another chance?"

Nick shrugged. "They'll serve dinner on the plane."

Diane feigned hurt. "You'd rather eat airplane food than mine?"

For the first time that day a faint smile flickered across Nick's face. He crossed the room and put his arms around her.

"No," he said and brushed his lips across her cheek, leaning against her the warm, welcome weight of his body. "I'd rather have your peanut butter sandwiches than any airline's plastic shish kebab. I just…I just…" He sighed, and tried again, "I just can't."

And Diane held him in her arms, rested her head on his shoulder, rubbed her hands up and down his back, and loved him with all the love of which she was capable. "I know," she whispered. "I understand."

THE HOSPITAL was another alien world. A world of stainless steel and disposable plastic, of beepers and monitors, of leads and bags and tubes.

What mattered here was not the merger of Feinemann Plastics with ABC Chemical, was not the questionable ethical compromise when XYZ took over RST, was not the cost and quality of fresh basil or the best year for *Asti Spumante*.

What mattered—the only thing that mattered—was Dominic Granatelli's life.

All the way home on the plane Nick had told himself his father would be all right. His mother had said he was stable, that he was "doing well," that things were looking better.

He made himself believe it.

He wasn't aware, though, of how very much he'd wanted to believe it until he walked into the Intensive Care Unit and saw his father at the mercy of all those machines.

This was "stable"? This was "doing well"?

This was a man on the edge of death, a man held back from the brink by heaven knew what tenuous threads.

As he walked toward the immobile figure lying on the high, steel-edged bed, Nick felt as if someone had punched him in the gut.

"D-dad?"

Slowly his father's eyes opened, focused on him, blinked. His lips moved but no sound came out.

"I'm here," Nick said softly.

Dominic's hand moved, and Nick reached for it, feeling the rough fingers curl weakly around his. He swallowed against the tightening in his throat.

"Nick. Good." Dominic managed something resembling a smile. "Take care of . . . rest . . . restaurant."

Nick rubbed his father's hand. "I will. Don't worry. I'll take care of everything."

Dominic's lips worked again, but no words came out. The few that he said had exhausted him. He, however, managed another smile.

It was his father's smile that Nick clung to over the next twenty-four hours. It was the memory of that smile that helped him leave the hospital when everyone else was coming so that he could do what he knew his father wanted him to do—go to the restaurant and keep everything running the way it should.

Granatelli's restaurant was the family's livelihood, its security, the one sure thing that stood between the family and economic peril.

As such it had to be cared for at any cost, even if it meant that while Frankie and Carlo, Vinnie and Paula and Sophia took turns going in with Teresa to see Dominic every half hour, Nick wasn't there.

The supplies had to be logged in, the orders made, the laundry delivery received, the dirty linens sent out. Little things. Big things. Necessary things.

So when everyone else hovered around waiting while Dominic went down for his heart catheterization the following day, when everyone else paced the hallways waiting for the doctor's verdict, when everyone else conferred about Dominic's scheduled surgery, Nick wasn't there.

SHE'D ASKED him to call.

He did. Once.

He sounded distant, vague. Not like Nick at all.

Diane worried, fretted, stewed. She finished her own papers, took her last finals, paid her library fines, picked up her cap and gown for Saturday's commencement exercise. But all the while, she worried about Nick.

She hesitated to call him. She didn't want to intrude, didn't want to distract him, didn't want to create pressure in a situation where there was clearly already more than enough.

But she did want to know. She cared what happened to Dominic Granatelli.

She loved Nick.

It was Jared who finally got some news and Annie who passed it on to Diane.

"He's on his way," Annie said without preamble, walking into the apartment.

Diane, who'd been trying to decide if she dared call her father and invite him to her graduation the next morning, thereby risking a confrontation between her father and her mother and stepfather or, worse, one between her father and grandmother, suddenly forgot them all. "Who?"

"Your one true love."

All her worries fled in the face of the news. "Nick? He's coming? Now?"

Annie nodded. "Jared said he called this morning."

For a moment Diane wondered why he hadn't called her. But then she realized she'd been gone all morning, spending one last tutoring session with her French students, so she wouldn't have been here even if he had.

"What else did he say?"

"Not much. His dad came through the surgery all right. Quintuple bypass, Jared said." Annie grimaced. "Sounds pretty rough to me."

It sounded rough to Diane, too. The one time Nick had called her, he had just found out that his father was going to have surgery. At the time he hadn't known when or how extensive it would be.

Still, Dominic must be doing well now if Nick was returning. For the first time since Nick had told her the news, she felt as if a weight had been lifted off her chest.

She smiled. She grinned. She closed her eyes, breathed deeply and then opened them again to a brighter, newer world.

"Thank God," she said.

She called Jared. "How's he getting home? When's he coming in?"

"He said he'd take a taxi. He should be getting here about ten."

"I'll meet him."

"You can't," Annie reminded her. "It's dinner at the Ritz tonight. Remember?"

Diane hadn't. In fact she'd totally forgotten her graduation dinner. At ten she would be in her parents' hotel suite visiting with Cynthia and Matthew and Gertrude who had come for her graduation.

There was no tactful way to get out of it. They didn't even know Nick existed, and the logistics of the family celebration dinner before her graduation had all been planned for months.

Matthew had, with his customary consideration, called her clear back in February to find out where she wanted to go to celebrate.

"I just want to be with all of you," she told him.

"Then we'll eat in the suite," he replied. "I think that's a fine idea. Easier on your grandmother, too."

Gertrude cultivated the notion that things should be made easier for her. She was, after all, she told them frequently, "not as young as she used to be."

Privately Diane didn't think age was slowing her grandmother down at all. But if she wanted to propagate the image of herself as a doddering septuagenarian, who was her granddaughter to oppose her?

"Sounds fine," she'd said to her stepfather. "I'm looking forward to it."

Since Nick had left, though, she'd all but forgotten it.

Now she groaned as the mantle of family obligation settled on her shoulders.

"Tell Nick . . ." She cast about for something appropriate and could think of nothing. She wanted to tell Jared to tell Nick she loved him. But so far she hadn't even told it to him herself.

"Tell him I'll call him in the morning or he should call me. All right? Tell him I wanted to be there, but . . ." She trailed off, helpless.

"I'll tell him," Jared assured her. "He'll understand."

Diane hoped so.

SHE HADN'T SEEN her parents or grandmother since Christmas. Five whole months. It seemed a lifetime. Yet her first impression, when her mother opened the hotel suite door that evening, was that none of them had changed a bit.

Diane had.

At Christmas she had been a child, smiling, blissful, innocent, unaware. Now she had awakened to the potential of her womanhood. She had fallen in love.

She stood motionless in the doorway wondering if they could tell.

Was her love of Nick written as clearly on her face as it was rooted in the depths of her soul?

Whatever showed on her face, Cynthia Bauer was obviously overjoyed to see it. She flung her arms around her daughter, hugging Diane for all she was worth.

Then, stepping back, she held Diane at arm's length, her blue eyes shining as she looked her over from head to toe.

Diane found that she was looking at her mother with new eyes, too. Though she was aware of having her mother's honey-blond hair and figure, she knew that her features were her father's. She had Russell Shaw's wide brown eyes, his slightly shy smile.

Did her mother see those things? Diane wondered. Did she ever think about him?

Had she loved him once the way Diane loved Nick?

And what about her love of Matthew?

They were questions she'd never really dwelt on before. Adult questions. She couldn't ask. At least not now. But seeing her mother and Matthew again, receiving their embraces, their love, made her wonder.

It also settled her debate about asking her father to her graduation.

She had learned to like the man who'd fathered her. She was, in a way, coming to love him. But she wasn't going to call him.

It would please her if he came to her graduation. But loving Nick had sensitized her more than ever to the feelings of others, and she knew that chances were too great that either he or Cynthia—possibly even Matthew—could be hurt.

She looked into her mother's face now, then her gaze shifted to Matthew who was smiling at her with equal love and pride.

"I think graduation is making a woman of our girl, Cynthia," he said to his wife.

Cynthia hugged her once more. "I think you're right."

Diane could have told them what had really done it. But she didn't—not then. That would come later, when the time was right.

She answered Matthew's questions about the ceremony, her mother's about where Annie was and if her parents had arrived. She crossed the room to where her grandmother sat in regal elegance, bent down and kissed Gertrude's lightly rouged cheek.

"You look wonderful," she told her grandmother.

"Ought to," Gertrude said tartly. "I work hard enough at it."

Diane smiled and sat down next to her when Gertrude patted the seat of the couch. The conversation became easy and general.

Diane, for the most part, contributed little. She sat back after the meal and listened while Gertrude held forth, while Cynthia added the occasional tidbit, while Matthew interposed a comment here and there.

Most of the time she thought about Nick, wondered if he was back yet, wondered how he was, how his father was doing.

Only when Gertrude raised her voice, did she attend carefully to the conversation.

"Flo's a scatterhead, if you ask me," Gertrude said now. "I know she's your sister, Matthew, but that's no excuse. It's outrageous. One never knows what she's going to do next."

"But she's wonderful with Diane, Mother," Cynthia said quietly. "And it's so kind of her to ask Diane to spend the summer with her."

"Probably wants her to carry the luggage," Gertrude sniffed. "Don't know why I let you talk me into it."

"It will be good for Diane," Matthew said with gentle firmness. "She needs a chance to spread her wings."

Gertrude fiddled with her glasses. "In my day girls didn't need to spread their wings," she said. "Did what they were told."

"Diane always does what she's told," Cynthia reminded her mother in a light tone.

Gertrude looked down her considerable nose. "Better than some, I suppose," she agreed shortly.

Diane saw her mother stiffen, but she didn't reply.

"Anyway, it's settled," Matthew said briskly, stepping between his wife and her mother, ending the discussion right there.

He was so good at that, Diane thought. Matthew could always diffuse the tensions that built up between the Hoffmann women. He never raised his voice, never argued, never fought. He just spoke, clearly and forthrightly, and even Gertrude didn't dare disagree with him.

Under the circumstances Diane didn't think that now was the time to tell them she'd changed her mind about spending the summer with Flo.

She would talk to them later, first Matthew, then her mother and, if necessary, her grandmother. Matthew would help her handle whatever problems arose.

She straightened her dress and stood up. "I really need to go," she told them. "I have a big day tomorrow."

Cynthia laughed. "Indeed you do. Are you sure you won't stay here?"

Diane shook her head. "Thanks, but it's sort of special, really. My last night with Annie as an undergrad. We've been together four years."

"I'll see you home, then," Matthew said.

"I'll be fine in a taxi," Diane assured him. "You stay here. You're tired. I know you are."

It was an indication of how very tired he was that her stepfather let her persuade him. But he did accompany her down and saw her into the taxi.

"Will we see you for breakfast?" He bent down and peered into the taxi.

"I don't think so. We've got to get ready." *And I've got to see Nick.* She gave Matthew an apologetic shrug and a quick smile.

He leaned down and pecked her cheek. "Then we'll see you at graduation, sweetheart."

The taxi pulled away, and Diane, already thinking about seeing Nick in the morning, already anticipating the feel of his arms around her and the touch of his lips on hers, didn't even look back as the cab turned the corner and drove out of sight.

Chapter Six

He had it all figured out.

He would dash over to Professor Riggs's office first thing, drop off the last case-study evaluation, which he'd been allowed to write up, then swing by his other professors' offices, get their comments, check his grades.

Not because it mattered now. Not even the paper mattered now.

But for purely academic reasons and just a bit of personal satisfaction, he wanted to know.

Then he'd come back and finish packing, say goodbye to Jared, hope to catch Diane and Annie and wish them well. Then he would head back for the airport and take off.

It was simple.

Organized.

The way he'd done everything lately.

The way he was running his life.

He did well, too, making the stop at Riggs's brief and perfunctory. His explanation about his situation was brief, too. If Riggs didn't understand, well, it couldn't be helped. Nick was simply doing what had to be done.

He did the same with Edmonds and Cooper. Their comments were favorable. His grades were good. They would, he knew, have served him well. He felt a momentary satisfaction. The regrets he wouldn't dwell on now.

He got back to the apartment just as Jared was waking up.

His roommate rolled over in bed and regarded him and then all the gear lined up by the door with one half-opened eye.

"You've already packed?" His tone was incredulous, and as they really hadn't had a chance to talk the day before, Nick couldn't blame him.

He consulted his watch. "Got to." He grimaced. "Flight's at one."

"Flight?" Jared sat up, rubbing his fists against his eyes. "You'll be leaving?"

"I'm leaving."

"Your father? Is he worse, then?"

Nick's smile was grim. "He's recovering. But it will be a long, long haul, and even then we don't know how much he'll be able to do." He shrugged and stuck out his hand. "I've left my share of the rent with Mrs. Patchin. I wish I could've hung on a bit longer, but—" He shrugged again.

Jared inclined his head briefly, then shook Nick's hand. "You do what you have to do," he said simply.

Their eyes met in complete understanding.

Nick nodded. "Yeah. That's it."

The last thing he had to do before he left was stop to see Diane and Annie.

He supposed he could have gone without taking the time. In the end, of course, it would make no difference.

Something else that didn't matter now, he thought as he lugged his gear down the stairs and left it by the front door.

But it was the right thing to do—the polite thing to do. So he would stop by, explain his plans and say goodbye before going.

It would be brief. Ten minutes. No more.

He opened the door and saw Diane coming up the walk.

She was smiling, her long hair streaming out behind her, her arms opening to him as she came.

Nick felt something twist in his heart.

And then she had her arms around him, her hair in his face. And he was drowning in the lemon scent of her shampoo and the soft, flowery freshness that was Diane alone. Automatic and unbidden, his arms came up to hold her close.

"I'm sorry I wasn't there last night. I wanted to come. I missed you so much. I— Oh, Nick!" And she kissed him full on the lips.

And whatever was twisting inside him tore then, as, for one desperate moment, he kissed her back.

Then he pulled away, looked down into her welcoming eyes, steeled himself, and forced a smile.

"I was just coming to see you."

She beamed. "I beat you to it."

A moment of silence, of expectation, hung between them. Then Diane took his hands in hers. "Your father? Is he better?"

"Some."

"I thought he must be since you're here." She smiled up at him again. "I'm so glad you're back. I don't begrudge them wanting you there, but I—"

"I . . . came to get my gear."

His words halted hers. A tiny frown appeared between Diane's brows as she looked at him. "What do you mean?"

"I'm going back."

"Back? To St. Louis?"

He nodded.

"When?"

"Today. I have a flight at one."

There was another pause while she digested that. "For the end of the year," she said. "You finished your paper? Turned it in?"

"Yes."

Traffic hummed past them as they stood on the sidewalk. Pedestrians pushed past them. A bus, chugging away from the corner, choked them with diesel fumes.

"Well, good," Diane said, mustering a smile. "Then you've finished everything up."

He nodded.

Now, he told himself. *Tell her now.* But he couldn't say it. Couldn't form the words.

He let go of her hands and stuffed his own in the pockets of his jeans. He studied the toes of his shoes, watched a gum wrapper blow past down the street.

"I'll be coming home in a week," Diane told him. Unable to take his hand, she laid hers on his arm. "I'll come and see you then. Maybe I can meet your father. I—"

"No."

Her eyes jerked up to meet his. "Only if he's well enough," she said hastily. "I won't intrude. I just—"

Nick shook his head quickly, desperately. "No. No, it's not that. It's—" He stopped, casting about for a way to express the inexpressible. He thought wryly of all those management classes, all the glib verbal footwork he'd been so good at in class. "Golden-tongued Granatelli," Ben used to call him.

But now—when it mattered—he couldn't say a word.

Diane was looking at him, her eyes wide and almost frightened now. There was a bewildered innocence in her face that made him ache.

But it was just exactly that innocence that made him press on with what he had to say.

He took a breath and began. "I'm not coming back next year."

"Not . . ."

"I can't! It isn't that I don't want to. I can't. I have to work now, full-time, at the restaurant. It's on my shoulders. All of it."

"Your father . . ."

"Is in for a long recovery. He's doing all right. But the doctor isn't making any promises about when or if he'll be back at work. He's got to live a whole new life-style. New diet, new behavior. No stress. And for him no stress means no restaurant." He met her gaze steadily, determinedly, almost defiantly.

For a long while Diane didn't speak. She bit down on her lip, obviously weighing his words.

"That doesn't mean we—" she began finally.

Knowing what was coming, he moved to cut it off. "It means, there is no 'we.' " He said the words harshly, with every ounce of determination he could muster.

And he meant them.

He'd done a lot of thinking during the last week in the wee hours of the night, which was just about the only time he had to think anymore. And the conclusion he had come to was that a future with Diane Bauer was a pipe dream.

Once it might have seemed remotely possible. Once, when an MBA was a probability, when a privileged future was a possibility, he had the right to consider it.

He couldn't consider it now.

She couldn't consider it now.

He thought about the night they'd gone to Jared's play, how astonished he'd been at gifts his roommate had that he hadn't even suspected, that hadn't had a chance to be revealed until Jared was given the opportunity.

It was the same with Diane. He thought how she'd blossomed the night of the Hamiltons' party, how she'd charmed every person she'd met. She belonged in an environment like that. She deserved opportunities like that.

He couldn't promise her any.

On the contrary, all he could promise her was a future on The Hill. It was all right for him. He'd been groomed for it. He understood it. It would simply stifle her.

"To love someone is to want what's the best for them," his grandfather had once told him.

Nick knew what was best.

"Forget me," he said gruffly when she didn't speak.

"Forget you?" Diane looked at him, aghast.

He shrugged negligently. "There are bound to be plenty of men willing to come along and take my place."

She looked stricken. "But I don't want any other man!"

Oh, hell. Nick's fists clenched in his pockets. His toes curled inside his shoes. He held himself rigid, controlled. "Don't be stupid," he said.

Diane's eyes widened. She opened her mouth, but no sound came out.

"Look," Nick said, desperate. "I'm not coming back. I'm not getting my MBA I'm going home to St. Louis and I'm going to be there the rest of my freakin' life. I have a family there and they need me! I have to go!"

She didn't even hesitate. She lifted her chin and looked right at him. "I'll come with you," she said.

For a split second he wanted to say yes. He wanted to grab her offer with both hands and hold it tight. He wanted to hold her tight, to close his eyes and believe that dreams might come true, that good might prevail, that a future for the two of them together might go on happily ever after.

He wasn't that much of a fool.

"Marry me, you mean?" he asked her now with gentle mockery.

There was a stricken pause, as if she had just realized what she was offering, as if she'd just noticed that, standing in the middle of a crowded sidewalk, she might actually have made a proposal of marriage. She hesitated, color rioting on her cheeks.

Nick wanted to reach out and brush his thumbs across them. His nails bit into the palms of his hands. He allowed himself a small smile as he said simply, lightly, "It wouldn't work."

Diane, obviously deciding that yes, she had proposed and meant it, lifted her chin. "Why not?"

"Think about it. Really think about it. Think about a future with me there. Would you be happy on The Hill for the rest of your life?"

"If you're—"

"Don't say, if you're there. It won't wash." He made his voice deliberately hard. "You're kidding yourself. You don't know what my life is like. You've had it easy, Diane. Anything you wanted, you got."

"That's not fair, Nick!"

He shrugged. "Life isn't fair. I wouldn't be quitting school if life was fair. But it isn't and I am. I have a job to do, a family to support, a life already laid out for me."

"Nick—"

"Listen to me. You don't even know who you are yet. You're only twenty-two years old. You've got your whole life ahead of you. You can do anything, go anywhere, meet anyone. You don't know what you want. And I'm damned if I'm going to wake up some morning with a discontented wife, a wife who thinks the world has passed her by because she's stuck with a guy running a restaurant for a living. I have enough on my plate without that."

She stared at him, her jaw slack.

"It was fun while it lasted," he said, moving in for the kill. "You're a nice kid. But it won't work. It would never work. I have my life all cut out for me. You don't fit."

Chapter Seven

New York City, September 1990

"Ma, no. Ma!" Annie could say it in her sleep now. "No, forget it." Pause. "I don't believe this."

This last, muttered to herself, wasn't true. Lucia D'Angelo's matchmaking attempts had become the one constant in Annie's otherwise unpredictable life. Still, it didn't mean she welcomed them.

"Ma..."

But Ma went on. And on.

Annie considered strangling herself with the phone cord, then wished her mother were closer so she could strangle her instead.

"Ma, I don't—" But it didn't matter what she didn't because Lucia D'Angelo was in full spate again. Annie glowered out at the brief summer thunderstorm that was making the rain sluice down the windows of her West Side apartment. Her mother's voice rose and fell on the other end of the line.

There was another pause. "No," Annie said into it. "How many times? How many men? I don't want you to send me any more men, Mother! I'm through with men!"

More cajoling. More plaintive guilt-inspiring lamentations emanated from her mother.

"I don't care if he's handsome, Ma." Annie banged her head softly against the windowpane. "I don't care if he's Italian. I don't—"

There was a sudden *brrrring* from the buzzer at her door. Annie frowned. Nobody had buzzed to be let in downstairs.

But then, she thought, when did that make a difference? With eight apartments in the brownstone where she lived, somebody was always letting somebody else's guests in.

Lucia, having taken her daughter's pause for the opportunity to get in more of her current hopeful's qualifications, rattled on.

There was a second ring. Sharp and insistent.

Annie crossed the room and peeked through the spyhole. Startled, she pulled back, frowned, then peeked again. Shaking her head, she hurriedly unlocked and jerked open the door. She stopped dead and stared.

Lucia kept on talking.

"Ma, I don't care. I don't want to know. Ma," Annie interrupted her, "I'm not interested in your handsome Italian hunks. Right here on the doorstep I've got one of my own."

And she hung up before Lucia could say another word.

"Nick."

It wasn't a question. There *was* no question.

It was definitely Nick, as large as life and as handsome as ever—if you discounted the several days' stubble on his cheeks—standing in the doorway looking back at her.

He wore holey sneakers, faded jeans and a St. Louis University sweatshirt with the sleeves cut short and the neck ripped out. And as much as he looked gorgeous, he also looked exhausted and rumpled. On the floor behind him were two navy duffel bags.

"Can I come in?"

There was a hesitancy in his voice that surprised her. Nick had never been short on self-confidence.

Of course, she hadn't seen him for a year and a half since cousin Mario's wedding. People changed, she thought grimly. She, of all people, should know that.

But she stepped back and waved him in, then shut the door behind him. "What are you doing here?"

"I'm running away from home."

HE KNEW IT SOUNDED melodramatic. Childish. Idiotic.

But he didn't know what else you could call it, really.

He had, in truth, run away from home.

And if he hadn't exactly stolen away in the dark of night or tied up all his worldly belongings in a bandanna and hitched a freight train north, he had still taken everything that mattered to him, loaded it silently and deliberately in the back of his '88 Toyota and, with his mother looking on in anguish, his brothers and sisters staring in amazement and his father caught in the middle of banging on the fender, he had driven off without looking back.

He hadn't said where he was going. He hadn't said when he'd be back. He hadn't said *if* he'd be back.

He wasn't sure he would be. Not at any time in the foreseeable future, at any rate.

"Does this mean you want me to hide you?" Annie asked him now, her expression curious and slightly bemused.

Nick flushed. "I don't think you'll have to, actually." His mouth twisted. "I doubt they're looking."

Annie's brows lifted. "You are Nick Granatelli, aren't you? Hotshot entrepreneur? Heir apparent? The whiz kid from Harvard who turned Granatelli's into the 'hottest spot on The Hill'? That's according to the *St. Louis Post-Dispatch*. The—''

"Stuff it," Nick said gruffly. He scowled and dug his toe into the worn carpet.

Annie gave him a quick smile and patted his arm. "Sorry. Just my flaky sense of humor getting the better of me." She slanted him a sideways glance. "You weren't kidding about running away?"

Nick sighed and shook his head.

She weighed that, then nodded. "So, you need a place to stay and you've come to Auntie Annie?"

He grimaced, then scratched the back of his head, feeling again like an idiot. He shouldn't have bothered Annie. He didn't know why he had. He'd been thinking of Jared when he'd headed this way. The summer he'd left Cambridge and returned to St. Louis, Annie and Jared had moved together to New York.

"You'll get lost there," Nick had warned them.

But Annie and Jared had shrugged happily. "It's a great city to get lost in," they'd told him. Besides, they had each other.

They were friends, Jared had told him. Colleagues. Yeah, sure, Nick had said, unable to believe that Jared's interest was only collegial. But all his speculation seemed to have been wrong.

Jared and Annie had, indeed, shared the apartment for a year. Then Jared had got a fantastic offer from Hollywood to star in a weekly adventure series about an Interpol investigator.

Nick had expected both he and Annie would go. It was a surprise, then, when Jared called him one day to talk about his new career and Nick had asked how Annie was.

"I haven't a clue," Jared had said.

"She isn't with you?"

"She isn't with me."

"But I thought—"

"Think again, my lad. Annie's an actress, remember? She has her own career in New York." If there was bitterness in Jared's voice, Nick wasn't quick enough to detect it. And as Jared had gone right on to talk about something else, that was the last overt reference either of them had made to Annie.

So they had been just good friends after all, Nick concluded. When Nick had seen Annie at her cousin Mario's wedding a year and a half ago, she'd confirmed it.

"Do you miss Jared?" Nick had asked her while they were dancing together.

She'd shrugged. "I have my work. And there's plenty to keep me busy in New York."

Perhaps it was the notion that there was plenty to keep one busy in New York that had drawn him to the city. Or maybe it was because, as he had told Annie and Jared earlier, one could get lost there.

Or maybe it was because Annie was the closest he could get right now to the person he suddenly found himself thinking about more than anyone.

The person he lay awake at night remembering.

Maybe he hadn't intended to come to New York at all. Maybe he'd just been passing through on his way to Cambridge when he came to his senses. Because, heaven knew, a part of him wanted to go back to Cambridge, to try to rethink things, to discover where he had gone wrong.

But there was no point in going on to Cambridge, he realized sometime on the third day of his wanderings.

You couldn't go back. You couldn't change things.

You simply had to go on.

"I—I drove around for a few days," he said when it became clear that Annie was waiting for an explanation. "I wasn't heading anywhere really. I...just ended up here. If you want me to leave—''

Annie rolled her eyes. ''Don't be a fool. Put your gear in the bedroom. You can sleep on the sofa. You're welcome to stay as long as you want.''

He hesitated, not having thought it would be that easy. But when Annie just waited expectantly, he nodded, picking up his duffel bags again and heading toward the bedroom. ''Thanks, Annie. You're a pal.''

''Oh, yes,'' Annie said dryly. ''Oh, yes.''

DIANE HAD BEEN STANDING in front of the restaurant for twenty minutes. Another five and she'd have to give up on Annie and head down to the Village lunchless. She never should have agreed to meet her given her schedule today, but when Annie insisted, one didn't say no.

At least Diane never had.

''Lunch?'' she'd said when Annie had called her at eight in the morning jolting her out of a sound sleep. ''You want to 'do' lunch?''

''Doing lunch'' was not an Annie D'Angelo thing. Annie was a pizza-after-the-matinee, BBQ-after-the-night-show sort of person.

''Yeah, lunch,'' Annie said. ''What's wrong with that? We've got to eat, don't we?''

''Well, yes, but...''

''I'll meet you at Fernando's at twelve.''

''Make it eleven-thirty,'' Diane had said. ''I've got a tour at one.''

But it was now nearly twelve and Annie was nowhere to be seen.

Pacing up and down in front of Fernando's was a questionable activity at the best of times. A Chelsea dive whose only redeeming feature was its Tex Mex dim sum,

Fernando's was not the best place for a single woman to hang out. Diane glanced at her watch once more before she moved toward the bus stop.

"Whoa! Wait! I'm here!"

Diane spun around to see Annie hurtling down the sidewalk toward her, waving madly. She stopped, looked at her watch, arched an eyebrow, tapped her foot.

Annie shrugged unrepentantly. "Sorry. I got caught in traffic. Should've taken the subway."

"I only have forty minutes," Diane told her as they went into the restaurant. "I have to be at Washington Square at one."

"What is it this time?"

"Writers' Paradise: lives, loves and landmarks of Village Literati," Diane recited as they slid into opposite sides of a cramped vinyl booth.

Annie grinned. "Very poetic. They ought to eat it up."

"They do."

"Business is booming?"

Diane nodded. She had been developing her own business in the last year—giving walking and bus tours to out-of-towners, in her case mostly non-English speaking tourists or business people.

She'd discovered the need during her work as a night concierge at a luxurious midtown hotel. She'd moved slowly at first, done some research, talked to people in the business—both the hotel and the tour business. Then, last April, when the walking tour season had begun again in earnest, so had Diane. She kept her concierge job for security for the time being. But Manhattan Meanderings was becoming an increasing success.

The waiter appeared with menus.

Annie waved him away. "Dim sum for both of us."

The waiter nodded and reappeared moments later with a cart laden with a variety of house specialties, half of them Chinese, half of them Mexican.

Annie made her choices with her usual rapid-fire intensity. Diane pondered a bit, then picked two.

"That's all?" Annie scowled.

"I'm not very hungry. I'm trying to think." Diane poked at her cheese enchilada, then broke off a piece with her fork. "I've got to come up with a way to make Greenwich Village writers relevant to Japanese teenagers. I'm distracted, I guess."

"You'll be even more distracted when I tell you the news."

The fork paused halfway to Diane's mouth. "What news?"

"Nick's here."

Normally Fernando's at lunchtime was a place in which a person had to shout to hear himself think. It seemed to Diane that at that moment a drop of water hitting the ocean might have easily been heard.

It was her imagination, of course. The noise level was just what it always was. Only in her head was there this pool of unending silence.

Annie speared a wonton, dipped it in salsa and waved it on the end of her fork. "He's in my apartment this very minute."

Diane's enchilada fell unnoticed to her plate. She set her fork down and knotted her fingers together in her lap. "Nick," she said, as if the word were in a foreign language, incomprehensible, difficult to get her tongue around.

"Nick," Annie repeated. "Granatelli," she added helpfully in case there was some mistake.

But Diane hadn't made a mistake. For her there was only one Nick in all the world.

"Oh," she said after a long moment.

What else was there to say?

Nick Granatelli was part of her past. A memorable part, to be sure. But not a part she dwelt on often. Not a part she wanted to dwell on now.

In actual fact she felt acute discomfort whenever she thought about him very much. It was far better to gloss over the months when she had been a naive young idiot who thought that all she had to do was wait and the world—and a husband—would drop comfortably into her lap.

Deliberately she picked up her fork again and speared the piece of enchilada she had dropped, putting it into her mouth, chewing slowly, concentrating on the bustle of humanity swirling through Fernando's, on the talk she was going to have to give in less than an hour, on the date she was going to have with Carter MacKenzie tonight.

"He's run away from home."

Diane choked, then spluttered.

Annie grinned. "Truly. That's what he said."

Diane gave her a skeptical look. "What does it mean?"

"That he isn't working at Granatelli's anymore, apparently. That his father is back running things. That he just . . . left."

Diane didn't think that sounded very likely. Granatelli's was in Nick's blood. Sometimes she'd doubted he had blood at all, suspecting that it was perhaps spaghetti sauce that ran through his veins.

No, that was unfair, she chastised herself. He was simply committed to the family enterprise. She'd known that, had accepted it, had wanted to be a part of it.

Had been turned down.

Not enough spaghetti sauce in the Shaw-Hoffmann veins apparently.

Annie seemed to be waiting for some further response, so Diane shrugged. "I hope he's happy," she said, then deliberately finished off her enchilada and began picking her way through her refried beans and cashews.

"Is that all you can say?"

"What am I supposed to say?"

Annie gave her an impatient glower. "Once you wanted to marry him."

"Yes," Diane said, proud of how indifferent she sounded. "But, as you'll recall, he didn't want to marry me."

She shoved her plate away, glanced at her watch and slid out of the booth. "Got to run," she said. "Tours wait for no one." She pulled her wallet out of her purse.

"This one's on me," Annie said.

"But—"

"You've fed me often enough. The least I can do is treat you to a couple of refried beans." Annie was smiling up at her, her expression compassionate, understanding.

Diane felt unaccountably like slapping her. She didn't want compassion. She didn't want understanding. She was past both where Nick Granatelli was concerned. She just wanted to forget him and have everyone else forget him, too.

"See you Tuesday at softball," she said over her shoulder. "Thanks for lunch."

"Don't mention it."

Diane wouldn't. She wished Nick Granatelli hadn't been mentioned, either.

IT WAS ONE THING to refuse to go for the bait. It was quite another to deny that the bait had been offered.

And if Diane hadn't asked Annie any questions about Nick, it didn't mean she wasn't interested in the answers.

She took her fifteen Japanese university students on a brisk Village walk, pointing out the former homes of writers like John Dos Passos, Sherwood Anderson, Henry James, Mark Twain, Edna St. Vincent Millay, e.e. cummings, Marianne Moore, Theodore Dreiser, and John Reed. She talked knowledgeably about their works, their lives, their loves, but her mouth was on automatic. Her mind was preoccupied with Nick.

It was curiosity, of course. Nothing more.

She hadn't seen him or heard from him in over two years. He had gone back to St. Louis and she had gone to spend the summer with Auntie Flo in Provence.

From there she had gone to the Sorbonne for a term, to Tokyo for a term, and then she'd come to New York. Nick, she presumed, had stayed in St. Louis. He had, he'd been at pains to assure her, intended to remain in St. Louis for the rest of his life.

So she couldn't help but be curious. She wanted to know about this "running away from home" business. It didn't sound like the Nick she knew at all.

But then, she asked herself in a moment of honesty, had she really known Nick Granatelli?

And the answer was, probably not.

Certainly she'd thought she had. In her youthful naiveté she had imagined that she had known his deepest desires just the way she had imagined he'd known hers.

He was right, she thought, when he'd intimated that she was a child. He was right when he had said she didn't know her own mind.

She ought to be grateful to him, she supposed.

Perhaps she even was.

But she certainly didn't want to see him again.

It was one thing to feel begrudging gratitude toward the man who had forced her to grow up. It was another to find oneself in a situation in which one felt one might be obliged to acknowledge it.

Well, she needn't worry, she told herself. In a city of eight million people, it was highly unlikely that their paths might cross.

Besides, she reminded herself, given the way they parted, given Nick's disparaging attitude toward her, it was unlikely he would want to see her any more than she wanted to see him.

The tour was not one of her best. She didn't add her usual crop of anecdotes as she led her gaggle of tourists through the narrow Village streets. Nor did she try to relate the writings of her selected Villagers to the sorts of writings her group might be familiar with.

For once she simply did the best she could with half a mind on the topic, then bowed and smiled them on their way, and sought refuge in her own apartment, intent on reordering her thoughts and keeping her mind on the present, not the past.

She should have known better.

ON HIS EIGHTH GRADE report card Sister Benedicta had written, "Dominic has purpose enough for two."

She should see him now, Nick thought. He didn't have any.

He was lost. At sea. Adrift.

Everything he'd been aiming for all his life had suddenly ceased to matter. Sometimes he wondered if it ever had.

"You're really not going back?" Annie asked him after a week during which he alternately stared out the window and pounded the pavement looking for work.

She hadn't asked before. It was as if she knew he wasn't ready to talk about it, as if she was giving him time to come to terms with life, to heal.

He marveled at her patience. It wasn't one of Annie's more notable attributes. But now, after a week of mooching off her, he owed her an answer.

"I'm really not," he said.

She was hemming a skirt, sitting in front of the window that faced the tiny garden four floors below, basking in the early-afternoon sun. Now and then she looked at him as he sat hunched over the newspaper, which was spread out on the bar between the kitchen and the living room. He had spent the last hour plowing his way through the want ads circling anything that looked remotely feasible.

"Did you hate it?" she asked him. "The restaurant business, I mean?"

He looked up, thinking back, trying to decide when everything began to go sour. "No. Not really. At least, I didn't at first. I wanted to get my hand in, to *do* something."

"According to my mother and dad you really made things hum."

Nick shrugged. "I did a few things."

"Picnic lunches," Annie said. "Ball game suppers. Pasta to go. Family reunion dinners. I'll say you did."

"You heard a lot."

"My mother is a great news source," Annie said dryly. "If a single Italian-American man accomplishes anything, I hear about it."

"Yeah." His mouth twisted. "Your mother isn't a lot different from mine."

"She's trying to find you single Italian-American men, too?" Annie grinned.

But Nick didn't smile. He shut his eyes and saw before him the future his mother had planned. "Not men. Women. One woman, in fact. Virginia Perpetti."

Annie's brows drew together momentarily, then her expression lightened. "I've met her. She was at Mario's wedding, too. Tall, slim, clouds of black hair and a Betty Boop voice. Porcelain complexion. Very ethereal looking."

Nick grunted. "Sounds like her. Frankie calls her Virginia Perpetua."

Annie laughed. "It's got to be the same girl. Your family wanted you to marry her?"

Nick shifted uncomfortably. "Mmm."

"And that's why you left?"

"Not . . . entirely."

She stopped hemming and looked at him. "Why, then? Entirely."

Nick chewed on his lower lip. His tongue traced a circle inside his cheek. "It's a long story."

"This is a long hem."

He smiled wryly. "All right. I guess I owe it to you."

"You do," Annie assured him.

But it was still hard to find the right place to start. With Ginny? With the restaurant? With his father and the rest of the Granatellis?

Finally he just plunged in. "You know how you were always fighting your family, trying to be your own person?"

"*Am* fighting my family," Annie corrected.

Nick shoved his fingers through his hair. "Yeah, I guess so. Well, I never did. I mean, I was a classic believer in 'Father Knows Best.' I bought it all—hook, line and sinker. I was Daddy's boy from the word go."

Annie didn't say anything, just nodded and kept poking the needle in and out of the fabric.

"I was the oldest son. The best student. The best athlete. You name it, I could do it better than any Granatelli born."

"Didn't your brothers and sisters hate you? I'd have hated you."

He shook his head. "No, oddly enough, they didn't. In a way I made it easier for them. Because I filled all the folks' expectations, they were pretty much free to do what they wanted. Sophia, my oldest sister, might've caught a bit of flak if she hadn't fallen in with the party line. But she and Aldo were going steady from ninth grade on. They were a sure thing. So the younger kids didn't have to toe the line the way we did."

"I thought Frankie once told me your father wasn't exactly thrilled about her hat shop."

"He wasn't. But she has the hat shop, doesn't she? He wasn't exactly thrilled about Carlo going into the seminary, either. But Carlo's there. And Vinnie—God Almighty—the old man sure hasn't controlled him. But he didn't need to. He had me." He paused, then corrected, "He used to have me."

He'd never been able to understand his brothers and sisters' reluctance to conform. He'd always wanted what his father did.

"I wanted him to be proud of me. I was proud of myself. We had it all figured out, how I would go to college, play baseball, go on for a business degree, then come back and set the restaurant world of St. Louis on its ear."

"SuperSon?"

Nick sighed and rested his chin on his hands. "You got it."

Annie cocked her head. "My father would have loved you."

"*My* father loved me. Past tense."

Annie's eyes widened. "Oh, come now."

Nick grimaced. "Oh, in an emotional sense I'm sure he does still. But in another emotional sense, I drove a dagger into his heart. I stopped being the son I'd always been."

"But how? Why?"

He sighed. "It was weird, really. His heart attack devastated me. I couldn't imagine functioning without him telling me what to do. He always had, you see. Even when he wasn't there, he was there. In spirit, even when I was at Harvard, I had him with me. Every case study I ever worked on, I used to do a separate accounting in which I'd apply it to Granatelli's. I lived and breathed that damned place."

"And obviously you did it very well."

Nick grunted. "I tried. But even with all that book learning, I was terrified when I got back there. Everybody was depending on me. My mom, my sisters and brothers. Aunts, uncles, cousins. My dad had always been the rallying point for the family. With him out of commission, they all turned to me."

Annie gave him a sympathetic smile. "You had your work cut out for you."

"I didn't have time to worry if I was doing things right or wrong. Decisions came so fast and furious it was all I could do to make them. I was lucky most of the big ones worked. And that made it easier in the beginning for my father. Once he was on the road to recovery, he didn't have to worry about providing for everyone else, so he had a shot at getting well."

"Which he did," Annie put in.

"With a vengeance," Nick agreed. He didn't smile.

Her gaze was quizzical.

"He wasn't the best of all possible patients. The doctor told him he had to take it easy, change his diet, his life-style. He did, but he grumbled about it constantly. He drove my mother nuts. She kept trying to get him into some bridge group or some bocce league. After a year he was a basket case. So was she. The doctor said that per-haps, for five or six hours a week, he could go back to work." Nick made a face.

"Too many cooks?"

"Amen. Five or six hours wasn't enough. He wanted more. He wanted the decisions back. He wanted to be the big cheese."

"And you were the big cheese."

A corner of his mouth lifted. "The biggest. Suffice to say, it didn't work."

"What did you do?"

"Damned near had a heart attack myself." He shook his head. "No, not really. But as time went on he spent more and more hours there, with the doctor's blessing. It was his 'lease on life,' the doctor said. The one thing he really cared about, that he could get his teeth into. But I couldn't work with him, and he sure as hell couldn't work with me."

Even now the memories of their confrontations made his fists clench, his jaw tighten.

"Everything I did, he had a better way, an older way, a more tried-and-true way. *His* way. And while he liked to get my suggestions when I was in Boston, he didn't want anything to do with them once I was working in *his* res-taurant."

"So what happened?"

"He decided it was time for me to go back to school."

"What?"

Nick shrugged. "I hadn't finished my MBA. He thought it was time for me to do it. And he and my mother both thought it was time for me to settle down with a family. I was twenty-nine. High time I got married, they said."

"I understand," Annie said with the voice of long experience.

It shouldn't have been a shock, for heaven's sake. He'd known three years earlier that Ginny Perpetti was on his parents' "short list" for potential daughters-in-law. At the time it hadn't mattered to him. At the time he'd been indifferent to all women as marriage material.

Afterward he compared them all to Diane Bauer.

But since he'd left her in Boston, he hadn't let himself think about her. For the better part of the past two years he hadn't had time to think about anything at all. It was only when his father came back, he'd had more time.

"Time for a wife," his mother had said.

"Time for a wife," his father said.

"Remember Ginny," Sophia said.

Everybody had. It was only a matter of time until they were fixing her up with Nick.

"It was like it was a given," Nick said now, still marveling at the events of the summer. "One minute I was taking her to her cousin Leo's kid's confirmation, and the next we were engaged to be married."

Annie stared. "You're kidding."

He shook his head. "There were a few intermediate steps. Not many. It just...happened. They had it all worked out. Nicky'd done his duty, saved the business, pulled the fat out of the fire, and now they didn't need him for a while. So they were going to set him up with a proper wife and send him back to Harvard until they needed him again."

"I doubt they were quite so calculating," Annie began.

But Nick slammed a fist down on the bar. "They damned well were! And I was stupid enough to go along with it!"

Annie had stopped hemming. She sat staring at him as if she'd never seen him before. "So why aren't you married? You didn't leave her at the altar, for heaven's sake?"

"Not quite. Ginny picked a date, a dress, a florist, colors, menus. All that rot. And...I guess it was the menus that did it."

He raked his fingers through his hair and gave a shaky laugh. "When I think about it, it terrifies me. Do you realize that I would right now be an unhappily married man, if it hadn't been for my allegiance to my grandmother's recipe for risotto milanese?"

"Say what?"

"I wanted it included on the reception menu. Nobody else did."

Annie just looked at him, mystified.

"Not a big deal, huh? But for me a very big deal indeed. I mean, I was going to be the groom, right? This was going to be *my* wedding. So I wanted my grandmother's risotto on the menu. I liked it. When I was growing up it was my favorite thing that she cooked. My mother has the recipe." He bounced off the bar stool and began pacing the floor.

"My sister Sophia said it was too hard to make. My father said we should have polenta instead. My brother Carlo said he thought any kind of risotto was unsuitable, too messy. My mother suggested potato salad! Even Ginny said she didn't want it. She wanted some pasta dish. I said, 'Let's have both. Let's have potato salad, too.' Hell, I didn't care." He reached the end of the room and turned and glared at her. "I was overruled."

"They said no?"

"They said no. So I said no, too. To the whole thing."

He did another complete circle of the living room, raking his hands through his hair.

"It wasn't the risotto, of course. It was what the risotto meant. It was that I didn't matter. Not me. Not Nick. Not the person I was. I only mattered when I was doing what they wanted in the way they wanted me to. And they were bound and determined I was going to fit in." He gave a bitter laugh. "When the risotto hit the fan, I started to think."

"And what you thought was that you'd pack it all in," Annie said quietly.

"I said I was quitting the restaurant. I said I wasn't going back to school. I told Ginny I wasn't ready to get married. And I left."

"What did they say?"

"A lot of things I don't want to repeat."

"They do sound a lot like my family." Annie plied her needle again. She waited until he settled back on the stool, then turned to look at him.

"So, setting aside all the things you thought you wanted and don't, what *do* you want for yourself, Nick?"

He gave her a faint smile. "That's what I have to find out."

Chapter Eight

Three days later he got a job managing a restaurant on Third Avenue in the upper seventies. The owner aspired to make Lazlo's to Hungarian cuisine in New York what Granatelli's already was to Italian dining in St. Louis.

Nick understood. He dug right in.

He studied the operation, checked the ordering system, visited all the suppliers, went over the books. He did all the things he'd done at Granatelli's. He worked himself to exhaustion and hoped it would bring him the satisfaction he was looking for.

It didn't.

Annie seemed to feel better once he had a job. She stopped looking at him worriedly all the time. She smiled more.

"You're looking a lot better," she told him after he'd been at Lazlo's two weeks.

It was a Monday, the only day Annie didn't have to work, and they were sharing a rare leisurely supper. Nick was going over to Lazlo's to supervise the new chef he'd hired, but he didn't have to be there until seven, and Annie had an hour until she had to leave for her ballet class.

Nick wished he could say he felt a lot better. He didn't feel much of anything. He worked, he ate, he slept. But a part of him was always outside looking in. And that part knew he was just going through the motions.

"You need a date," Annie said.

Nick rolled his eyes. "Yes, Mother."

"I'm not trying to marry you off," Annie protested. "I'm just trying to broaden your horizons."

"Broad being the operative word?" Nick grinned.

Annie flipped a strand of spaghetti at him. "I know a really nice girl who works at Zabar's. You'd have something in common right off the bat."

"I don't think so."

"Zabar's deals in food."

"I mean, I don't think I want to meet her."

"Well, you don't know what you're missing. Laurie's really sweet. I have another friend, who works in midtown. Very intense corporate type. A climber."

Nick grinned. "What am I, a trellis?"

"A pain in the rear, more like," Annie told him. "Her name is Wendy, and—"

"No."

Annie pushed away from the table and went over to the desk, picking up her Rolodex, flipping through it. "What about Daphne? She's got a litter of puppies and an apartment in Soho. I wouldn't think you two would—"

Nick laughed. "No. No, no, no."

Annie looked at him, offended. "Picky, picky, picky. I don't have a limitless supply of unattached women friends, you know. How will you know which one's right for you if you don't meet them?"

"What if I already have?"

Annie's eyes narrowed. "What?"

He shoved the spaghetti around on his plate, debating the wisdom of what he'd said, then deciding he couldn't deny it any longer. He lifted his eyes and met her gaze. "What if I already have met her?"

Annie's frown deepened. "Her who?"

"Diane."

She stared at him. "Diane . . . *Bauer?*"

Nick nodded.

Annie shook her head quickly and firmly. She pointed her fork at him. "You dumped Diane Bauer," she reminded him.

"I had obligations. She was a kid. It wouldn't have worked. She wouldn't have been happy."

Annie just looked at him.

"Could you see her stuck in St. Louis the rest of her life, living with me and the entire Granatelli clan on The Hill? Forget The Hill, cripes, she didn't even come back to St. Louis at all. I don't even know where she is!"

"Just as well," Annie muttered.

It was Nick's turn to frown. "What did you say?"

"Nothing. Listen, Nick." Annie perched on the edge of her stool. "Forget Diane. You can't go back. You can't change things."

"I know that, but—"

She shoved the Rolodex under his nose and riffled through the cards. "Pick one. Any one. And forget Diane Bauer."

DIANE BAUER wished she could forget him.

Some days she damned Annie for telling her he was in the city. Other days she was extremely glad Annie had. It kept her from appearing at Annie's unannounced the way she used to. It kept her from calling Annie on the phone.

In fact, the only time she saw her friend now was when they played softball on Tuesday or Thursday afternoons.

The first time she'd seen Annie again after their dim sum lunch she'd asked cautiously if Nick was still with her.

Annie had said he was. She hadn't said more than that, and Diane hadn't asked. If perverse curiosity wanted to know, common sense did not.

At subsequent ball games, she never mentioned his name. Nor did Annie.

After four weeks of silence and of never running into him even though her own apartment was only eight blocks from Annie's, Diane began to breathe easy again.

Then she looked in from her position at second base that hot afternoon in late September, and there he was.

THE FIRST TIME Nick heard about Annie's softball league was when some guy called Bruno phoned and left a message that the rain-out date had been changed to Friday.

"Rain-out date for what?" Nick had asked her when he delivered the message.

"Softball," Annie said absently. She was doing sit-ups a mile a minute, her feet tucked under the sofa, a hot pink leotard outlining her curves.

"You play softball?"

She stopped mid-sit-up. "What's wrong with that?"

"Nothing." He was still grinning. "It just doesn't go with my image of you."

"What is your image of me?"

"Oh, you know. Intense, committed, artistic type. No sense of humor."

"That's me," Annie said. "And I play to win." She began her regimen again.

Nick laughed. "I'll bet you do. Can I come watch?"

She jerked to a stop. "No!"

He scowled at her vehemence. "Why not?"

"Because I don't like an audience."

"You play in Central Park."

"So?"

"So, people must watch you."

"Not people I know." She was exercising again now, but she wasn't going as fast, and she had a frown on her face.

"I won't tell anyone I know you," Nick offered.

She stopped moving entirely. "No. Please, Nick. Just don't come, okay?"

"But—"

"I'm very self-conscious."

"You're an actress."

"I'm a *good* actress. I'm a lousy softball player." Her look implored him. "Please."

So he hadn't. Not at the rain date. Nor at the next three games she played.

She was, after all, doing him an enormous favor letting him stay with her. He was helping with the rent now, but that didn't give him the right to ignore her request. It wasn't as if it was important.

He never would have stopped at all if he hadn't been walking across the park midafternoon that Thursday, coming back from a morning of working on the books at Lazlo's.

Through the trees he glimpsed a game in progress, and the uniforms looked a great deal like the one that turned up in the laundry every week.

Curious he angled his path through the trees, wanting only to catch a glimpse, to see if Annie was really there.

He didn't know what position she played. And so he stood scanning the entire field, trying to pick out the ones with long dark hair, the ones that might be Annie.

But the women had their hair pulled back or stuffed under their caps and it was hard to tell.

He moved closer, squinting against the bright sunlight, watching as the woman at bat hit a grounder through the infield. He followed its progress, saw the right fielder practically throw herself on it, her enthusiasm knocking her hat off.

He smiled. Annie.

She didn't so much field the ball as smother it. But at least, he thought, still smiling as his eyes followed the ball, she threw it to the right base.

And that was when he saw Diane.

HE SHOULD HAVE KNOWN better than to follow her.

He probably should have known better than to stand and watch, let alone shadow the second baseperson home.

But, damn it, he wanted to see her.

He *had* to see her.

One tiny part of him—the part that dreamed impossible dreams—believed that the past two and a half years had been nothing more than a bad dream that seeing Diane again would banish.

He had to know. He had to try.

He still couldn't believe that she'd been right there under his nose the whole time. But there was no mistaking her, even with her honey-colored hair obscured under a cap.

"Diane?" He'd said her name aloud. But his voice was breathless. He sounded stricken.

Not surprising. He was.

He was torn between joy and fury. Joy at having found her here of all places. Fury at Annie for having never told him that she was.

When he'd left her in Boston he told himself it was best not to know anything more. It was over, after all. What could come of it but pain?

Still, she'd been nagging at the back of his mind for the last two and a half years. Always there when he'd slowed down long enough to let himself think.

It hadn't taken long for his resolve never to look for her to die.

After all, it wasn't as if he was going to go after her, he told himself.

He was simply curious. He wanted to know what had happened to an old friend.

At first he assumed she'd returned to St. Louis. So when the bug first bit him, he scoured the society pages, looking for some mention of her. He found nothing.

Periodically, holding his breath, he checked the wedding announcements. He breathed again only when he was sure he wasn't reading hers.

He'd even asked Annie when they danced at Mario's wedding, but the music was loud and there were people everywhere. She hadn't heard his question.

For two and a half years, he'd heard nothing.

From society deb to vanished woman, Diane Bauer was nowhere to be found. He felt as if she'd dropped off the face of the earth.

She certainly hadn't dropped out of his dreams.

In fact during the last few months, especially since his engagement to Ginny, she seemed to appear nightly, smiling at him, taunting him silently, reproaching him for his foolishness.

He'd tried to ignore the dreams; he'd tried to forget her. He'd focused desperately on the life he'd chosen.

It hadn't worked.

It had taken him some time to realize it, of course. He was not, Nick thought wryly as she hurried away from him down the street, a quick study.

One might call him a lot of things—many people, not least, Ginny Perpetti had—but a quick study he wasn't.

He stayed in the shadow of the pizzeria on the corner, watching as Diane ran up the steps of a brownstone midway down the block. She'd taken off from the game as if all the devils in hell were behind her. He'd tried to catch her then, but it hadn't worked.

He'd shot a glare at Annie. She glared right back at him. "Why didn't you tell me?"

"I told *her,*" Annie said. "Don't you think if she'd wanted to see you, she'd have come by?"

"She's going to see me," he said flatly and started after her.

Annie called after him, "Nick?"

He glanced over his shoulder. "What?"

"Think about someone else for a change." Then she turned her back and was gone.

Think about someone else for a change? As if he hadn't, two and a half years before! Damn her, anyway.

He practically ran after Diane's fast-disappearing form, then decided against catching up with her on the street. He didn't want their meeting to be a momentary encounter. He slowed his pace and followed her discreetly.

He hung back now, watching until she went inside. Then, taking a deep breath, he followed.

There was a tall, bespectacled man coming out of the brownstone as he went in. Nick smiled his most disarming smile. "I'm going to Diane's," he said.

He didn't know whether to be glad or not when the man gave him a knowledgeable shrug and held the door for him.

According to the mailbox she was in apartment three. He headed up the steps. It was three flights up, and that he was winded had nothing to do with the climb. He took a deep breath and pressed the bell.

The door opened almost at once.

"You're early," she began, then stopped dead, the color draining from her face. "Oh," she said tonelessly. "It's you."

Not precisely the reaction he'd hoped for.

Nick swallowed, then wiped suddenly damp palms on the sides of his jeans. He had rehearsed a few little opening speeches on the way over here. One for every occasion, he'd told himself. From the one where she threw the lamp at him to the one where she threw herself at him.

Words deserted him now.

She was still wearing her softball uniform. Her hair, no longer covered by the cap, lay damp and golden against her shoulders. Her face was devoid of makeup, and yet the exertion of the ball game had given it a radiance that other women spent hours trying to duplicate. She was not smiling.

She was still the most beautiful woman he'd ever seen.

He licked his lips, cleared his throat, offered her a hopeful smile. "Diane. Hello."

Still unsmiling, Diane nodded. "Nick." It was an acknowledgment, nothing more.

Silence rose around them like a rapidly rising flood. Nick raked a hand through his hair, shifted from one foot to the other, groped for something—anything—to say. "I—I'm visiting Annie. I saw you at the game. I—I thought I'd say hi."

In his worst nightmares, he'd never ever thought he'd come face-to-face with Diane Bauer and there would be nothing to say.

It was inconceivable.

The night they met they'd spent hours talking nonstop. Subsequent dates had been the same. There had never seemed time enough for them to get it all said.

It wasn't that way now.

Nick scratched the back of his head. "It's...been a long time."

"What do you want?"

To start over? To take back all the stupid things he'd ever said? To make her love him now the way she'd loved him then? Given an ounce of encouragement, he might have said such things. But her stolid, unwelcoming stance precluded any such confessions.

He shrugged awkwardly, managed a smile. "I checked out the society pages now and then. I expected to see you in there—that you'd gone to a party or—" his voice roughened "—got married or something."

"No."

"No," he repeated. Then with false heartiness, he asked, "So, what have you been doing?"

"Finding out who I am."

The words came at him like an unexpected body-blow. He winced, remembering all too well when he'd suggested just that to her. He rubbed a hand across his eyes. "I was an ass. I never should have said—"

"On the contrary," Diane cut across his apology. "You were right. Absolutely right. I'm very grateful."

She didn't sound grateful. She sounded as if she'd like his head on a plate.

"That's...great," he said hollowly. And then, because she didn't volunteer anything else, he asked, "What did you do? I mean, how..." He felt like an even bigger ass asking.

Diane hesitated a moment, as if she were debating what to reply. "I looked around and decided I had to make some decisions of my own."

"You didn't come back to St. Louis at all?"

"No."

"You went to Provence?" It was what he expected.

"I went to Provence, then to Paris. Then I went to Tokyo."

"Tokyo?" Nick's eyes widened.

Diane's chin lifted. "Why not? I'm good with languages. I wanted to be better. I studied Japanese language and culture there for six months."

That he hadn't expected. "Good for you."

"It was. I learned a lot. I'm my own person now," she told him, confirming his thoughts. She met his gaze almost belligerently.

Nick was the first to look away. He tucked his hands into the pockets of his jeans. A corner of his mouth lifted in an ironic smile. Her own person, huh? More than he could say for himself. "You're lucky."

Diane frowned. She didn't speak for a moment, then opened the door a little wider. "I need a shower, but it can wait. You might as well come in for a few minutes as long as you're here."

As invitations went, it wasn't the most welcoming he'd ever received. But under the circumstances it was more than he had any right to expect.

"Thanks."

Her apartment was larger than Annie's, in a slightly better block. It was a floor-through up three flights in a brownstone not far from the Park. The furnishings were Crate and Barrel modern. Piles of gaily colored pillows on the floor and on the brown-and-white striped sofa softened the atmosphere. Diane herself softened it even more.

"Sit down." She gestured politely toward the sofa. "Would you like something to drink? Tea, milk, soda, or cranberry juice? Or I could give you a glass of wine."

"No wine," Nick said quickly. But he needed something to assuage the dryness in his mouth. "How about juice?"

"I'll be right back." She disappeared through the doorway to the kitchen in the center of the apartment. Nick could hear her taking out glasses and opening the refrigerator. He wished he could follow her. Instead he sat down on the sofa and tried to figure out what he was doing here.

Diane reappeared moments later carrying a tray with juice, napkins and a plate of cookies. Homemade oatmeal with nuts and raisins.

Nick's brows lifted. "Did you make them?"

Diane shook her head and sat down at the opposite end of the sofa. "I have a friend who owns a health food store. He keeps giving them to me. They're very good for you." She smiled. "That's what he tells me, anyway. I don't know how he'd know. He never eats them."

He.

He, he, he. Four *he*'s in the space of five seconds. And a smile to boot.

Nick felt a primitive twisting deep in his gut. Had he really expected she wouldn't have male friends?

Had he actually imagined that she had spent the last two and a half years pining away for a man who had thrown her love back in her face?

She set the tray on the coffee table, then handed him the glass of cranberry juice and offered him a cookie. He took one. Sawdust had more flavor.

Diane nibbled on one, too. Then she smiled reflectively. "I can see why he doesn't eat them now," she said. "You don't have to finish it."

"It's fine." Nick took another bite. It was penance. A small price to pay for all his years of being a fool.

"So," Diane said. "What are you doing in New York?"

He was glad he had his mouth full. It gave him a chance to think. Not to Diane was he going to offer the glib "I've run away from home," though she, more than anyone perhaps, deserved to hear it.

He couldn't. It sounded too childish, too foolish. God knew it was, of course. *He* was. But there was a limit to a guy's humility, for heaven's sake.

"I'm on vacation." It was, in its way, true. It was the first vacation he'd had in his life—the first time since he was eleven that he hadn't had school or work or family hanging over his head, determining his every move.

"How's your father? Well, I imagine, or you wouldn't be on vacation."

"He's fine. Better than fine. He's fantastic. Back at work."

"Full-time?"

"And then some." He gave a harsh laugh.

"So, if he's running things, what are you doing?"

The question of the year.

So much for dissembling, Nick thought.

"That's what I'm trying to figure out."

For the first time he thought he detected a flicker of concern on her face. She started to say something else when the doorbell rang. "Oh, heavens!" She glanced at her watch, then looked in dismay at the uniform she still wore. "Excuse me," she said to Nick and got up to answer the door.

It was not the sort of scene a guy wanted to witness.

The man—whoever he was—grabbed Diane up in a bone-crushing hug, then spun her around once and kissed her soundly before settling her back on her feet. "Early for once," he said smugly. "How about that?"

"Amazing," Diane said. "As you can see, I'm not. I have a visitor."

She took his hand and drew him further into the living room so that his gaze collided with Nick's.

He was a little taller than Nick with shaggy dark auburn hair and the most truly patrician nose that Nick had ever encountered. He wanted to break it on sight.

"This is Nick Granatelli," she said to The Nose. "He's an old . . . friend. From school."

Nick saw her link her fingers with The Nose's before she added, still smiling. "Nick, I'd like you to meet Carter MacKenzie."

She didn't have to explain who Carter MacKenzie was. It was all too obvious.

IT WAS OVER.

It was over. She said it again and again like a mantra. Over. Over.

She had seen him. She had talked to him. He was gone. It was over.

" . . . with me tomorrow?" Carter said.

She didn't reply. She stood in the middle of Central Park and stared at him dumbly.

He bent and peered intently into her face, a whimsical grin teasing the corners of his mouth. "You are in there somewhere, aren't you, Di?"

Diane gave herself a mental shake and managed a wan smile. "Sorry. I was . . . thinking about . . . work."

"Work," Carter grumbled, beginning to scuff along the path again. He squeezed her fingers gently. "The bane of my existence."

Diane laughed. "Why don't you quit then? Live off the family millions?"

Carter frowned and pushed his hair off his forehead. "Can't," he said.

"Why not?"

"If I did, Daddy would think he could tell me what to do."

"No one could ever tell you what to do, Carter," Diane told him with absolute certainty. If ever she had met an absolutely dedicated free spirit, it was Carter William MacKenzie, IV.

"Try telling him that," Carter said. He shook his head and laughed. "No, don't. I don't even want you to meet the old man." He paused, considered, then changed his mind. "On second thought, maybe I do."

Diane stopped where she was. Surely he couldn't be serious. Carter MacKenzie had told her the first time she met him that theirs would be a frivolous relationship.

"Fun and games, how about that?" he'd promised her the night of Auntie Flo's party, when he had followed her out onto the balcony of Flo's apartment and tried to charm the serious, unsmiling young woman she'd been then.

She had rebuffed him at once, still unwilling to get involved with anyone, even though she'd last seen Nick Granatelli a year and a half before.

When he'd persisted, she'd said flat out, "I don't want a boyfriend. I don't even want a date. I want to be left alone."

He'd feigned horror. "Forever? Well, in that case, I have the name of an absolutely delightful Mother Superior."

She couldn't help smiling then. And his continued gentle teasing had nudged her into a conversation. From there it was a small step to agreeing to meet him for a walk in the park, then a hot dog from a street vendor, then a tram ride to Roosevelt Island.

He didn't come on to her again. He simply smiled at her and tried to get her to smile at him.

They had been smiling at each other for almost a year now. But this was the first time he had intimated that he might want to take her home to meet his family.

It was a serious step. It didn't help that he thought of it the very day she'd confronted Nick.

Nick.

Even now, faced with Carter's hint of something deeper, something stronger, she was thinking about Nick.

She wanted to say he hadn't changed. And in some ways, of course, he hadn't. He was still ruggedly handsome. His thick brown, sun-streaked hair still made her want to twist her fingers in it. His firm jaw still made her want to reach out and touch it.

But in other ways she sensed a difference in him. She couldn't put her finger on it, but it was a mood more than anything else.

If she'd had to describe the Nick Granatelli she knew in Cambridge in five words or less, she would have picked *intense, determined, committed, purposeful.* Also *sexy.* Only the last still seemed to apply.

But, she reminded herself, what did she know? She'd seen him for less than an hour. They had barely begun to talk when Carter had appeared.

There had been little talking after that.

She, who could make small talk with the best, found herself floundering in a sea of surly stares and monosyllabic mutterings.

"You're not listening again," Carter chided her.

"I know. I'm sorry. I—"

"Is it really work bothering you?" Carter asked. "Or is it your 'old friend' Nick?" He put a twist on the words that made them spin in the air.

Diane scuffed at the dirt underfoot. She'd never lied to Carter, never pretended with him. She sighed. "It's Nick."

Carter nodded glumly. "Figures."

Diane gave him a sidelong glance. "Why do you say that?"

"Always happens."

"What do you mean?"

"Me and women. I spook 'em." He shrugged philosophically and hunched his shoulders against the wind.

Diane caught his arm. "It has nothing to do with you."

"Oh? I could have sworn I was the one in the room with you and friend Nick today."

"Of course, you were. But it goes back a long way. A very long way."

"Ah."

It was an all-knowing "ah." An all-seeing "ah." It made Diane nervous.

"What do you mean by that?"

"You have a 'past.'"

Carter could invest a word with more meaning simply by his tone of voice than anyone Diane had ever met. He made "past" sound deep and mysterious, intriguing. Not the way Diane remembered it at all.

"*We* have a past," she agreed flatly. "I was in love with him and he told me to go away and grow up."

"The more fool he," Carter said promptly. He towed her over to a bench and pulled her down next to him.

Diane shook her head. "Not really. I was a naive little jerk in those days. I thought the world was my oyster. And he was the pearl in it, just sitting there waiting for me to come along."

"I wouldn't mind being your pearl," Carter told her.

She smiled at him and brushed a lock of hair off his forehead. "Shows what you know," she said, but she smiled.

"See? You're brushing me off."

"I'm not!"

"No? Sounds like it to me. And believe me—" He grimaced "I'm an expert on it."

"Then you pick the wrong women."

He sighed, stretched his feet out in front of him and crossed them at the ankle. He contemplated his toes. Then he raised his head and looked sideways at her. "Have I this time?"

Diane didn't know.

So PENANCE was going to be more than an oatmeal cookie that tasted like sawdust.

Somehow Nick wasn't surprised.

It would have been too much to hope for, just as it had been too much to hope that his interest in Diane Bauer had died when he cut her out of his life three years ago. He'd told himself he'd quickly forget her. And if she'd stayed a girl, he might have done so.

She had become quite a woman.

Even in her dirt-streaked softball uniform she was beautiful. Obviously she was successful, too.

He hadn't stayed long once Carter had arrived, but in the course of what conversation they'd had, her job as a concierge had come up. So had her fledgling tour business. She didn't make a big deal of it. She didn't have to. She was clearly a person in her own right, just as she had said.

She had taken his words seriously.

It was odd, really, because even though the words were true enough when he'd said them, he'd meant them more as self-defense than as a condemnation of her.

He'd wanted her, and yet he'd been afraid of what the future might have brought the two of them. It was too uncertain. He had too little confidence in her—in himself.

He didn't know, at the time, what else he could have done.

So now he had to live with it.

Diane Bauer had a full, successful, self-determined life. And a boyfriend.

He had zilch.

Annie was at the apartment when he got back. She was eating macaroni and cheese and a lettuce salad, and though he knew she was dying to say something else, what she said was, "There's enough for two."

"I'm not hungry."

Annie looked at him critically. "You're getting too skinny. Women won't drool over your manly bod if you don't eat."

Nick threw himself down on the sofa and folded his arms behind his head. "I don't want them drooling over me."

Annie's eyes widened. "No? None of them?"

Nick scowled and made a disparaging noise.

There was a pause. Then, "Did you see her?"

"Yes."

"And?"

"She wasn't thrilled."

Annie had the grace not to say, "I told you so." She gave him a sympathetic look and went on eating.

"Who's her friend?"

Annie frowned. "Friend?"

"Carter somebody. God's gift to women." Nick cracked his knuckles irritably.

Annie laughed. "I'm sure he'd be delighted to hear you say so. His name is Carter MacKenzie. I can't believe Diane didn't introduce you."

Nick scowled. "She did. I wasn't listening."

"You should," Annie said. "Carter is worth knowing about."

Nick gave her a doubtful look. "So, who is he?"

"Carter William MacKenzie IV, heir to the MacKenzie Metal fortune, also to the Blalock Oil Conglomerate, also to Taft Chemicals." A pause. "Proprietor of Jack Sprat's Health and Wellness Store."

Nick blinked. "Jack Sprat's . . . ?"

Annie shrugged. "Carter is his own man. He's also been many women's man. But never for more than a month. He dumps them or they dump him."

Nick brightened. "Then he must be on his way out with Diane."

"Don't count on it."

"Why?"

"It's a funny thing about Carter and Diane. At first no one thought they were a couple. When Carter has a woman, it is generally a very high-profile affair. But he was never high profile with Diane." She stood up and carried her plate to the sink to run it under the tap. "They went for walks together, they cooked pancakes together. Once, she told me, they walked across the Brooklyn Bridge together."

Annie laughed, saw Nick's face and stopped at once. She shrugged awkwardly. "Anyway, I don't think you could say he's on his way out with Diane. On the contrary, what they have seems really different than anything

Carter's ever had with anyone. You might say they're just getting started."

Nick sat up. "She's serious about him?"

Annie lifted one shoulder. "I don't know." She fixed him with a level stare. "Why?"

He hunched his shoulders. "I . . . just want to know."

"Why?"

"Because I care," he said irritably.

"Why?"

"Damn it, Annie, because once she loved me."

"Loved," Annie repeated firmly. "Past tense. For all the good it did her."

Nick winced. "I know." He shut his eyes.

"You hurt her."

"I hurt us both."

"And you're not going to hurt her this time?"

"I don't want to!"

"But will you, Nick? That's the question."

Nick sat with his head bent. He studied his toes, flexed them, watched as they pushed against the rubber tips of his sneakers. He sighed and shook his head slowly, recognizing the justice of the question at the same time that he recognized his inability to answer it.

He lifted his gaze to meet Annie's. "I don't know."

Chapter Nine

When he was little, Nick had had a guardian angel. His *nonna* had told him so. It hovered somewhere right behind the headboard of the bunk beds he and Carlo shared.

He'd wanted to know if they shared the angel, too. But *Nonna* said no. Nick was surprised; they shared clothes, toys, bats, balls, books, friends and everything else. Still, it was a good thing, he'd thought.

He couldn't imagine any angel being energetic enough to be able to keep both of them out of trouble, let alone see that anything good came their way.

In recent years he hadn't given a lot of thought to guardian angels. The theology courses he'd taken at St. Louis University didn't focus on them. At Harvard he hadn't had time for one. And since then, it seemed, his family had determinedly taken over all the angel's duties. For the last two and a half years the Granatellis had definitely overseen his life.

But in New York he was on his own.

He hadn't thought a lot about guardian angels there, either, until the Sunday afternoon four days after he had seen Diane at the softball game.

He was in the midst of helping the bartender restock the bar at Lazlo's right after the Sunday brunch rush was over, and the door opened.

In walked Diane and her tour walkers.

Nonna would have said, "You see, I'm telling you. You got to trust and you got to wait. Your angel, he knows what you need, Nicky."

Nick needed this.

Diane didn't see him at first. The bar was in the shadows on the far side of the room, and she was busy talking to her group, telling them a bit about the history of the Yorkville area while she herded them toward Carla, the hostess.

"I'm Diane Bauer, Manhattan Meanderings. I called earlier about bringing my tour by."

The hostess beamed. "Of course. Come right this way."

Nick didn't move. He vaguely remembered Carla saying something to him about a group coming in this afternoon for a taste of *konyakos meggy,* a Hungarian dark chocolate, sour cherry and cognac specialty. He'd never imagined it might be Diane's.

Now he sent a prayer of thanksgiving winging heavenward. *Nonna* would have been pleased.

Diane's back was to him when she sat down, and she was still speaking to her group. There were twelve of them, men and women ranging in age from twenty to seventy, all listening intently. Nick moved closer and discovered she was speaking German.

His German was basically nonexistent. And he was relieved a few moments later when she switched to English, detailing the history of the Hungarian community that had settled on the Upper East Side after 1905. Nick edged slightly closer so he could listen, too.

Using anecdotes to illustrate the history as she talked, Diane had no trouble capturing his attention. And only the arrival of the promised treat and cups of steaming coffee with whipped cream distracted her listeners, even those whose English was not the best.

Fascinated by her talk, Nick had to remind himself that he was a fool if he didn't take advantage of the chance.

He waited until they were eating before he made his move. And then he simply walked up alongside her and asked politely, "How is everything today?"

Startled, Diane spluttered into her coffee.

"Wunderbar," the lady seated next to her said when Diane couldn't seem to catch her breath.

"Delicious," seconded the man at the end of the table. "Just like my mother used to make."

Nick smiled at him. "I'm glad. Can I bring you more coffee?" He addressed the question to the table in general, nodded as they made their replies, then dropped his gaze to meet Diane's.

"And you, miss?"

She wiped the crumbs off her mouth and gave him a wary look as she struggled for composure. "Er, I don't think so, thank you." She glanced at her watch. "We really shouldn't be spending too much longer here. We have quite a lot more to cover in the next hour and a half." She looked as if she might bolt right then.

"I'll be right back with the coffee," Nick said and returned to pour it before she could mobilize her troops.

The coffee poured, he left them alone. For the moment it was enough to let her know he was there. He busied himself behind the bar again, straightening the bottles on the shelves, putting the new stock away.

She ignored him, concentrating with great determination on the questions her tourists asked her, charming them, Nick could tell.

When they were about to leave he slipped up beside her again. "May I come along?"

She frowned at him. "You're at work."

He shrugged. "It's Sunday. I'm just helping out."

"You don't want—"

"I do want," he cut in. "That's why I'm asking."

"You want to learn about the history and development of Yorkville?" The look she gave him was scornful.

But Nick nodded. "Yes, I do. Lazlo's developed out of the culture in Yorkville. I don't know much about it, and that means I'm at a disadvantage marketing it."

"And you think following me around will help you?"

"It's worth a try." He gave her a guileless smile.

She still looked doubtful. "Suit yourself."

Nick would have liked to have walked alongside her but instead he hung back. He knew he made her nervous, could tell from the swift little glances she darted his way. He managed to look politely interested, not obsessed. It wasn't easy.

In fact, he was studying her every move, analyzing the ways in which she had changed and the ways in which she hadn't changed at all.

She still had the ready smile and look of fresh-faced innocence he had seen the first time he had met her. But her eyes were knowledgeable, her poise even greater than before, her maturity evident.

She knew her stuff and didn't hesitate to show it.

As they walked, she spoke in German, then repeated herself in English. There were several third- and fourth-generation Hungarian-Americans in the group as well, all asking questions about the culture and how their grandparents and great-grandparents had coped with American ways.

She was as comfortable with the German-American history of Yorkville as she was with the language, expounding on their history as she led her charges up Third Avenue.

She talked about the changes in the neighborhood, pointed out the new high-rise developments and those establishments that had been in the neighborhood for years.

"A neighborhood is a living thing," she told them at the end as they stood on the corner of Eighty-sixth and First Avenue. "It is born, it grows, and if it isn't infused periodically with new blood, with new businesses, with new people, it dies. What you see around you is a neighborhood in the process of revitalization. Appreciate it. Enjoy it. Walk through it with your eyes and your ears open. You will be amazed at what you discover. And if you find any particularly fascinating spots, I'd love to hear about them so I can pass the word to others. A tour has to develop and grow, too."

Then she handed them each a list of a number of local businesses and restaurants in the neighborhood whom she had personally dealt with.

"And I don't get a kickback," she promised them with a smile. "I just think you might enjoy some further contact with the local people and the local businesses, and these are all establishments I deal with myself."

Nick, scanning the sheet, discovered that Lazlo's was on it. He raised his brows.

"I've been there several times," she said in answer to his unspoken question. "It's improved enormously of late, so I just included it."

She turned then, making a point of answering the question of one of the tourists who was waiting.

The others were wandering off, studying the sheets Diane had given them and looking around the neighborhood with new eyes.

The middle-aged woman, who had asked Diane a question about Yorkville during the Second World War, smiled her thanks and moved off. Nick waited patiently until she was finished.

Diane looked at him standing there. "Was it useful?"

"Very."

She nodded. "I'm glad." She started to leave.

"Wait." He caught up with her. "Have coffee with me."

Her fingers knotted around the strap of her purse. She seemed about to shake her head.

"One cup of coffee . . . to say thanks for the plug."

"I said, 'no kickbacks.'"

He rolled his eyes. "All right. Not for the plug." His eyes met her, compelling her. "For old times' sake, then."

Still she hesitated.

"Please."

She sighed. "One cup of coffee."

He didn't take her back to Lazlo's though they were only a few blocks away. Lazlo's would distract, and he needed no distractions.

He had one cup of coffee's worth of conversation promised; he wasn't about to waste it solving kitchen problems or helping fold napkins before the dinner crowd came in.

He steered her into a hamburger joint on Second Avenue. It was noisy, culturally insignificant, and had just the right nonthreatening atmosphere Nick was looking for. He would have preferred someplace dark and intimate and full of tiny discreet tables for two. The sight of one, he knew, would send Diane Bauer heading in the other direction so fast he probably wouldn't be able to see her move.

So he opted for bright awnings and plate glass, an old-fashioned soda fountain and a flashy black-and-white checkerboard linoleum floor.

"Do you want anything else?" he asked her when they'd taken a table by the windows.

Diane shook her head. "I'm still full."

"Two coffees," he said to the waitress, then turned back to Diane. "I've never seen you at Lazlo's."

"I never saw you, either," she said quickly.

"You mean you didn't put it on your list because of me?"

Diane gave him a long-suffering sigh.

It reminded him of the sorts of sighs he used to provoke when he teased her. He grinned. "Somehow I didn't think you had."

A faint blush touched her cheeks. She folded her hands primly. "How long have you been there?"

"Three weeks."

"Are you the new manager?" she asked, and when he nodded, she said. "I knew there was a difference recently. I try to check places out fairly frequently. There's been a big improvement in three weeks. But then, I suppose you're very good at that."

He shrugged. "It's a job." The server brought the coffee and Nick stirred a bit of milk into his.

But he didn't want to talk about his job. It was just that, nothing more. He wanted to know more about Diane. "So, tell me more about your tours. How long have you been doing it?"

"I'm just starting out really. It's a seat-of-the-pants operation, not a Harvard Business School sort of project."

Nick snorted.

Diane shrugged. "It's not. It just fills a need I saw. I mean, I know there are other, doubtless more qualified, tour guides in New York. There are people who have made it their life's goal to know as much about the history and the development of the city as they possibly can. I've gone on a lot of their tours and, believe me, they know what they're talking about. But mine are usually tailored to specific needs—very often language needs. I do the French, Italian and German ones myself. And I can give a sort of basic Japanese tour if I have to. But I try to farm those out. I have several students and other free-lance guides who help me.''

Nick was impressed. "How'd you get started?"

She sipped her coffee. "When I came back from Japan, instead of going home to St. Louis, I came to New York to stay with my Aunt Flo. You remember me telling you about Aunt Flo?''

He nodded. "The Bauers' black sheep?" He grinned, recalling her description of her renegade aunt.

Diane laughed and she looked again like the Diane he remembered. His heart ached.

"The one and only," she said. "But Flo is terribly respectable in terms of society, you see. She 'married well.'" Diane gave the phrase all the dignity it deserved. "And to my grandmother that is a paramount consideration. So she could hardly object when Flo offered me a chance to live with her. After all—'' Diane grinned, too ''—Who knew? Flo might've found me a baron, too.''

She'd done just as well with the heir to every damned company in America, Nick thought grimly. He didn't say it, of course, but he felt it there, looming in the back of his head.

"I got a job fairly quickly working as a night concierge at the hotel where my aunt and uncle used to stay when they just visited New York. It's sort of European. The baron liked that.''

Annie, when grilled, had told him the name of the hotel. It was an expensive one on the Upper East Side, very elegant and cosmopolitan in fact as well as in reputation.

"It was family connections that got me the job," Diane admitted. "The 'old baron's network,' I guess. But it was a trial only, and they made sure I knew it. That was all right with me. I didn't want it if I couldn't handle it. I thought I could, though, and I worked like crazy because I loved what I was doing."

"And they were pleased?"

"Yes, they were. They liked my languages and my willingness to learn, I guess." She gave a blithe shrug. "Anyway, they seemed happy with me. And the first Christmas I was there, they sent me to Munich for a month to work in a hotel there while I practiced my German."

"It's very good," Nick told her.

"Better than it used to be, that's for sure. The second Christmas they sent me back to Japan because they'd been getting lots of Japanese business and I was the only one who could talk to them."

"Lucky woman."

"Good business for them, too. You'd be amazed how much return business they get because they have someone who can speak the language of the guests. They've found, too, that guests bring their families if they feel someone is looking out for them. That's my job." She smiled at him then. A confident smile. A proud smile.

And Nick, looking at her, saw how much she'd changed, how much she'd grown.

It made him glad, in a way, that he'd walked away from her. It had been the right thing to do.

So why, he asked himself, did it have to hurt so much?

"And what about the tours?" he asked. "That's your own, not the hotel's right?"

"Right. But they're the reason I got going in the tours,"
Diane went on. "Families that came along wanted to know
about different areas of New York. So I started to learn
about various neighborhoods, different parts of the city or
life-styles. I took guests on tours of neighborhoods, first
as a part of the hotel's services. Then, with the management's encouragement, I went out on my own."

"And you like it?"

"I love it."

Nick managed a smile. "Sounds like you've done well
for yourself."

"I'm happy," Diane told him. She looked him squarely
in the eyes as if daring him to dispute it.

He didn't. He couldn't. His gaze slid away.

The waitress came and poured more coffee into their
cups, then drifted away.

"Do you see your family much?" Nick asked.

"I go home once or twice a year. My mother comes here
now and then. Matthew, my stepfather, died almost two
years ago."

"I'm sorry."

Diane nodded. "I still miss him. So does my mother,
naturally. I wish she'd find someone else. But I don't suppose she ever will."

"What about your father?"

"He comes into the city every few months and we have
dinner." She smiled. "I like him more and more."

Nick remembered her telling him about Russell Shaw,
the poor boy who'd swept Cynthia Hoffmann off her feet,
married her and given her a daughter, and then, a few
months later, unable to give them what he thought they
needed, had disappeared.

Two and a half years ago Nick had taken Russell Shaw as an object lesson and had refused to do the same thing to Russell's daughter.

"So everything's worked out swell, familywise and workwise," Nick said, summing it up for both of them.

For a moment a shadow seemed to pass across Diane's face. But then she smiled. "I guess you could say that, yes." She shoved her hair back away from her face and met his gaze squarely.

"What about you, Nick?"

Nick was afraid they'd come to that.

Indeed, what about him?

For a man who'd had everything going for him, who'd had enough purpose to lead an army, Nick didn't think he'd accomplished much. In fact, compared to Diane, he'd accomplished damned little.

He shrugged. "I worked at my folks until my father was back in harness, then I left."

It summed things up, of course. It told nothing of the pain, of the sense of desperation he'd felt, of his increasing despair at the tangled mess his life had become.

But those were things he couldn't tell Diane. Not now. Not under circumstances like these. Once he might've. Now he had no right.

"Well," she said brightly after a pause, "you seem to be doing fine. Your taking the job at Lazlo's must mean you've decided to stay."

"I guess."

"Are you enjoying it?"

"Could be worse."

"You don't sound very enthusiastic."

"I'm not, especially."

"I thought restaurants were in your blood."

"Once I thought so, too. Now I wonder. Sometimes at night when I'm sitting there with all the damned orders and the invoices and the columns of figures it feels like I'm going to drown in them. And instead of digging in, I just start to daydream." He slanted her a glance and saw her smile.

He shoved his fingers through his hair. "I remember things that happened when I was a kid. The good times, you know? The baseball games. The days we played hooky and went fishing. Those times I used to work with my grandfather.

"Do you know, sometimes I'd be sitting there, trying to make sense of these damned orders and I'd be rubbing my thumb along the side of my other hand, and all of a sudden I'd realize what I was doing—in my mind I was sanding wood." He gave a self-mocking half laugh. "Maybe it's sawdust, not restaurants I've got in my blood."

Diane smiled.

"But it doesn't matter, either way," Nick said heavily. There was no workshop now. His grandfather's tools were stored away. There was nothing left but the memories that crept up on him when he sat, unsuspecting, and made him want to run his fingers through his hair.

"I don't know what I want anymore." He smiled wryly, then sighed and pushed back his chair so he could stretch out his legs. His eyes met Diane's. He remembered so many other times in the past when their gazes had caught, when they had looked at each other with perfect understanding, with sympathy. With love.

He wanted that now, wanted it desperately. And knew he had no right to it.

He saw concern in her eyes. Even a vague sort of sympathy, which only made him feel worse. But he didn't see love. Where love had been, there was a wall now. A wall that Nick himself had built.

He hadn't expected it to fall at once, of course.

But right now it seemed the height of presumptuousness to expect it to fall at all.

He felt suddenly at sea, swamped with a depression he'd never known before. When he had worked, he'd had purpose; when he'd left, he'd had anger, determination.

Now, for the first time, he felt he had nothing.

It had seemed so simple days ago—even minutes ago—to get to know Diane again, find his place in her life again, start over again.

Yet now it didn't seem simple at all.

What was he doing walking back into her life, expecting her to accept him back?

Why should she?

If he'd had little to offer her three years ago, he had, as Jared would have said, "damn all" to offer her now.

And if he had nothing, Conrad—or Carpenter or whatever his name was—had everything on earth. Hell.

"What *is* his name?" he asked her irritably.

Diane blinked. "Whose name?"

He scowled. "That guy. The one in your apartment." His fingers clenched against his thigh.

"Oh. Carter."

"Yeah," Nick said grimly. "Carter."

Diane's eyes widened at his tone. "He's a good friend."

Her assurance did nothing to make him feel better. A good friend? Nick bet he was. He didn't want to think how good.

"Mmm."

Diane gave him a challenging look. He knew what it meant. He knew she dared him to object. He knew he couldn't. He, of all people, had no right to voice any objection whatsoever.

He closed his eyes, suddenly wanting to get out of there, to live the life of a hermit, to forget the past, the present, the future.

What future? he asked himself.

There was no future—not, at least, like the one he once had hoped for.

You can't go back.

And of course he knew that, had always known it.

It had been folly to ask her to join him for a cup of coffee. Folly to have followed her back to her apartment last week.

Folly to dream. Folly to hope.

He shoved his cup away decisively and stood up. "Thanks for joining me," he said. "Don't let me keep you."

Diane looked up at him startled, then scrambled to her feet. "No, that's fine. You're right. I really should be going," she said hastily.

Nick dropped some money on the table and stood back to let her precede him out the door. He held it for her, then stood on the sidewalk outside and shoved his hands into his pockets.

Diane looked at him, at the ground, then at him again. He didn't know what she was thinking now. She looked distant. Remote.

Passersby jostled them as they surged past. A bus rumbled away from a stop, spewing exhaust.

Nick pulled a hand out of his pocket and held it out to her. He managed a smile. "It was nice to see you again."

She took his hand. Her touch made him burn and he steeled himself against it.

"Yes," she said. She gave him a smile that he was certain her grandmother Hoffmann would have been proud of. "I enjoyed it, Nick. I'll be sure to bring my tours by Lazlo's again, too."

Nick kept smiling. "You do that," he said and let go of her hand.

He had been going to stand there and watch her as she left. But he couldn't do it. He turned abruptly, even before she did, and walked quickly down the street.

"How's Nick?"

Annie stopped midway down in a plié. "What?"

Diane, who kept right on going up and down with a grace owed to long years of apprenticeship at St. Louis Youth Ballet, repeated the question.

It had been haunting her—*he* had been haunting her—for the past two weeks, ever since she had run into him that Sunday on her tour of Yorkville. It had been an afternoon she'd dissected over and over.

At first their meeting had disconcerted her. She'd been embarrassed to show up in what was clearly his territory. She didn't want him to think she'd planned it. And she'd been reluctant to allow him to come along. But short of being rude, she hadn't seen how to stop him.

But then, when he had come, and when he'd followed her every move with such interest, she'd been determined to show him just how good at her job she was.

She'd been the consummate professional. And she'd been a warm, caring, effective guide at the same time. She hoped she had impressed him. She sure as heck impressed herself.

His invitation to join him for a cup of coffee hadn't been much of a surprise. What had been was the way their time together ended.

He'd been rapt in his attention. He'd listened when she'd talked just as he always had. And Diane had had to be careful not to allow herself to bask in his approval the way she had done in the past. Nick's approval didn't matter now, she reminded herself. She was her own person, not his.

She was sure she'd made that point, too.

She had even dared to ask about him. That was when the mixed signals had started coming her way.

It surprised her. Nick had always been so straightforward, so focused. Now he seemed—was it possible?—lost.

Certainly he'd given her little to go on. "My father came back to work, so I left." That was it in a nutshell.

But there was plenty there between the lines—unhappiness, aimlessness, melancholy. All emotions she'd never in her life associated with Nick Granatelli.

And no matter how much she tried, she couldn't seem to stop thinking about him.

She'd have thought that Lazlo's would have given him the perfect chance to do what he'd been training for, what he'd been doing, what he wanted to do.

And yet he seemed to show little interest in it at all. "It was a job," he'd said.

That wasn't Nick, either.

She sensed a hesitation in him, a doubt.

And, at the end of the conversation, when he had asked her about Carter, she sensed something else. Anger? No. Maybe that was putting it too strongly. But irritation for sure.

Was he jealous?

It didn't seem likely. Nick had had a great deal more of her three years ago than Carter had now. He could have had all of her, and he hadn't wanted her.

It was Nick, not she who had walked away. He wouldn't be regretting that. Why should he?

No, he wasn't jealous.

He probably, she thought, had just decided that they'd dawdled long enough over their cups of coffee, that there was nothing much else they had to say to each other, that he had spent quite enough time catching up with a woman he must simply count among his old friends.

Still, she worried. Sometimes, when she took a group of people around Yorkville, she considered dropping in for *konyakos meggy*.

But she didn't want him to think she was chasing him. She wasn't.

But she did, heaven help her, care.

She wondered how he was doing, if he was any happier than he'd seemed that day, if he had made his peace with whatever had driven him away from Granatelli's, if he'd come to terms with New York.

She didn't want to ask him, of course.

Finally she asked Annie.

Since softball had ended, she and Annie met at a health club equidistant from their apartments. They ran laps around an indoor running track on Mondays. They did ballet on Wednesdays.

Diane never had enough breath left on Mondays to do more than gasp.

On Wednesday, two weeks and two days after she'd run into Nick at the restaurant, she found the courage to ask.

"He's okay," Annie said now, midcrouch. She gave Diane a searching look.

"We had coffee together a couple of weeks ago."

Annie frowned. "You did?"

Diane extended her leg along the barre, then leaned toward her pointed toes. "I was taking a tour around Yorkville." She gave Annie a brief rundown of their encounter, ending it by saying, "He didn't seem very happy."

"He's not."

"Because of leaving Granatelli's, you mean?"

Annie considered that for a moment. "I guess," she said at last.

"It's too bad."

Annie nodded. "It is."

"Maybe he just needs some time to adjust."

"Maybe."

"And a few friends."

"Mmm."

"You don't sound too sure?" Diane gave Annie a quick searching look.

Annie brushed her hair out of her face. "No. I agree," she said quickly. "He probably does need friends. Heaven knows, I'm certainly not enough. I'm gone so much."

"Maybe I'll call him."

Chapter Ten

Paprika was to Lazlo's what basil was to Granatelli's. And if basil had caused his father's problems, paprika, it seemed to Nick, was going to do him in.

There was Hungarian paprika and there was Bulgarian paprika. There was Spanish paprika and Moroccan. There were paprikas in varying shades of red and brown. There were paprikas that were sweet and paprikas that were pungent. There was paprika that suited one recipe and paprika that suited another.

Most of all there was paprika that his chef liked and paprika that he loathed.

It wasn't immediately apparent from an order form which paprika, the likable or the loathable, Nick was dealing with.

He never knew until it got here, and then he heard loud and clear. The diners unlucky enough to be eating in Lazlo's at the time, heard, too. There had been another outburst yesterday evening. It made him want to tear his hair.

It wasn't that he didn't appreciate his chef's problems. He knew what happened when you used oregano in a recipe that called for thyme. He knew the difference between poplar and cherry, chestnut and oak.

He could sympathize with the creative process, damn it.

It was trying to come up with the materials sight unseen that was the problem. It was so tedious, so thankless, so bloody boring. Some people, he conceded, might consider it a challenge. Not him.

It was his day off and he'd been in the office since seven. It was one now, and he still had plenty of work to do. He pored again over the order sheets, trying to decipher the codes and descriptions, forcing himself to concentrate, to finish up so sometime today he could go home.

But when the phone rang, he grabbed it. Any distraction would do.

"Want to play hooky and go fishing?"

His eyes widened. He dropped his pencil. "D-Diane?"

"Yes. Remember what you said about daydreaming you were fishing? Well, a bunch of us are going on Saturday, staying the weekend, actually. And I...wondered if you'd like to come along?"

He thought she sounded slightly breathless. He felt as if she'd knocked the breath right out of him.

Diane calling him? To go fishing?

"Er, yeah, sure," he managed, impulse setting in before common sense reared its ugly head.

"Great. We'll pick you up at seven-thirty, okay?" And she hung up before he knew what hit him.

"DO YOU SUPPOSE I could build a casket?" Annie asked when he got home.

"Mmm?" Nick's mind was miles away. Fishing.

"I've tried everything," Annie went on. "No undertaker will part with one for less than four hundred dollars. Four hundred dollars we don't have, naturally. And I don't know what else to do. So, do you?"

Nick, smiling, still turning over in his mind the invitation that had come out of the blue, blinked at her. "Do I what?"

Annie rolled her eyes. "Think I can make a casket?"

What she was asking registered for the first time. "What in hell do you want to do that for?"

"For my play," Annie explained patiently. "We're doing a wake simulation this month. *The Wake of Archie O'Leary.* And we had a perfect one. Unfortunately the director's uncle died and got himself buried in it this morning."

Nick nodded dutifully, not even thinking it was strange. He'd lived with Annie long enough now to know she acted in some pretty far-out things. But her recent spate of simulated dinner parties, wakes and weddings was proving to be popular with theatergoers, so who was he to say?

"Have you ever built anything?"

"A paper-towel holder in seventh grade."

He grinned. "I think you might need a bit more expertise than that."

Annie looked glum. "Maybe Jack could help me," she said. "Or Frances."

Her downstairs neighbors, she meant. Nick had met Jack Neillands and his wife on the stairs a couple of times. Jack was a model and Frances, a writer.

Nick said he didn't see how either occupation qualified them for making a casket.

Annie shrugged. "Well, maybe Jack has a saw at least."

"You get a saw and I'll build you a casket."

"You?" Annie goggled at him.

"Of course, me." Damn right, me, he wanted to tell her. He found that his fingers tingled at the prospect.

"What is there about being a restaurant manager that qualifies you to build a casket?"

"Not a thing," Nick admitted. "But being the grandson of Vittorio Cardona qualifies me for a lot."

Of course he needed more than a saw. He needed a plane, a level, a miter box, and more. Not to mention wood. But even offering made something spark to life within him. He wanted to do it, wanted the challenge. Paprika be damned.

Annie, galvanized by the possible solution to her problem, was already on the phone. Minutes later she turned to him. "The wood will be here in an hour."

Jack, serendipitously, turned out to have some of the things he needed in the basement workshop he and Malcolm, the owner of the brownstone, shared.

And when Nick walked into the narrow, low-ceilinged shop with its long, broad workbench and its wall hung with clamps and tools, and breathed in the smells of sawdust, turpentine, varnish and linseed oil, even though he'd never been there before, he had the oddest sense of belonging.

"You don't mind if I work down here?" he asked Jack, who had brought him down.

Jack shook his head. "It's Malcolm's really. But he and Julie have gone to Europe for a month. Before he left he was helping me work on a cradle for our coming addition." He grinned at his very pregnant wife who had followed them downstairs. "But now I'm on my own. I'm not all thumbs, but I've got maybe six of them, so if you want to offer some advice, it's welcome."

Nick, spotting a cradle lying against the far wall, went over to crouch down and look at it with interest. He ran his fingers along the curving oak. And as he did so, it was almost as if he could feel his grandfather's presence in the room.

He felt calmer, safer, more settled. He felt as if he'd come home.

"I'll take a look," he promised.

The casket didn't have to be professional quality, Annie had told him. It only had to look as if it were. To Nick, once he started, it was the same thing.

He measured, he mitered, he joined, he sawed. Things he hadn't thought about in years occurred to him. Memories he hadn't known he had, resurfaced, sometimes making him smile, sometimes causing a lump in his throat. Things his mind wasn't sure of, his fingers knew.

And always, there was the wood.

He forgot about Lazlo's, about the books and the orders, about the price of paprika, Hungarian or otherwise. He forgot the fumble-fingered waitress and the cashier with the sticky hands.

He forgot about what had led him to Lazlo's in the first place—about Granatelli's, about his parents and Sophia and Ginny Perpetti.

He even forgot about going fishing with Diane.

He became wholly consumed with his work, with the wood beneath his fingers, with the precision of the tools in his hands.

"A simple pine coffin," Annie asked him for.

A simple pine coffin was what she got. But for all that it was simple, it was beautifully made.

Its corners were true, its top was level. He had sanded it until it was as smooth as glass. And when he lifted the lid and lowered it, the hidden hinges moved without a whisper.

It was a job Vittorio Cardona would have been proud of.

He worked the rest of the day, into the evening. Into the night. And when Annie came down after she got home from her performance, she stopped on the bottom step and stared, amazed.

Nick looked up from the stool where he sat. He had finished half an hour before. But he hadn't left. He hadn't wanted to leave.

The smell of the sawdust soothed him. The feel of the wood under his fingers was as seductive and enticing as a woman's flesh. Not as exciting, of course. But as he sat and rubbed his fingers again and again along the wood he held, tracing the grain of the piece of scrap pine in his hand, he felt for the first time in nearly two and a half years a sense of peace.

"Nick?" Annie's voice was almost a whisper.

He looked up and brushed his hair off his forehead, then gave her a rueful smile. "Oh, hi. Back already?"

She glanced at her watch. "It's almost two."

"Is it?" He'd lost all track of time. He shrugged. "Well, I finished it. What do you think?"

She came all the way into the room and walked around the casket, which sat in the center. She touched it gently, running her fingers along the edge of the lid.

"Open it," Nick said.

She lifted the lid. It went up soundlessly. She slowly lowered it back down. "You did all this today?"

He nodded.

"You're amazing."

"I was possessed." And saying it, he knew it was true.

She looked at him, still marveling. "Your grandfather taught you all that?"

"Yeah. It's all right, then?"

"It's marvelous," Annie assured him. "I'll stain it to-morrow. One of the costumes girls can do the liner on Saturday. It'll be perfect." She threw her arms around him. "You saved my life."

"Yours, maybe," Nick agreed, giving a sidelong glance at the casket. "Not Archie's."

Annie grinned. "Archie won't mind in the least."

Nor did he. The director was equally pleased.

"D'you suppose your friend would look at that table we've got that keeps cracking?" he asked Annie.

"Sure," Nick said when she asked him. "When?"

"Oh, sometime next week. No hurry. Besides, you're busy this weekend, aren't you?"

He had forgotten about that.

Had he really said he'd go fishing with Carter and Diane?

HE HAD. He did.

Diane wondered at first if it had been a mistake to invite him. Carter was, to be sure, less than thrilled.

"You what?" he demanded with as much asperity as she had ever heard from him when she told him she'd asked Nick to spend the weekend with them.

"Why not?" she said with more confidence than she felt. "You asked Jack and Frances."

"That's different. They're friends."

"Nick's a friend."

"Is he?" Carter looked at her doubtfully.

Diane steeled herself against his doubt, against her own. "Yes," she said. "And he needs friends right now. He seems so...I don't know...lost."

Carter still looked doubtful, but he only said, "He went to Harvard Business School, right?"

Diane nodded.

"Then he's got more direction than a compass. I know the type. Runs in my family."

"He's not like your family," Diane said.

"We'll see," was all Carter promised.

But however unenthusiastic he was, Carter had had a childhood of proper manners drilled into him, and he was far too much of a gentleman to show any reservations at all when they picked Nick up Saturday morning.

It was an hour-and-a-half drive to Carter's family home in northern New Jersey. In the past it had always seemed relaxing to Diane.

Now, even with Carter behaving impeccably, it seemed fraught with peril. For one thing, she found that her desire to be friends with Nick might be academically sound. Emotionally it had more cracks than a three-egg omelet.

Her panache seemed nonexistent. Her savoir faire *n'existait pas*. She couldn't think of a thing to say beyond the mundane, and when she managed even that, Carter's contributions were polite platitudes and Nick seemed disinclined to do more than mumble.

Why had she bothered? It wasn't as if Nick wanted her to. It was obvious he couldn't have cared less.

He wasn't rude. But she could feel a distance between them, a wall that kept him apart from her now. It was as if he wasn't the Nick she had once known at all.

She should have left well enough alone. She should have accepted his abrupt departure the day they'd had coffee for what it was—a dismissal, a desire to have nothing more to do with her.

Heaven knew she didn't need any more to do with him.

Still, she had done it and he had accepted.

So they were stuck with each other—and Carter was stuck with both of them for the next two days.

Please God, the time would pass quickly.

"How's your family?" she asked finally as they sped along the highway heading west. They had already talked about the weather, about softball, about walking tours, about Carter's health food store.

She turned toward the back seat and caught Nick's gaze momentarily. He shrugged, unsmiling. "I got a letter from Frankie last week. She's the one with the hat shop."

"How's she doing?"

"Fine. She got what she wanted and she's making something of it."

"Good for her," Diane said.

Nick's mouth twisted. "Yeah. Good for her."

His gaze shifted abruptly and he lapsed into silence, turning once more to stare out the window.

So much for conversation.

Diane didn't think she wanted to try again.

Carter's family owned a colonial mansion, a stately brick pile with a curving driveway leading up through manicured grounds. If it looked as if it could have graced the cover of *Architectural Digest,* it was only because it had. Diane sensed Nick's skepticism at once.

"You *fish* here?" he said as they pulled up in front and piled out. He looked around disbelieving, as if the catches of the day could only be caviar, lobster and fillets of sole.

Carter laughed. "Just wait."

Diane knew what he meant.

The immaculate order of the house and its front grounds gave way to totally uncontrolled woods behind. She waited, too, for Nick's reaction.

His amazement was obvious when they led him through the subdued elegance of the house to the back and pointed out the dense foliage not twenty yards from the porch.

"Voilà," Carter said. "The forest primeval." He waved an expansive arm. "Nobody's been there since Washington's troops in 1778." At Nick's astonished look, he grinned. "Just kidding. The stream is about a hundred yards down that path." He nodded his head toward a narrow break in the foliage.

Nick looked from Carter toward the woods and back again. He also looked as if he might finally believe it. "Did you fish here as a kid?"

Carter gave a shake of his head. "My folks didn't buy this place until '83. They used to have a country house in Massachusetts, but my dad wanted to be close to the city. They come out a lot during the summer, but now they head to Florida every chance they get."

"Nice work if you can get it," Nick said dryly.

"I never thought so," Carter said.

Nick's brows rose.

"Carter is the family black sheep," Diane said.

"Not wholly black," Carter grinned. "Just sort of a dirty gray. Diane's working on reforming me."

"I am not," she protested at once when Nick's gaze sharpened.

Carter laughed and gave her a quick hug. "You couldn't even if you tried." He dropped a kiss on her forehead before turning to Nick. "Jack and Frances will be along later. You've met them?"

Nick frowned. "You know them?"

"I went to college with Jack. We go back a long way," Carter said. "And I'll be damned if I want Jack to catch the biggest trout. I'd like to get a jump on him if I can. Are you game?" He gave Nick a conspiratorial grin. It was the first offer of friendship he'd made. Diane prayed it would be reciprocated.

She saw Nick hesitate. His eyes flickered from Carter to Diane and back again. Then, at last, he nodded. "Sure. Why not?"

And for the first time that day Diane heard a flicker of enthusiasm in his voice.

JACK CAUGHT the biggest trout and several more besides. Nick caught three medium ones and a carp.

Carter caught an old boot.

"It's my father's, too, wouldn't you know?" he grumbled as he tossed it back. "Too bad the old man isn't in it."

Nick, who'd had similar thoughts about his own father over the past few months, shot him a sympathetic grin.

It was well past midday now. The sun was shining, bathing the woods and the river in a warm Indian summer glow. They'd been fishing for most of the day, first he and Carter, then later with Jack.

Every once in a while he told himself he would wake up and find himself back at Lazlo's going over invoices. But so far he hadn't. He was beginning to believe his whereabouts might be real.

They sat in the silence of the woods, and far from being plagued with doubts about the wisdom of his decision, Nick found that he was enjoying himself.

Diane had walked down to the river with them, but had declined to fish. "Frances won't," she said. "I'll just keep you company till Jack comes."

She stayed a little more than an hour, sitting quietly, her back against a tree, her face tilted upward to catch the gentle autumn sun. Nick looked at her from time to time with hunger, with regret, with resignation.

Carter caught him staring once and he felt unaccountably guilty. But the other man didn't speak, just tugged a little on his fishing line and shifted his feet.

When Diane left to go wait for Jack and Frances, Nick braced himself, expecting Carter to warn him off. But Carter just watched her go, his own gaze a little wistful. He didn't speak.

He lay back against a tree trunk, letting his line drift, his eyes closed, content merely to fish.

When Jack came he stirred himself to be a genial host. He joked with Jack, scowled at the almost immediate success of his friend who caught a trout within minutes of arrival. Nick, watching them, was reminded of his own relationship with Jared, with his brothers. Something he missed. And when Carter made a point of including him in the conversation, he roused himself to make an effort.

That was when Carter caught the boot.

"Wouldn't you know," he said. "The old man is determined to get me."

"You have trouble with him?" Nick asked.

Carter shrugged, his mouth twisting into a parody of a smile. "We get along," he said. "As long as he goes his way and lets me go mine. I can't work with him, that's for sure." His eyes met Nick's, frank and open.

Nick nodded. "I understand."

Whatever differences they had, whatever competition they felt over Diane, they were in complete accord on this.

"Right," Carter said.

"My old man's a peach," Jack said bluntly. "When I grow up, I'm going to be just like him."

Carter turned a baleful stare on him. "Go soak your head."

Jack just laughed, hoisted his full string of trout, stood and stretched, then thumped his chest in a modest Tarzan imitation. "Let's go back. Maybe supper will be ready."

"Dreamer," Frances said when he got there. "Supper will be ready when you cook it." She smiled seraphically up at him from a chintz-covered armchair.

Nick thought she looked cozy and maternal and extremely well loved.

"Like that, is it?" Jack growled as he bent over her.

She giggled and reached up to pull his head down so that their lips met. "Just like that."

And Nick, watching them kiss, felt a sudden ache course through him. His gaze went at once to Diane. Their eyes met, their minds remembered. Whether their hearts both jolted or only his did, Nick couldn't have said. But Diane's eyes flickered away and a flush stained her cheeks. She moved quickly to Carter's side and hooked her arm through his.

"Come on," she said, looking up at him. "Let's you and I put the meal on." She was already drawing him away with her. "What do you have in the kitchen?"

"Trout," Carter said equably, allowing himself to be drawn. "Acorn squash. Salad fixings. An old boot."

"A what?"

He grinned and tugged at her ponytail. "Come on. I'll show you."

Nick watched them go, the ache still there. It took a determined effort to refocus, to remember that there wasn't anything left between Diane and him anymore.

Still, even concentrating on the present didn't completely solve his problem. He hovered in the doorway, unsure where he'd be more superfluous—in the kitchen being the third wheel between Diane and Carter or in the den where Jack and Frances hardly needed a chaperon.

Before he could decide, Frances pulled Jack down so he sat on the arm of the chair beside her, while she asked Nick, "How did you know Diane?"

"When I was at Harvard," he said and, at Frances's encouraging smile, he came into the room and sat down. "I went out with her roommate once."

He gave them an abbreviated and not entirely accurate account of their friendship at Cambridge. He played up the camaraderie. He played down the passion. He forced himself to sound cheerful and hail-fellow-well-met. And by the time Diane reappeared to say that dinner was served, he felt reasonably comfortable with the story he'd told.

Diane's behavior certainly corroborated it. She was a wonderful hostess, making sure that everyone had everything they needed. She was solicitous of Frances, teasing with Jack, and she treated Nick with the genial concern of an old friend.

She occasionally reminisced about something that happened back during their year at Harvard. And when she did, if he caught her eye, she gave him a conspiratorial smile.

"Nick remembers, don't you?" she'd say.

Nick always did.

After supper he and Jack washed the dishes while Frances, Diane and Carter ate chocolate cake. Then, as he and Jack finished and joined them in the living room, Carter got up to add a log to the fire and the discussion turned to firewood.

Diane beckoned the two of them, a smile on her face. "Come sit down," she said to both of them, but her eyes were on Nick. "Surely you have an opinion about the relative merits of various types of wood."

Nick shook his head. "Not for burning, I don't. Only for working with."

"Building with, you mean? As in houses?"

"No, furniture."

Carter turned. "You build furniture?"

Jack grinned. "Does he build furniture!"

Nick shrugged, embarrassed by Jack's enthusiasm, yet still enthusiastic himself. Even lying on the riverbank today, he'd found himself thinking how much he'd enjoyed building Annie's casket. "I built a casket for Annie."

Diane looked horrified. "A casket? For Annie?"

Nick laughed. "For the theater company."

"You should have seen it when he finished," Jack said. "It'd be a privilege to be buried in it."

"Jack!" It was Frances's turn to sound horrified.

Jack shrugged negligently. "It would."

Carter looked up from the fire. "Do you do other stuff? Do you do bookcases?" he asked.

Nick hadn't, but he found the idea appealed. "What sort of bookcases?"

"I want some built into my living room." Carter finished with the fire and got to his feet. "It's a great barn of a place, all wall, no storage. And I have a lot of books." He shrugged, looking embarrassed almost. "No big deal. I just wondered. I mean, if you don't—"

"Can I look at it?" Nick asked.

"You would?"

Nick nodded, unable to mask his eagerness.

Carter grinned and stuck out his hand. "As soon as we get back."

"It's a deal." Nick grinned, too.

"There are some upstairs in the library that I really like," Carter said now. "Want to see them?"

Nick said sure.

Later, when he had time to think about it, as he lay awake, but not sleepy, in the high mahogany bed that lay like a brocade-covered whale in the bedroom he'd been assigned, he was amazed.

The day had turned out quite differently than he'd imagined.

When he'd contemplated coming along with Diane and Carter, he'd thought it would be tense. Carter was her boyfriend, after all. He'd be making claims by the minute and Nick would be there to watch.

But, having agreed, even though he'd told himself he was crazy, he had also told himself it would be an exercise in discipline, in getting his head on straight once and for all.

Instead it had been great fun.

He had relaxed and enjoyed himself as he hadn't done in ages.

Being around Diane had gradually become easier. The wall between them seemed to have crumbled a bit. She had treated him casually, comfortably, just as she might an old friend.

They were old friends, Nick reminded himself.

And he had tried to treat her the same way.

Carter had made it easy by not trying overtly to lay a claim to her. He hadn't behaved jealously or proprietarily. After an initial coolness, he'd been warm and mellow and funny, treating Diane more like a kid sister than an impassioned lover. Nick couldn't have disliked him even if he'd wanted to.

He found he didn't want to.

Carter might have the woman Nick had once loved, but he hadn't taken her away. He'd been there to pick up the pieces.

And, Nick thought ruefully, who could blame him?

No, there was nothing about Carter Nick disliked. In fact, the more he saw of him, the more he found he wanted Carter for a friend.

He found, as well, that he had stopped looking forward to the weekend being over. He was looking forward to morning, to sharing the cooking duties with Frances, to going for a drive through the small northern New Jersey towns, as Diane had suggested, to looking through the shops, buying some apple cider, then enjoying a bit more fishing before they left for home.

He thought about the bookcases Carter had shown him. He thought about the living room Carter had described, about finding some walnut to work with, about maybe buying a few tools of his own.

He hopped out of the bed and paced around the room, stood by the window, stared out into the moonlit night and smiled.

For the first time since he had slammed out of his parents' house, thrown his bags in the car and headed east, he felt as if the knotted skein of his life was beginning to sort itself out.

For the first time since he had told his father he didn't want to be part of Granatelli's anymore, he had found something that gave him a sense of satisfaction.

For the first time since that night back in Newport before his father's heart attack, Nick went to bed again with a smile on his face.

It was ironic, he thought, that he owed it to Diane.

Chapter Eleven

Against all odds, they became friends.

The three of them. Diane. And Nick. And Carter.

"The three musketeers," Annie called them.

It wasn't far from the truth.

Where one was, the other two weren't far behind. They jogged together, they swam together, they fished together. They cooked and talked and played cards together.

Nick built Carter's bookcases, and while he did, Carter and Diane offered moral support, meals and a bountiful supply of St. Louis beer. They also offered praise and congratulations when the job was complete and well-done.

When Diane needed a tour guide through Little Italy for a group of Italian tourists, it was Nick who found himself reading up on the neighborhood's history until three in the morning, then spouting it all forth the next afternoon in the Italian he hadn't used in four years.

"They loved it," Diane told him afterward. "They loved *you*. Do you want a job permanently?"

She was kidding, of course, but Nick was pleased.

"I liked doing it," he told Diane as they sat together in her living room while Carter made mulled wine in the kitchen. "It opened my eyes."

She rested her head against her arm, which was propped on the back of the sofa. Her eyes were wide and warm and watchful as she smiled at him. "How?"

He felt the stirrings of desire and promptly squelched them. She was his friend now, that was all. Deliberately he focused on answering her question. "I don't know if I can explain it really. It just made me recognize the pressures my folks were under, the ones they put me under..." He gave an awkward shrug. "It helped," he said simply.

Diane nodded. "I'm glad."

There was a look in her eyes that warmed him. It made him want to kiss her, to touch her, to feel once more the closeness that long ago they had shared together. But she was on the couch, he was in the chair, and before another moment passed Carter reappeared bearing a tray with glasses and pitcher, pungent and steaming, filled with wine.

"All hardworking men and women deserve a brew like this," he said, setting the tray on the table and sitting down next to Diane. He leaned over and casually kissed her on the mouth, then turned back with equal casualness and began to pour.

Nick sucked in a careful breath and let it out slowly.

That was the way it was, he reminded himself. They were friends, yes. But if there was more than friendship here, it was between Diane and Carter now. They were the ones who had the future.

He had no part in it—deserved no part in it, he told himself forcefully. He'd had his chance.

Still, sometimes the present mingled with the memories and somewhere deep inside he hurt.

BECOMING FRIENDS with Nick Granatelli was turning out to be the easiest—and the hardest—thing Diane had ever done.

It was easy because once she'd loved him, and all the many things she loved about him were still there.

It was hard for exactly the same reasons.

Still, she couldn't regret it happening. She thrived on the afternoons they spent playing touch football in Central Park, the evenings Carter would invite them both over for a meal and they would play Monopoly after. Both Nick and Carter battled to the death over their various monopolies, while Diane, with the luck of the indifferent, seemed more often than not to win.

She liked watching Nick work with wood. Sometimes, in the mornings when she didn't have a tour to prepare for, she would stop by Annie's to see if he was there. More and more frequently she found him in the basement workshop, humming softly to himself while he worked on whatever project was current.

He did fantastic work. She remembered him mentioning his grandfather's workshop while they were at Harvard. She hadn't given it a lot of thought until she saw him in one of his own.

There was a sense of peace about him when he was there. He exuded a purposefulness that made her simply enjoy watching him. It was quite different when she watched him at Lazlo's.

Of course, it was a different type of work. He never sat still when he was at Lazlo's, unless he was trying to sort through orders or balance the books. He was dealing with people and crises and everything was in flux. He handled it well, unflappably, she would have said.

But he didn't smile much.

And whenever she asked him how things were going at work, he never did more than shrug.

Sometimes, when he wasn't in the workshop, she'd catch him sitting in the apartment, his feet on the coffee table, a pile of Lazlo's papers spread out on his lap, his eyes shut, an expression of stark weariness on his face.

She wanted to ask him if he was all right. But once she did, and his eyes snapped open and he said, "Of course I'm all right," in such a gruff tone that she backed off at once.

"I just thought you looked . . . unhappy."

"I'm tired," he said sharply. "My bloody maître d' quit without notice. I have a cashier I think has her hand in the till, and half my suppliers don't seem to give a damn whether they get their stuff there when I need it or not. I have a right to be tired."

"Of course you do," Diane agreed soothingly.

But privately she thought he was more than tired. She learned not to speak of it, though. Their friendship didn't seem to allow for that.

Another thing their friendship didn't allow for was discussing his family.

When they were at Harvard he'd been full of stories about his father and mother. Though she'd never met Dominic and Teresa Granatelli in person, she had a very clear idea of the robust, determined man and the strong, capable woman who were Nick's parents. She also had a pretty clear picture of his brothers and sisters, from the managing Sophia to the slightly flaky Vinnie.

But whenever she asked about any of them, he shrugged her off. He might offer a tidbit of information, but nothing more. It didn't even seem to Diane as if he knew much more. She found herself wondering if his "running away" meant that he wasn't even communicating much with them.

But when veiled, curious hints aimed in that direction produced nothing but curt, monosyllabic responses, once again she backed off.

She wished he would share with her the way he used to.

But, she reminded herself, things were not the way they used to be.

They were friends now.

She wasn't asking for more.

But she wondered just exactly when it occurred to her that sometime she might.

IT HAPPENED—she could actually put her finger on it—the day Frances and Jack invited everyone up to their place in Vermont for the Thanksgiving weekend.

Without even stopping to think, she found herself asking Frances at once, "What about Nick?"

"He's invited," Frances assured her, knitting needles clicking away, most of the already-finished blanket draped across her increasing belly.

The happiness Diane felt at hearing it was far beyond what it should have been if Nick had been only her friend. She felt a great burst of joy deep inside her.

Then, aware of how intense she sounded, she looked away quickly, staring out the window as if the Federal Express truck double-parked in the street below was of all-consuming interest.

"Did you think I wouldn't ask him?" Frances asked her. "I like Nick a lot."

"Yes."

There was a pause. Then Frances asked, "What do you think about him and Annie? As a couple, I mean."

Diane's head jerked around, all pretense gone. "Nick and Annie?" She shook her head. "No way."

Frances's needles slowed down. "Why not? They're living together. He came to her when he left St. Louis."

"They're friends," Diane said firmly. "Just friends. They have been for years. Besides, matchmaking between them has already been tried."

Frances gave her a skeptical look. "If you say so," she replied after a moment, her knitting picking up speed again. "You aren't, perhaps, protesting just a bit too much, are you?" she asked with a sly smile.

Diane knew her cheeks were reddening, but she shook her head anyway, unwilling to admit to anyone else what she only dared to hint at to herself.

"I dated Nick for a while," she admitted after a moment. "But that was a long time ago. A very long time ago."

Whatever finality there was in her voice must have been convincing, for Frances shifted the blanket on her lap, then nodded. "All right. Anyway," she said hopefully, "now there's Carter."

Diane managed a smile. "Yes. Now there's Carter."

But nothing was likely to happen between herself and Carter, she thought. If anyone was just friends, they were. Good friends, dear friends. They loved each other in their way, but not the way she and Nick once had.

Or, she amended, touching reality tentatively, she'd thought they had.

"I'm really glad about you and Carter," Frances went on now. "You're the best thing that's happened to him since I've known him."

She was looking so pleased that Diane felt unaccountably guilty. "I don't think ... I mean, it's not ... Carter's a friend, that's all," she said quickly.

"Carter needs a friend," Frances said and smiled an enigmatic smile.

Diane wondered if perhaps, in Frances's eyes, she'd also protested a bit too much about that.

SHE DIDN'T WONDER too long, however. She spent most of her time when she wasn't consumed with work, walking around smiling, pleased at the notion of spending a holiday weekend with Nick.

It didn't seem to matter if other people were going to be at Frances and Jack's—even if she loved them dearly. It only mattered that Nick was.

Perhaps, she found herself thinking, it would reawaken the feelings they'd once shared. Perhaps it would be the start of something new. Perhaps...

She had a million "perhapses"; they all came to naught.

Nick wasn't going to Vermont.

He had to stay in New York, he told her, and work at Lazlo's instead.

She wanted to protest, to say he should forget Lazlo's, that he should quit Lazlo's since he didn't like it anyway, that he should please, *please* just come.

She didn't, of course, say a word.

Instead she bit her tongue, smiled and said, "Enjoy yourself here, then," as brightly as she could when he waved them off the Wednesday afternoon before the holiday.

Nick smiled. "Sure."

She looked at him closely to see if she might find a few signs of regret, some slight hint that he wished he were coming along. He was giving nothing away at all.

Sighing inwardly, Diane gave him another smile and a blithe wave as Carter bore her off in his baby-blue '56 Thunderbird.

"We'll bring you some turkey," Carter said.

Nick nodded. "Do that."

Her last glimpse of him was of him standing on the sidewalk, the brisk November wind ruffling his hair as he stared after them. His hands were tucked into the pockets of his jeans, his shoulders were hunched, but he wore a perfectly bland, have-a-nice-time smile on his face.

She had, in fact, a terrible time.

Not that anyone knew.

If there was one thing Diane knew how to do, it was be a good guest. She was a lovely guest. She walked through the hills with Carter, helped Frances stuff the turkey, and played backgammon with Jack.

She helped out when she was asked and sometimes when she wasn't. But just as she wasn't reticent, she wasn't pushy, either. She participated when it was required and disappeared when privacy seemed the order of the hour. But wherever she was, whatever she was doing, her heart was with Nick.

She wondered what he was doing every hour of every day.

She wished she were back in New York, eating Hungarian goulash at Lazlo's, watching Nick fret over his invoices, interview his candidates for maître d', charm his guests.

And even though everyone else bemoaned their return to the hustle and bustle of the city, she was delighted when Sunday evening rolled around and they were finally on their way home.

THE FIRST WEEK in December Frances had her baby. Jack, normally the most relaxed of men and reputedly the best coach in Wednesday night Lamaze, panicked and promptly forgot everything he'd learned.

"It's happening," he blurted the moment Nick opened the door to his middle-of-the-night pounding.

He was a Jack Nick barely recognized, his chest still bare, his hair disheveled, his jeans half-zipped. There was a light of desperation in his eyes as his gaze darted about the room.

"*What's* happening?" Nick asked him, fairly certain, but wanting a moment to get his bearings.

He'd been in the midst of a dream he had no business having and he needed to readjust, to get his feet back on the ground.

He'd told himself it was a good thing he had to work at Lazlo's over the holiday. He'd tried to convince himself that not spending time with Diane was the right thing to do.

And he might be right; but it didn't help him get through the day with fewer thoughts of her.

Nor, as witness the dream just interrupted, was he sleeping any better than he had been.

"It's Frances!" Jack said now. "She's having it! The baby!"

Nick yawned and rubbed his eyes. "Now?"

"Now!"

Annie, peeking out from the bedroom, saw Jack and echoed his panic, her face turning white. "Oh, my God."

Nick gave her a withering look. "How far along is she?" he asked Jack.

Jack shook his head. "I don't know. She woke me up a few minutes ago. She just rolled over in bed, poked me and said to go get the car. What should I do?"

"Go get the car."

Jack raked his fingers through his hair. "But I can't leave her. I—" He stopped, looking at Nick helplessly.

It was a look Nick had seen before. His brother-in-law, Aldo, the sanest and most mellow of men most times, fell apart whenever Sophia went into labor.

"It's sympathy," he'd told Nick.

"It's idiocy," Nick had countered. But he understood. There was always the worry, the helplessness, the sense of having set in motion something that was now out of one's control. He knew deep in his gut that if it were Diane, he'd feel the same way.

"Never mind," he said, holding out his hand. "Give me the keys. I'll get the car. You bring Frances downstairs when I pull up in front."

"What about me?" Annie demanded as Jack departed. "What shall I do?" She was stuffing her left foot into her right shoe even as she spoke.

Nick took one look at her and said, "Go back to bed."

When he drove up out front fifteen minutes later, Jack was there, ready to bundle Frances into the car. Frances, smiling, her face flushed, was far calmer than Jack.

"You're a dear to be doing this," she said as she eased her considerable bulk into the seat. "Isn't he, Jack?"

"Dear," Jack muttered, tucking her in solicitously, shutting the door gently, then clambering into the back and slamming that door. "Step on it," he said tersely.

Nick did.

At the hospital it didn't matter what Jack did, it was out of his hands. "I'm coming with her," Nick heard him insisting to a doubtful nurse.

"He is," Frances agreed. "He helps me breathe. He keeps me calm."

The nurse snorted. "Him?"

Frances smiled, her fingers tightening around Jack's as another contraction began. "Very definitely him."

And Nick watched almost wistfully as the skeptical nurse led them through the swinging doors and toward the elevator to maternity. When they had disappeared, he sat down to wait.

It was odd sitting there, waiting. It was like being on another planet, another plane of reality altogether. People scurried to and fro, all purposeful and intent. They walked past him, deep in conversation, unseeing. He might as well not have existed. He certainly didn't matter.

Would he ever matter to anyone? he wondered.

He remembered the hours he'd spent sitting at the hospital in St. Louis, fretting over his father.

He had mattered then, of course, but not in the way he wanted to. He'd mattered because he was the one who could keep things going, who could keep the family on an even keel, who could make the restaurant work. Nick Granatelli, the person, hadn't mattered a whit.

And now?

Now everything had changed.

No, not true, he corrected himself. The Granatellis hadn't changed.

But he had. He'd changed a lot.

"There you are." He heard a voice and turned to see Carter and Diane coming toward him. They looked concerned, but rumpled, as if they'd staggered out of bed to get here.

Had they been in bed together?

Nick shoved the unwelcome question away as quickly as he thought it. It wasn't his business, he told himself. He didn't want to know.

Determinedly he dredged up a smile. "Did Annie call you?"

Diane nodded, sitting down beside him. "And then went back to sleep. She has a matinee today, but she said to call as soon as we heard. How's Frances?"

"Doing fine. I think it's Jack we should be worrying about."

Diane rolled her eyes. "Jack will just have to cope."

"He will," Carter said. "He always does." There was a split second's pause, then he shook his head as if he'd just remembered evidence to the contrary. "No, not true. Not when it comes to Frances."

"They'll both be fine," Nick said firmly. "And so will the baby."

"Please God," Diane breathed, and before Nick realized it, she had taken his hand in hers and was holding on.

Nick's mouth twisted at the bittersweet sensation of her hand in his. He shut his eyes briefly. "Please God," he muttered.

But it wasn't simply Frances and the baby he was praying for. Though what it was for, he couldn't have said.

JASON DANIEL NEILLANDS was born at 6:37 a.m., dark-haired and robust with a healthy set of lungs.

"The spitting image of his father," Frances told Nick, Diane and Carter from her bed shortly thereafter.

She was smiling and pale as she looked up at them. Her freckles stood out against her ivory complexion and her gingery hair was curly with sweat, but Nick didn't think he'd ever seen her look lovelier.

"His mother's son," Jack said, his voice breaking. His hair was still tousled, his eyes red. And though he couldn't stop grinning at his friends, he didn't even for a second, let go of his wife's hand.

"Have you seen him yet?" Frances asked them.

They shook their heads. "He wasn't ready for visitors yet," Diane told her. "They said to come back in a few minutes."

"He's lovely. Beautiful, just like his father," Frances said. "Of course, I'm prejudiced."

"Just a bit." Carter grinned. "I'm ready to be prejudiced too though, since I'm going to be his godfather."

That, Nick remembered, was something they'd asked Carter last week. Carter had seemed a bit doubtful at the time, questioning their good sense.

"What kind of role model are you looking for?" Carter had asked them.

"You only have to be yourself," Frances had assured him.

Carter grinned. "Foolish of you," he said. But he'd looked extraordinarily pleased.

Nick wondered if they'd ask Diane to be godmother, but Frances had said almost at once that an old friend of hers from Vermont was going to be godmother. Nick had looked at Diane, curious to see if she was miffed.

She didn't seem to be. She had smiled brightly. "Good idea."

Nick thought so, too. And if it had anything to do with jealousy, he wasn't ready to admit it.

"I hope you don't mind," Frances had said to her a bit worriedly.

Diane had shaken her head emphatically. "Not at all."

Now she looked at Frances and Jack—at the way they were looking at each other—and turned to Carter and Nick, taking them each by an arm. "Come on, guys. Let's leave these two alone."

Jason Daniel was both the spitting image of his father and his mother. He was beautiful. He had Jack's features in newborn form, but he had Frances's long, elegant fingers and, when he opened his eyes, though they might not focus yet, Nick definitely got the feeling that when they did, they would look at everything with the same curiosity and intensity that Frances's eyes did.

But it wasn't Jason who captured the bulk of Nick's attention.

It was Diane's reaction to this tiny newborn child.

She stood there, transfixed, absolutely silent and unmoving, her attention wholly caught by the child before her. Behind them breakfast carts rattled by, telephones rang, the intercom called for Dr. Washington to come to Emergency.

Diane, it seemed, heard nothing, saw nothing, beyond the child in the bassinet. She stood, her forehead pressed to the glass, and stared.

Finally she blinked, then swallowed. Her eyes went from the baby sucking his fist, first to Carter, then to Nick, silent tears rolling down her cheeks.

"Are you all right?" he asked her softly.

Biting her lip, she nodded her head helplessly and turned back to the child.

Nick, smitten with an ache he couldn't put a name to, didn't ask anything else.

In the face of the miracle of new life, what, after all, was there to say?

NOTHING MADE Diane regret more the loss of her love with Nick than the birth of Jack and Frances's son.

She thought she'd reached the depths of pain years before. She thought she'd come to terms with it. She thought, even as she began to hope they might get back together again, that she hoped in moderation.

She found out differently when she stood in the nursery and looked at Jason and then at Nick.

All the "might have beens" came rushing back, inundating her, swamping her, destroying her hard-won equilibrium. All she could think was how much she would have loved a child with Nick, how, had things worked out between them three years ago, they might have had one—or even two—by now.

Instead they stood side by side and looked down at the sign of another couple's love for each other. And when their eyes met, it was in silent pain; with words they could say nothing at all.

But it wasn't just the two of them, she realized. Even Carter, normally voluble, seemed struck dumb in the face of the child before them. He stared at Jason, swallowed hard, then leaned his forehead against the glass and stared some more.

Finally, dazed and disoriented in a way that Diane had never seen him, he shook his head.

"Holy cow," he muttered. "A baby."

"You were expecting maybe a rhinoceros," Jack said, coming up behind them.

"I wasn't expecting anything," Carter said with complete honesty. "I never really thought about it. I mean, Frances kept getting fatter, but I never thought..." His voice trailed off and he stared once more with awe at the newborn child. "Amazing."

"Yes," Jack said simply, and he sounded no less awed than Carter. He looked down at the child again, a smile lighting his face. "My son."

"A big responsibility," Carter said gravely.

Jack cast him a sidelong glance, a furrow deepening between his brows, as if Carter's words surprised him. "It is," he agreed after a moment.

"You'd better do a damned good job," Carter continued.

"I'll try." Jack was smiling, but Carter wasn't. His gaze was fixed on his best friend.

Diane watched them both, curious at the interchange, amused at Carter's unsuspected gravity. Her gaze flickered to Nick, wanting to share the amusement. His face was just as grave.

"He might be your son," Nick said suddenly, "but he's his own person, too. Don't forget that."

Jack's gaze met his as if he heard the unspoken message in Nick's words. "No," he promised. "I won't."

Diane, seeing Carter about ready to extract another promise, leaped to Jack's defense.

"I'm sure he'll do fine," she said. "Let's give the man a chance." She gave Jack a quick hug, then turned to Carter and Nick. "I think we should be going," she said. "I have to give a tour of Yorkville at ten."

They followed her willingly enough. Both still seemed slightly dazed. They caught a cab in front of the hospital, and for the better part of thirty blocks not one of the three said a word.

Carter got off at 72nd, mumbling something about walking the rest of the way to the health food store, needing the air to clear his head. Nick and Diane continued on across the park toward the Upper East Side, she to her office, Nick to Lazlo's.

When Carter left them it seemed as if the silence grew to fill the space.

Diane looked at Nick, sitting there hard against the opposite side of the cab, staring out the window, his eyes focusing on heaven knew what, and she had to say what was in her heart.

"He's lovely, isn't he?" she asked. "Jason, I mean."

"Hmm?" Nick seemed to struggle back to her from far away. When at last he had, he attempted a smile. "Oh, yeah. He is."

"Makes me envious," Diane ventured.

Nick's eyes met her's briefly, then skated away. "Yeah."

"Do you ever wonder..." she began, then faltered. Should she do this? Did she dare? "I mean, if we... I mean, it could have been..." She stopped, panicked, then threw caution to the wind and plunged ahead. "Have you ever thought... we might have had a child by now?"

Their gazes collided again, hers frightened at her audacity, his surprised, at first bleak, then changing to— To what? Diane wasn't quite sure.

But he didn't look away. And even when the cabdriver pulled up in front of Lazlo's, he didn't move. Blue eyes searched her brown ones, and what he saw she wasn't certain. But finally he nodded his head, a smile more wistful than bitter on his face.

"Yeah," he said, his voice heavy. "I have."

Chapter Twelve

I have.

It wasn't much, granted, but it was enough to give Diane fantasies that wouldn't quit.

She sat at her desk at the hotel late into the night and remembered the fathomless look in Nick's eyes, the slightly rueful curve of his mouth when he had said those two words, acknowledging the present that might have existed had things been different.

What if...

What if, indeed? she chided herself. That was then; this was now.

But still, she couldn't seem to help it. She couldn't stop imagining that things might change now, that their friendship might turn to something more, that they might come together again.

She didn't know what Nick thought.

In the beginning, she admitted to herself somewhat ruefully now, he had been still interested in her. His following her home from the softball game had proved it.

But back then she'd been terrified. She'd shrunken from any contact with him at all. Nick reminded her of all her inadequacies, recalled all too well for her the innocent child she had been.

But once she'd got over her initial panic, once she realized that she did in fact have some feelings left for him, she took stock. Three years had passed, and she had changed. Part of her reason for becoming friends with him again was to gain an opportunity to prove it.

She thought, in fact, that she had proved it.

But to what end?

The more she had proven herself competent, talented, a woman to be reckoned with, the more it seemed Nick had withdrawn into himself.

If he still felt passion for her, she couldn't tell. If he had been interested in her in September, he didn't seem to be now. Except as a friend.

He seemed, she thought grimly, quite content to be her friend.

Yet now and then there was still that something in his expression—a longing she saw once in a while when she caught him looking at her, that wistfulness she hadn't experienced alone at the sight of Jack and Frances's son—that made her think there might still be something there.

An ember. A tiny, weak, flickering flame.

God, how she wanted to fan it to life again.

But how? *How?*

"ST. LOUIS?" Nick strove to keep the dismay out of his voice as he echoed Diane's words. His fingers tightened around the rung of cherry he'd been sanding. He'd thought he was simply going to have to endure another session of being near her while she watched him work. He didn't realize he was going to have even deeper issues to cope with.

Her words shouldn't have been surprising, of course. Where else, he asked himself glumly, would she be spending Christmas?

He guessed he'd been hoping she'd spend it here. He guessed he'd been hoping she'd spend it with him. Or at least with him and Carter.

But no. He'd dropped it into the conversation quite without thinking, saying something about the holidays, and she'd looked momentarily baffled, then said rather hesitantly that she wouldn't be here.

"No?" He'd paused in his work and looked up at her. "Why not?"

Her brown eyes widened and she said, "I'm going to St. Louis."

Then, even before he got over hearing that, she'd added, "Aren't you?"

The question stopped him cold. Him spend Christmas in St. Louis? He hadn't even considered it. Didn't *want* to consider it. He didn't want to think about St. Louis at all.

Diane, apparently seeing all those thoughts writ large on his face, said quickly, "I just assumed...I mean, I didn't..." She flushed. "I'm sorry."

Nick shook his head quickly. "No need." He gave a wry grimace. "It's just that it wouldn't be a very happy holiday for anybody if I did."

"But your folks—"

"My folks have plenty of other kids and grandkids to keep them busy," he said, trying to sound nonchalant.

"It's not the same."

"It'll have to be," he said shortly. Because he certainly wasn't going, though he had to admit that only part of the reason now had to do with the rift between himself and his parents. The rest had to do with Diane.

The more time he spent with her, the less he could imagine himself in St. Louis with her now. Before there had been economic issues, even class issues, if you would. But now there was, he thought grimly, the success issue.

Diane was. He wasn't.

It was as simple as that.

Hell, yes, he'd thought about the fact that they might have had a child by now. The thought could, if he dwelt on it, almost kill him with pain.

So he tried not to think about it. He tried to get by, day by day. And it wasn't getting any easier.

"I wouldn't be going, either," she told him, "except one of my friends is getting married." She sighed and smiled. "Actually she's more the granddaughter of one of my grandmother's friends, but—" she gave an expressive shrug "—you know how those things go."

Nick did and he didn't. He knew about family obligations, God knew. He had enough of his own.

But he didn't know about blue-blood society weddings, and if Diane's grandmother had anything to do with it, that's what this one would be.

He gave a noncommittal shrug. "Sure," then bent his head and concentrated again on the chair rung he was sanding.

He expected she'd leave then, but she didn't. She stood watching him wordlessly, unmoving. It unnerved him.

The first time she'd come he'd thought it was a whim, that she'd been curious. He'd shown her around, told her what he was working on, then had thought she'd leave.

She hadn't. She'd just said. "Do you mind if I watch?" and he'd looked at her so blankly that she'd colored and said, "I won't disturb you, I promise."

Nick didn't see how she could promise any such thing, since her mere presence did incredible things to his mind, his heart, his loins. But he'd shrugged, saying, "Suit yourself." And while he tried to concentrate on sawing a straight line, Diane had stood and watched.

He'd been aware of her every breath, had wondered what she found so fascinating, had not been able to ask. He'd been unable to even formulate a sensible question for the rest of her visit, and he'd breathed a sigh of relief when she'd left.

He was astonished when she showed up to watch yet another day. And another.

At first he'd offered to stop, but she'd shaken her head. "No. Don't mind me," she'd say. "I won't bother you."

She had, of course. Sometimes, like now, he found her presence distinctly unnerving and felt as if he ought to say something to fill in the silence, to justify her being there. But at other times he became absorbed in his work, discussed what he was doing with her, and without realizing it at first, found that he liked having her there, moving about quietly, reading, watching, making the occasional comment or asking a question.

It gave him hope where, as far as he was concerned, there was damned little reason for any.

"Is this for Carter's father?" she asked now. Carter's father had seen the bookcases Nick had recently finished and had commissioned a project of his own.

Nick nodded. "A whole set of dining-room chairs. Twelve of them. Solid cherry."

"You must be pleased."

"Yeah."

"But you're still going to hang on at Lazlo's?"

He scowled at the censure in her voice. "What's it to you?"

"You're my friend."

"And friends find fault with their friends?"

"No." She paused, then apparently reconsidered. "Maybe they do. Maybe when they see their friends wasting their lives doing things they don't like, walking around like they're half-dead all the time because they have no enthusiasm about their work when they could be doing something about it—''

''Yeah? What?''

''Quit!''

Did she think he hadn't considered it? Ever since their talk before Thanksgiving, he'd toyed with the idea, tossed it and turned it in his mind while he did his own tossing and turning in bed at night.

But the conclusion he came to was always the same. ''There's the little matter of eating. You want to support me?''

''I will,'' she said without missing a beat.

''The hell you will!''

''I'm successful enough.''

''Too damned successful,'' Nick muttered, his head bent.

''What?'' She stared at him, aghast.

He twisted the chair rung, strangling it. ''Nothing.''

But Diane had heard what he'd said. ''Does it bother you that my aunt knew the people who gave me the concierge job?''

''No, of course not!''

''Then what does bother you?''

But he couldn't tell her that. It was buried too deeply, it mattered too much.

''Nobody handed me my tour job,'' she went right on.

''I know that!'' Nick gritted his teeth. ''We can't all be as successful as you are, I guess,'' he said bitterly and turned back to the wood he was sanding.

Damn her, anyway. *Quit Lazlo's,* she said. Just like that. Just as if other jobs were there for the taking that would make him her equal. Once he'd had that chance. Not anymore.

God knew he thought about it. He couldn't help himself. He entertained the hope almost every night when he lay in bed and stared at the lights in the high-rise apartments in the next block.

If only he could quit Lazlo's.... If only he could get some jobs lined up.... If only he could feel secure enough about getting something steady with the woodworking, then maybe, too, he and Diane could—

He blotted the thought out now as he did then.

Once he'd been a dreamer. Once he had dared. Never again.

He could feel Diane's eyes boring into him. He hardened his resistance to the needs they evoked. "Have a nice time in St. Louis," he made himself say.

"I will," she said flatly. There was a moment's pause, and she added, "Too bad you won't come."

"Can't," Nick corrected, flicking her a glance.

Diane gave a small snort.

Nick glared at her, then shifted uncomfortably under her unblinking stare. "Maybe next year," he muttered.

"You're afraid."

His head jerked up sharply. "The hell I am!"

"What would you call it?" Her eyes flashed fire.

He'd never seen her like this, combative, irritated. "I'd call it doing what *I* want for a change instead of what my family expects me to do!"

"And you want to stay in New York?" she mocked.

"Yes," he said, tightly.

"Work all day at Lazlo's? You love it so much." She was smiling, infuriating him.

"It's my job, damn it! It's what I have to do!"

"Is it?" Her voice changed suddenly and she sounded almost sad.

It was the hint of pity that undid him. "You don't have to feel sorry for me, damn it!" he said harshly.

Whatever sadness he'd heard vanished in an instant. Diane bristled like a hedgehog right before his eyes. She tossed her hair and lifted her chin, then looked at him down her version of the Hoffmann nose. Her brown eyes glinted.

"I wouldn't dream of it," she said with biting scorn. "You're feeling sorry enough for yourself."

"JENNIFER'S HAVING ten bridesmaids, you know," Gertrude Hoffmann said, stirring sugar into her tea.

"Ten bridesmaids?" Diane, who'd been staring blindly out at a pre-Christmas snowfall, looked at her grandmother, aghast.

Gertrude Hoffmann calmly sipped her tea and ignored her granddaughter's outburst. It was the way she handled everything, ignoring what she didn't want to see or hear, plowing straight on, determined to make the world over in her own image of it.

"All in blue silk, Minna says," she went on as if Diane had never interrupted. Minna, Jennifer's grandmother, was quoted frequently these days.

Gertrude had been nattering on for the better part of an hour now about Jennifer Naylor's wedding, and Diane had been half listening, making what she hoped were coherent noncommittal responses—always the best kind where Grandmother Gertrude was concerned.

But she'd been preoccupied then, as she had been ever since she'd come home, with thoughts of Nick.

She anguished about the angry accusation she'd flung at him. She fretted that it might be the last she'd ever see of him. Yet more than once she stopped her fretting and her anguish to tell herself it might be good riddance if it were.

It was true, what she'd said about him feeling sorry for himself. It was true that he was hanging on to a job he hated for the least sensible of reasons. He was so much happier when he was making furniture or refinishing woodwork. He was more like Nick.

Try telling him that, she told herself.

And, of course, she had. For all the good it did her. He had taken her flaring accusation with stony silence, never even looking up when she'd stamped her foot and flung herself across the room and up the basement stairs.

He didn't call her after her outburst, either. And he hadn't been at Carter's the next evening when they strung popcorn and cranberries. He didn't even call her to say goodbye.

And now it was Christmas Eve, and though she knew better, she couldn't help wondering in spite of herself how he was and what he was doing today.

It was her preoccupation with Nick that had caused her to express her honest astonishment at what seemed an excessive number of bridesmaids. Normally she wouldn't have said a word.

But it didn't matter anyway as Gertrude, as usual, chose not to acknowledge it. "Graduated shades from ice to indigo," her grandmother went on. "Stunning, I should think. Pity you couldn't have been one of them."

"I don't know Jennifer that well," Diane reminded her.

Gertrude looked down her nose. "Pish."

Diane shrugged helplessly. "We were only at cotillion together one year."

"She could have asked you, regardless," Gertrude maintained. "Matthew was one of her father's dearest friends."

"Perhaps Jennifer wanted her own friends."

Gertrude gave an elegant snort. "What does that have to do with it."

It wasn't a question. It was a statement. In Gertrude Hoffmann's world friendship had little to do with such things. Social obligation was all.

"You'll like her brother," Gertrude continued. "He's finishing a residency at Johns Hopkins this year, Minna says. Cardiology."

"Mmm."

"A fine field, cardiology," Gertrude said. "And he'll soon be wanting a wife. A man like that needs a wife." She brightened as if the idea she'd been leading up to for the last half hour had suddenly, miraculously occurred to her. "Derek would be absolutely perfect for you, dear. And vice versa, of course."

That demanded more than a noncommittal response. "I don't think—"

"Of course you don't think," Gertrude snapped. "You never think! And you never meet anyone appropriate in that ridiculous job of yours! That's why I arranged for you to dance with him. I—"

"Grandmother!"

Gertrude gave her a look of purest innocence. "What dear?"

"You asked this man to dance with me?"

"I mentioned it to Minna. Heaven knows, he needs you as badly as you need him."

"I don't need—"

"*I* know what you need, my dear. And you would do well to pay attention. I haven't gotten to be seventy-four through sheer stupidity."

"I know that, but—"

"So you will dance with him. Smile at him. Talk to him. And who knows?" Gertrude smiled her cat-eating-canary smile. "Maybe next Christmas you'll have ten brides-maids, too."

It was no secret that Gertrude would like her married off—and married off well. She had been parading eligible men in front of Diane since she'd graduated from eighth grade.

Cynthia had objected, of course.

"She's a child, Mother," Diane had often heard her say.

"One can never start introducing one's child to the right people at too early an age," Gertrude said flatly. There was a pause, then, "I clearly should have started earlier with you."

What her mother answered to that Diane never heard. She did hear, moments later, the slam of a door.

"Oh, Mom," she'd whispered, and she'd felt the hollow aching sensation in the pit of her stomach that she always felt when she confronted the memory of her mother's ill-fated marriage to the man who had fathered her.

Gertrude was determined not to let such a mismatch happen again. She would do everything she could to prevent it.

Diane smiled as she wondered what Gertrude would have thought if she'd married Nick.

And there she was . . . right back at Nick again.

She had to stop thinking about him. There was no point. The next move—if there was a next move—would have to be up to him.

"Tell me about this cardiologist," she said to her grandmother. And she settled back against the sofa and pretended once again to listen.

CHRISTMAS in New York. In the minds of most it conjured up the leg-kicking Rockettes at Radio City Music Hall, the sight of skaters whizzing past the brightly lit tree in Rockefeller Center, the smell of roasting chestnuts and pine trees, and the sound of Salvation Army bell ringers.

For Nick it conjured up the legs of a hundred Chicken Paprikas, the sight of thirty *Dobosh Tortes*, the smells of dilled zucchini and roast duck and goose, and the sound of five waitresses calling in sick so they could spend the holiday with their families.

He nearly went berserk.

He got to the restaurant at seven on Christmas Eve morning, he didn't leave until eleven in the evening.

When he finally dragged himself back to Annie's empty apartment—even she had gone home for the holiday—he was exhausted.

He stumbled up the stairs, and fell onto the sofa facedown.

He had given up St. Louis for this?

Even the thought of confronting his family, armed as they would undoubtedly be, with a dozen rounds of guilt, didn't seem as bad as going through the day he'd just experienced. He rolled over, kicked off his shoes and loosened his tie.

"Come have a drink with us. Or even better, dinner," Carter had said to him. "My family's quite tolerable on state occasions. They rise to them."

But Nick couldn't rise to it, and he knew it.

He knew where he wanted to go. He knew whom he wanted to be with. It wasn't on the Upper East Side and it wasn't the seasonally well-behaved MacKenzies.

His gaze lit on the reindeer Christmas card propped up on the desk. The one that had come yesterday morning with a St. Louis postmark. The one with no other message than a signature.

"Diane," he muttered, closed his eyes and pulled the pillow over his face.

WHEN THE PHONE RANG it was well past midnight. He'd fallen asleep on the couch, the pillow still on his face. He groaned and groped for the receiver only because one tiny molecule in his brain wouldn't believe she'd given up on him.

But it was a gruff, masculine voice demanding, "Where's Annie?" on the other end of the line. Nick frowned, disconcerted, then recognizing the accent, amazed.

"Jared?"

There was a moment's pause, then, "Nick?"

In spite of his weariness, Nick found he was smiling. "Damn right."

If it wasn't Diane—and had he really expected it would be?—to hear from Jared Flynn on Christmas was the next best thing.

No one had ever been as good a friend to him as Jared.

So he was a little surprised at Jared's fierce "What in hell are you doing there? Are you—" There was a pause, then, "Where's Annie?"

There was a wealth of sudden suspicion and irritation in his tone. Nick could hear it. And once more he wondered just how platonic this relationship between Annie and Jared had been.

He didn't ask.

Instead he said quickly, "Annie isn't here. She went home for the holidays."

Jared breathed what sounded rather like a sigh of relief. "Ah, well, that's a surprise. They closed down for the holiday, then?" His suspicion was gone, but there was an edge to his voice and a tone Nick couldn't quite put a name to.

"Just for today. But she won't be back till the weekend. Director's orders. He thought she needed a break."

"Ah." It was a weary, all-knowing sound.

"Do you want her number?" Nick asked.

"Doesn't matter," Jared said brusquely. "I...only thought, since it's Christmas, you know, and us having been friends and all..."

"Friends?" Nick couldn't help querying.

"Drop it," Jared said.

And Nick, with pains of his own along those lines, did.

"So, how are you? What are you doing in New York, then?" Jared asked. "There's a story behind it, to be sure."

"A long story," Nick said wearily. "Have you got a while?"

"As it happens, I have," Jared replied, and there was a kindred weariness in his tone that made Nick wish his friend weren't a continent away.

"I've the whole bloody night," Jared said. "Tell all."

So Nick did.

He didn't intend to, really. He didn't want to burden his friend. But he'd forgotten how much he and Jared had once shared, how close they once were, how they'd bolstered and supported each other when their dreams and their hopes had once been all either of them had had.

And so when he began talking, he couldn't seem to stop.

He told Jared about his father, about the family's expectations, about his increasing dissatisfaction with it all. He told him about Ginny, about her expectations, about his inability to be the man everyone wanted him to become.

"So I split," he finished hotly. "I got tired of fulfilling everyone else's expectations. I wanted, for once, to do what I want to do!"

"And are you?" Jared asked him quietly.

And are you?

Three simple words. So simple they caught him off guard. So blunt they made all his arguments and rationalizations meaningless. So direct that for once they elicited an honest answer.

"No," Nick said. "I'm not."

And as he spoke, the angry heat that had been building up within him seeped from his voice. In its place the weariness crept back.

And with it came the pain, the loneliness and all the other emotions he fought, like tigers, day and night. Most of the time he vanquished them. Not tonight.

"You have to," Jared said.

Nick didn't say anything. He remembered Diane telling him he ought to quit. He remembered her telling him he was afraid. He remembered her scornful dismissal of his qualms, her accusation that he was feeling sorry for himself.

And he knew she was right.

Just as Jared was right.

What he enjoyed was working with wood.

He was good at it. He liked it. It gave him a personal peace and satisfaction that even Granatelli's never had.

Diane said he should try it professionally.

And he'd dismissed it out of hand.

Why?

Because, and here she was also correct, he was afraid. Afraid of failing.

He never had. In his whole life Nick Granatelli had never failed. He'd never even worried about it. Life had always been, if not easy, then at least quite manageable. He was clever, capable, a good student, a good athlete, and he had all the Granatellis behind him, cheering him on.

Nothing he set his hand to ever crumbled under it. Nothing he'd set his mind to ever slipped away.

"My son, the success," Dominic used to call him and clap him on the back.

And while Nick had laughed, he'd always known the pride that had come with his father's approbation. He'd basked in it, in fact.

If his natural abilities had given him a head start on success, family approval had always been his safety net.

But he didn't have that approval anymore.

If he tried woodworking, he was trying it on his own.

It was scary. It wasn't by any means a sure thing. But if he didn't do it, he knew now with certainty he'd regret it all his life.

And if he did risk it?

A faint smile began to dawn on his face. If he did risk it, he could take other risks—like trying to get back together with Diane.

"I will," he said to Jared now.

"I'm a fine one to be telling you." Jared sounded almost sheepish.

Nick didn't know what he meant. It seemed to him that Jared had every right to tell him. He had pursued his own dream in the face of obstacles Nick couldn't even imagine. Now a big-time Hollywood actor, he'd succeeded beyond his wildest dreams. But even as he thought it, Nick realized something else.

"Didn't matter who else told me," he said with sudden insight. "It only mattered when I told myself."

CARTER CALLED on Christmas morning. Annie called. Jack and Frances called. There was no call from Nick.

Was she surprised? Diane asked herself.

No.

Disappointed?

Oh, yes. Because for all the pep talks she gave herself reiterating how not seeing him was for the best, she couldn't control her fantasy life. She couldn't forget. And she couldn't squelch entirely the fledgling hope that somewhere inside the unhappy man she knew now was the Nick he'd once been, the Nick who had been her soulmate, her friend. The man who had come closer than anyone to being her lover.

She knew she'd made him angry that last day in New York when she'd come to his workshop. She hoped she'd made him think. At first she'd worried about it, regretted it. Now she wished she'd said more, not less.

She was almost sure she hadn't been wrong about the way he'd looked at her the day Jason was born. She was almost certain he still felt something for her. Perhaps if she'd goaded him, challenged him, told him how she still felt . . .

But she hadn't.

And he hadn't written or called.

Yet even in the face of silence, she clung to a hope. Maybe, with patience he could be brought around. Maybe, she told herself with inveterate optimism, he was already.

But so far she'd had no sign.

She got through the day on social grace alone. She smiled when required, said thank-you when appropriate, and passed the turkey on cue.

She didn't feel much of anything until late Christmas evening when the phone rang and Cynthia answered, then held it out and said, "It's for you."

It was Carter. Again.

"I'm missing you," he told her.

She missed him, too, but not the way he meant. That worried her, too, the little hints Carter seemed to be dropping lately, the way he looked at her, the sense that to him there was getting to be more than friendship here.

"Did you have a good Christmas?" she asked him.

"Not bad. The old man didn't even show up."

"What about your mother?"

"Oh, she was there. Hanging in. She ought to dump the bastard," he said with as much savageness as she'd ever heard from Carter.

"That's for her to decide," Diane said gently and heard him sigh.

"I suppose. Anyway, it isn't much of a Christmas topic. How was yours?"

"Fine. Everyone showed up at least."

He told her about calling Frances and Jack. She told him about talking to Annie. And then she had to ask.

"Did Nick come for dinner?"

"No. I don't know where he is."

"He didn't even stop by?"

"Nope. I tried to reach him. He's not at work. He's not at Annie's. Or Jack's. Maybe he went home for Christmas, after all."

"Do you think?" But even as she voiced the question, Diane felt the hope inside her burst into flower.

Of course he had. He was a Granatelli, wasn't he?

A man like Nick, even one who'd run away, wouldn't let a holiday keep him away. He'd come back. She was sure he would.

And if he'd come to St. Louis to see them . . .

She smiled all over her face.

He'd made a move.

WHEN GERTRUDE had suggested—no, demanded—she get a new dress and hat for Jennifer's wedding, Diane had been indifferent. When Minna suggested a little hat shop called The Mad Hatter not far from Neiman-Marcus she'd manufactured several reasons why she couldn't go.

But now all her reasons had vanished. She not only went to The Mad Hatter, Francesca Granatelli, Prop., she was smiling as she walked in the door.

Up until this moment she'd only thought of the Granatellis in the abstract. She had known the remarkable influence they'd had on Nick, but she'd never encountered any of them.

Suddenly she wanted to.

The smiling blond woman who waited on her had Nick's eyes, Nick's smile. She was so friendly, so welcoming, so correct in her assessment of just what Diane would need for Jennifer's wedding, that Diane liked her at once.

And as the woman wrapped her purchase, Diane found herself asking with as much casualness as she could muster, "Are you by any chance related to Nick Granatelli?"

She might as well have dropped a bomb. The woman's head jerked up and her words, which had been flowing so easily, dried up. Her mouth formed a silent O, and for a moment there was only silence.

Then slowly she nodded, her expression, once merely friendly, was now intently curious. "His sister."

"Frankie?"

The woman shook her head. "No. I'm Sophia. It's Frankie's shop, but sometimes I take over so she can work on her hats and I can get out of the house." She gave Diane a cautious, still curious, smile. "Where do you know Nick from?"

"I . . . live near him in New York." That seemed enough to say for now.

"You're not from St. Louis?"

"Yes, but I live in New York now. I'm home for Christmas." She paused a millisecond, then dared to ask, "Is he?"

"Home?" Sophia snorted. "Not Nick."

Diane frowned. "But I thought...I must've been mistaken."

"Must've." Sophia concentrated on wrapping the hatbox, then sighed and asked, "Have you seen him recently?"

"About a week and a half ago."

"How is he?"

Diane wasn't sure how to answer that. She'd obviously misread one sign. She wondered about the others. "He's...all right," she said finally. "Working hard."

"At what?"

Surprised that he hadn't even told his family, she shrugged. "He's managing a little Hungarian restaurant on the Upper East side."

"He could be managing *our* restaurant," Sophia said gruffly.

Diane didn't know what to reply to that. She shifted from one foot to the other, wishing she hadn't come.

"He'd better come to his senses pretty quick," grumbled Sophia. "Ginny isn't going to wait forever."

"Ginny? Who's Ginny?"

Sophia blinked. "Ginny? Ginny Perpetti. Why, she's Nick's fiancée, of course."

It came out of the blue, the fatal left jab when you had the wrong side covered. Diane felt her mind reel. "His...f-fiancée?"

"For the moment anyway," Sophia said grimly. "She's a saint, Ginny is. But I don't know how much longer she'll sit around waiting for him. Stupid man."

Stupid man? No stupider than she was, Diane thought dazedly, her dreams evaporating even as she stood there.

Nick Granatelli? Engaged? Oh, God.

"I...d-didn't realize," Diane stammered. "He never said."

Sophia looked disgusted. "Figures. Just goes to show how crazy he's behaving. Arguing with Papa. Fighting. Carrying on. Acting like an idiot. I couldn't believe it when he took off. It doesn't make sense. He's got everything—*everything*—going for him—the restaurant, Ginny, the folks' house even, if he wants it—and he acts like it's a disaster!"

A disaster, Diane thought, was exactly what it was. For her.

"It's a good thing Ginny is so understanding. Not many women would wait," Sophia went on.

"I guess not," Diane said hollowly. She took one last stab. "Is she...sure? That he's coming back, I mean?"

Sophia stared, then rolled her eyes. "Of course he's coming back! It's a momentary aberration, that's all. He's a Granatelli, isn't he?"

He's a Granatelli, isn't he? Diane had asked herself the same question last night. She knew the answer.

She held on to the edge of the counter for support. Her mind tested the "momentary aberration" idea and found it all too likely. She felt sick.

"There've been a lot of demands on him these past few years." Sophia said. "Papa's heart attack, his having to leave school. He took over too soon, I suppose. He never really got to sow any wild oats, I guess." She smiled and shrugged, as if the explanation were that simple.

Perhaps, Diane thought grimly, it was.

She'd never thought of herself as a wild oat before. The idea wasn't comforting. It was, however, probable.

Sophia finished tying a red bow on the hatbox. "He'll come around," she went on. "It's just a matter of time. It's all here waiting for him. The family, the restaurant, Ginny. Papa knows he had good ideas. He's ready to make some concessions. And Ginny will, too. Did he tell you about that business with the menu?"

"No, he—"

"I knew it. I knew he'd regret it. Probably embarrassed to even mention it. Imagine throwing away a life over a little bit of risotto." Sophia laughed and shook her head. "No. He's a loyal guy, our Nick. He won't let us down."

Diane took the hatbox wordlessly and smiled a bleak smile. "No, I suppose he won't," she said in a voice that sounded to her own ears as hollow as a drum. "Thank you very much."

"You're quite welcome." Sophia walked her to the door. "Are you going back to New York soon?"

"Right after New Year's."

"And you'll see Nick?"

"Probably." Though she'd love to avoid it.

Sophia smiled. "Good. When you see him tell him Papa's waiting. Tell him Ginny's waiting. Tell him a June wedding would be nice."

Chapter Thirteen

He handed in his resignation at Lazlo's the day after Christmas. It wasn't much; but it was a start.

He owed them two weeks' notice and he'd give them that. But the die was cast. He was out of the restaurant business forever.

He was now Nick Granatelli, woodworker and furniture restorer, pure and simple. He was also, for all intents and purposes, unemployed.

As he walked out into the lead-gray afternoon, he felt a moment's panic, a throat-choking fear of the unknown, and then, quite suddenly, the sharpest surge of exhilaration he'd ever known.

He felt, for the first time, as if he were truly his own man.

He took a deep, cleansing breath, not even caring that it was ten parts car exhaust. Then he headed back across the park, feeling expansive, liberated, alive.

His only regret was that Diane was still in St. Louis, that he would have to wait until she came back to tell her of his decision.

He could have called her, but he knew he wouldn't. He was on the right track now and he knew it. He wanted to see her face when she knew it, too.

He did go to tell Carter. He stopped at Jack Sprat's on his way home, needing to tell someone, to share his good news.

Carter was in the back room, sitting at his desk, scratching his signature across a stack of invoices in front of him while a lullaby played in the background and he rocked a baby buggy with his foot.

Nick halted in the doorway and stared.

Carter kept right on flipping through the invoices, unaware that he was being watched, unaware of any outside interference at all until the lullaby ended and there was a tiny whimper from the buggy.

Then he was on his feet in an instant, bending over the buggy and crooning softly to the child within.

Nick shifted from one foot to the other, then, finally and loudly, cleared his throat.

Carter looked up startled. "Oh, hi." His gaze flickered from Nick to the baby buggy and back again. "I'm babysitting," he said unnecessarily and with none of the sheepishness Nick might have expected from him.

The whimper turned into a hesitant wail, then a full-throated yell. There was no hesitation on Carter's part. He picked up the baby at once, cradling Jason in his arms with an ease of familiarity, rocking him gently as he swayed back and forth, humming in tune with the melody as he did so.

Nick watched them, amazed.

Jason hiccuped, let out one more tentative whimper, then managed to focus on the man holding him. Nick thought he might as well not have been there. They saw only each other.

Finally he cleared his throat. "Where're Jack and Frances?"

"Jack had an assignment this morning and Frances had a meeting with her editor. Brief, but necessary, she said. I don't think she trusts me with him for too long." Carter gave him a rueful grin.

"She should," Nick said. "You're a natural."

"You think so?" Carter looked inordinately pleased.

A corner of Nick's mouth lifted. He rocked back on his heels, considering man and child. "Yeah," he said. "I do."

Carter dropped a kiss on the baby's forehead. "So do I." He looked down at Jason again, then lifted his eyes to meet Nick's. "What brings you here in the middle of the day? Run out of paprika?"

Nick shook his head. "I quit."

Carter's eyes widened. "At Lazlo's? Why?"

"I talked to a friend of mine in California the other night. A guy I knew when I was in Boston. A guy who had even fewer possibilities to do what he really wanted than I did. But he didn't give up. And now he's doing it—with a vengeance. It made me think."

"Thinking can be dangerous," Carter said softly, his eyes drifting once more to regard the child in his arms.

"I know."

"It makes you want to take risks."

"Yes."

"And do things you never dared think of doing."

"Exactly," Nick said.

It was uncanny how Carter's words were reflecting his thoughts, his dreams.

"It's funny the way things work out," he said slowly, groping his way, looking for the right words in which to tell Carter how he felt about his future now, about his past. About his love of Diane.

"Sometimes," he said carefully, "you know you'd like to, it's just that the time isn't right. Or the circumstances. For what you want, I mean. For woodworking, for example."

"Or getting married."

Nick stared at him, amazed. Carter had really picked up his drift. "Yeah, right, or getting married. Sometimes, you know, the right person can be there under your nose for ages but you're . . . afraid to take the risk."

"I know."

"Afraid to make the commitment, afraid to ask her to commit to you . . ." He looked at the other man hopefully, and was relieved to see Carter nod vigorously. It was the one thing he'd dreaded, telling Carter how he felt about Diane.

"I know exactly what you mean," Carter said. He looked down at Jason again, still smiling. He touched the baby's cheek.

"And then something wakes you up, makes you look around," Nick went on. "And you realize what you should have done a long time ago."

Carter nodded. "Uh-huh."

"You understand?" Nick couldn't mask the hope he felt. It would make things so much easier if Carter understood about the past, understood about the circumstances, understood that even though he and Diane were friends, Nick was the one who loved her, who wanted her to be his wife.

"Of course I understand," Carter told him. "Didn't I just say so?"

"Yeah, but—"

"And I owe it all to him." Carter nodded at the baby in his arms. "He woke me up. Made me take a look at where my life was going. Who I wanted to spend it with. Made me realize what I really wanted." He was looking at Nick now, his gaze steady, his eyes smiling.

"What's that?" Nick asked.

"To marry Diane."

JENNIFER Amelia Naylor married Anthony Ward Beecher II with all due pomp and ceremony two days before the New Year. Diane Bauer and six hundred and twelve more of their closest friends were witnesses to the marriage.

They were wed at the new cathedral, attended by a veritable regiment of beautifully dressed attendants, feted at LaClede's Landing, and, after champagne toasts, a sit-down supper and a night of dancing, whisked off in Jennifer's father's private jet to their Bermuda honeymoon destination.

It was, according to Gertrude, the most perfect wedding she had ever seen, even more beautiful than Cynthia and Matthew's. It set a standard to strive for. To outdo if possible.

"When you get married..." she started every third sentence she said to Diane. "When you get married..."

Diane wasn't listening.

Diane didn't give a damn.

She was mulling over Carter's marriage proposal.

IT HAD HAPPENED last night. She'd been sitting there in quiet misery, watching the evening news with her mother, pretending vast interest in the state of the world, when the phone rang.

When Cynthia handed it to her, Diane had answered almost absently.

"Oh, hi, Carter," she'd said when she'd discovered who it was.

"Hi." Just the one word sounded different, as if there was a suppressed excitement in him—a newer, more enthusiastic Carter, struggling to get out.

"What's new?" she asked.

"My goal in life."

It was an answer designed at least to attract her attention. As far as Diane knew, Carter had never *had* a goal in life, beyond, perhaps, annoying his family by his free-spirited pursuit of irresponsibility with regard to the family fortunes and expectations. "Say what?"

"You asked me what was new, and I said—"

"I heard you. I'm just surprised. What is it?"

"I want to get married."

"Married?" God, Carter, too? Her knot of misery twisted tighter.

"Married," he confirmed. She could definitely hear it now, the excitement threading through his tone.

She curled her feet under her and found herself smiling in spite of her own unhappiness. "What brought this on?"

"Jason. He made me realize what I've been missing out on. Fatherhood. Family. Marriage. It's a long story."

"I guess it is." She'd hear it sometime. She couldn't bear it now. "Well, I'd say it's an admirable goal, Carter."

"I'm glad you think so."

"Oh, I do. I do."

He laughed. "That's what I hope you'll say."

"What? When?"

"At the wedding. Will you marry me?"

SHE SHOULD HAVE been expecting it. She'd seen it coming, after all.

She'd seen the way he'd been changing recently, the way he'd stopped teasing Jack for his devotion to his wife, the way he'd sought opportunities to be around them, especially since the baby had been born.

But she'd just said to herself, "Isn't that nice? Carter's mellowing in his old age. How about that?"

She hadn't thought beyond that because she hadn't wanted to. She'd been too busy thinking about Nick.

And now what?

What in God's name was she going to say?

No?

It wasn't that easy. They'd been friends—close friends, dear friends—too long. Maybe, she thought wryly, it was all those damnable social graces she'd been endowed with. No matter what she felt, she couldn't turn him down flat. Not without some compassion, not without gentleness, not without, however difficult, some explanation.

So she'd laughed, hemmed, hawed, stuttered, mumbled. She'd hedged and stammered.

And finally Carter said quietly, "I know. It was rotten of me. I never should've sprung it on you over the phone."

"It doesn't—"

"I'm a jerk."

"You're not a jerk, Carter. You're just . . . impetuous."

"And in love."

"No."

"Oh, yes, I am. We've been friends for a long time, Di. More than friends. And we've even been heading in this direction for a long time, too, haven't we?"

"Well . . ." But she couldn't absolutely deny it. She remembered the kisses, the warm, comfortable embraces all too well. And if they hadn't had the passion of Nick's, still there had been something there.

"You're just as slow as I was. Maybe even slower," he said, shaking his head. "It's because we've been content with the status quo. We've never really thought how much more there could be."

"I—"

"But I, for one, have been thinking lately. And I've decided: I want to marry you."

She hadn't said no.

She'd let him ramble on. She'd let him excuse her from answering right then. She'd let him tell her he'd see her at the airport when her plane landed and ask her in person. She'd let him hang up after he'd said, "I love you."

And she hadn't said no.

She'd sat through the rest of the newscast. She'd eaten a light supper with her mother. She'd dropped by her grandmother's for a quick visit.

And she hadn't heard a word.

She was busy turning over and over the predicament her life had become. Nick was going to marry someone else. Carter wanted to marry her.

She went to Jennifer and Anthony's wedding the next day, her mind still spinning, still trying to make sense of the upheaval of the past two days.

She looked stunning. She acted charming. It just went to show, she thought grimly, how deeply ingrained her social graces were.

She watched Jennifer and Anthony, saw them look at each other with tenderness, saw them laugh, saw them kiss. And she thought, *I will never do that with Nick. Carter wants to do that with me.*

And for just one instant, she let the pain of it surface, blinked her eyes furiously, sucked in a deep breath, and went back to smiling as if she were the prototype Wedding Guest Of The Year.

Jennifer and Anthony certainly never noticed her lapse. Nor did her grandmother or six hundred and ten of the other people who were present at the wedding.

The only one who noticed was her mother.

Cynthia didn't comment. Not then. She did her own fair share of smiling, hand-shaking, cheek-kissing and platitude-prattling.

Diane didn't even know her faux pas had been detected until late that night when she was getting ready for bed. She was removing the last of her makeup when there was a discreet tap on her door.

Answering it, she found Cynthia, already in her robe, standing there with a tray bearing a pot of tea and two cups.

"I thought we'd toast the bride and groom," she said and stepped into the room.

Diane hovered by the door uncertainly. The last thing she wanted tonight was to think about happy wedding couples.

"Come sit down, darling." Cynthia set the tray on Diane's dressing table, then sat down and patted the bed.

Smiling halfheartedly, Diane did. But she sat where she could see the mirror and continued removing her eye shadow, not wanting her mother's scrutiny. Cynthia very often saw too much.

Cynthia poured out the tea, added sugar to hers and milk to Diane's.

Diane concentrated on dabbing at her eyelids, steeled for whatever platitude served as the toast.

But Cynthia didn't speak until Diane's eyes met hers in the mirror. Then she raised her cup, a poignant smile on her face as she said, "To Jennifer and Anthony, may their good times be many and their bad times be few. And may they always be there for each other no matter what."

Then, blinking several times very rapidly, Cynthia bent her head and took a long sip from her cup.

Diane, shutting out the thought that it would never be that way for her and Nick, did the same.

I should drink to Nick and Ginny-Whoever-She-Is, she thought.

But nothing in her could make her do it.

"You were sad today." Cynthia was watching her, a gentle smile on her face.

It could have been a question, a guess, but Diane knew it wasn't.

She gave a tiny shrug. "Weddings sometimes do that to me."

Cynthia's mouth lifted at one corner. "Wishing?"

Diane finished removing her eyeliner, then sighed. "Maybe."

"Someone special?"

"Mmm."

"The man who called last night?"

"Carter?" Diane couldn't keep the surprise out of her voice. "Not . . . exactly."

"He's been very attentive," Cynthia commented. "He's called you several times."

"Yes."

"Is he the one you met at Aunt Flo's?"

"Yes."

"But he's not the one who matters." That wasn't a question, either.

Diane smiled sadly. "He matters a lot," she said, but without any real force.

Cynthia's smile was gentle. "I'm sure he does. But he's not the right one."

"I don't feel for him what I feel for—" Diane broke off suddenly. She'd never talked about Nick to anyone in the family, had never even mentioned his name except as a friend she'd met through Annie. At first it had been too special, later it had hurt too much.

She didn't imagine she was fooling Cynthia into thinking there wasn't a man responsible for some of her irritability three years ago. Her mother was far too astute. She was also circumspect, and she didn't pry. Unlike her own mother, Cynthia never demanded her daughter's confidences. Diane was grateful for that.

And she was discovering gratitude again tonight when faced with her mother's gentle perception and the comfort she so delicately offered.

"You don't feel for Carter what you feel for..." Cynthia prompted softly after a moment.

Nick. She would never feel for any man what she felt for Nick.

Had it been the same for Cynthia?

Diane looked at her mother and saw not simply the woman who had raised her, who had bandaged her cuts and scrapes, kissed away her petty hurts, baked her birthday cakes and attended more mother-daughter functions than anyone should have had to.

She saw as well a woman who understood the joys and pains of relationships—a woman who had had two marriages. And two losses.

She saw a woman who would understand.

She took a deep breath and began. "For Nick," she said. "Nick Granatelli."

And once she said his name, she couldn't stop. She needed to talk to someone about Nick.

She told her mother about their time together three years before, about how he'd seemed like a gift from God, the perfect man to fulfill her fantasy.

She saw Cynthia smile, a painful smile, as if perfect men were something her mother, too, had thought about.

She told Cynthia about Nick's father's heart attack, about Nick dropping out of Harvard and returning to St. Louis. She even, swallowing gamely, told her mother that she had volunteered to come with him.

"He said no," she admitted in a tiny voice. "He said I hadn't grown up yet. That I wouldn't ... fit."

Even now it hurt to say the words, and she ducked her head, dug her toes into the thick ivory-colored carpet, twisting a tissue in her fingers.

"Oh, Di—"

Diane shook her head. "He was right."

"Was he?" Cynthia said, surprising her.

Diane's gaze lifted and met her mother's, saw there compassion and understanding and heaps of love.

"I had nothing to offer him," she said. "I *was* a child."

"You were," Cynthia agreed. "But I think you did have something to offer him. You had a great deal of love—all for him."

"He didn't think love was enough."

Cynthia's gentle smile twisted slightly. "No—" her voice was a bare whisper "—sometimes men don't."

There was something in her voice—some deep, terrible pain—that Diane couldn't ignore. "My father, you mean?"

She rarely spoke of her father to Cynthia. When it came to speaking of Russell Shaw, Diane could never get beyond her mother's reserve.

It wasn't that she hadn't told Diane about him. When Diane had thought he was dead, she had always simply accepted the praise and the generalities that had made her father a shadowy benevolent figure in her past. She had hoped, after she'd discovered he was alive, that she would learn more about him, about his relationship with her mother.

It hadn't happened. Russ had been forthcoming enough about his own recent past. He'd even told her quite a bit about his growing-up years. But all he had said about his relationship with her mother was that, except for Diane, it had been a mistake.

"She's a wonderful woman, your mother," he'd said to Diane. "She deserved better than me." And that was all he'd said.

Cynthia had said little more about him.

But now she nodded, chewed briefly on her upper lip, then nodded again. "Yes, dear. Like your father."

"You...really did love him, then? It wasn't just..." But how did you ask your beloved mother if you were simply the product of a brief infatuation, a terrible mistake.

But she didn't have to say it. Cynthia understood.

"I loved your father more than anyone on earth," she said with a fierceness that left no room for doubt. "Don't you ever, *ever* believe otherwise!"

Diane couldn't help smiling. "My mother, the tigress."

Cynthia flushed. "I loved your father," she said. "And you'd better believe it."

"I do."

"He was good, and kind, and loving," Cynthia went on firmly. Her gaze drifted away and she stared unseeing across the room. "And when he left—" her voice broke "—he left because he was all those things."

"What do you mean?"

"He didn't want to be selfish. He wanted for us what he could never provide. He tried. God, how he tried. But it was too much for him."

"He could have loved us," Diane said, her voice thin, aching almost as much as her mother's.

"He did," Cynthia said quietly. "Never doubt that, either. And I loved him." She closed her eyes and added in a voice Diane could scarcely hear. "For all the good it did me."

"At least," Diane said, reaching for her mother's hand, "you had him for a while."

She had never had Nick. Except in her heart.

"I did," Cynthia agreed. "And I had you."

Their fingers squeezed and their eyes met with a warmth and a solidarity that made Diane sorry only that her father had missed out on sharing it.

"Also," Cynthia went on quietly, but firmly. "I had Matthew."

Matthew. Matthew Bauer. Kind and loving Matthew. The solid support on which both Diane and her mother had depended. The man who had shared in what Russell Shaw had left.

"Did you . . . love Matthew?"

Diane had always loved Matthew dearly herself. She could never have asked for a more wonderful father. And she'd always assumed her mother had loved him, too. But the fierceness of Cynthia's answer to her question about whether or not she had loved Russ suddenly gave her reason to wonder.

"Absolutely." There was no hesitation in Cynthia's reply. She smiled. "Matthew was the finest man I have ever known. He taught me that there was more to love than passionate yearning. He showed me how many various, wonderful facets of it there were. He was there for me when I needed him. He loved me as selflessly as ever a man could love."

It was true. Diane believed it. She knew that Matthew, too, had been married before and that his first wife had died. She couldn't help asking, "So . . . passion isn't necessary?" She didn't know if she felt more doubtful or hopeful.

Cynthia smiled. "Passion is . . . wonderful. Marvelous. Beautiful. But it is not everything. It is a part, not the whole, of love."

"And you were happy with Matthew?"

"I was happy with Matthew."

"And . . . my father? Are you sorry—?"

Cynthia smiled. "I will always be sorry we don't live in a perfect world, a world in which mad and impetuous love finds a safe haven. But I'm an adult now. I learned a long time ago I couldn't have everything the way I wanted it. Sometimes—" and here she smiled at her daughter "—sometimes I think I am a far luckier woman than I ever deserved to be."

She set her teacup down on the tray, got up and came to stand behind Diane's chair. She laid her hands on her daughter's shoulders, meeting her eyes in the mirror.

"I consider myself a very fortunate woman," she said and dropped a kiss on Diane's hair. "I have been blessed. I wish the same for you."

I LEARNED a long time ago I couldn't have everything the way I wanted it.

Some of us, Diane thought ruefully as she snuggled back into the airline seat and shut her eyes, are not such quick studies.

Some of us rail against fate far too long. Our expectations are unrealistic. Our demands too great.

We need to make adjustments, to compromise. We need to be grateful for what life offers us, not bemoan the loss of what we can't have.

We need to learn to love the men who love us.

And not, Diane thought as the plane hurtled down the runway, taking off toward New York and La Guardia and Carter, the men we can never have.

CARTER had been whistling the whole damned afternoon. Tapping his feet. Humming little snatches of love songs. Driving Nick to distraction without even trying.

"What is it with you?" he snarled finally, glowering at Carter from where he sat in the dining room, sanding the door to the built-in buffet. It was his latest project, refinishing all Carter's woodwork to match the bookcases he'd built.

"I'm in love," Carter said through a mouthful of corn chips. "Love makes everyone happy."

"Does it?" Nick muttered and rubbed the sandpaper even harder against the wood.

"You're just jealous." Carter grinned.

Nick bent his head over the door. "Yeah." Trust Carter to nail him right where it hurt and not even realize it. He sighed and wiped a hand across his face.

"Her plane is due in an hour," Carter said now. "You want to come to the airport with me?"

"No, I don't want to come to the airport with you."

"Hey, I just asked. No need to get sharpish. What's the matter? Worried about work? I'm sure some will come through. My uncle said—"

"No, I'm not worried about work." Work was the least of his problems. The biggest was how he was going to get through the rest of his life with one of his best friends married to another best friend who just happened to be the woman he loved.

Carter raised his hands defensively. "Right. Work isn't a problem." A pause. "Then what is?"

Nick shrugged irritably. "I don't know. The weather maybe?"

"It's a nice night," Carter said. "Clear. Cold. No storms in sight."

Nick scowled. "So maybe it's not the weather."

He wished Carter would leave, would take his cheerful countenance and his tapping feet and get the hell out.

"Well," Carter said, "it sounds to me as if you've got a bug up your butt about something. But if you don't want to talk about it, it's all right with me."

"I don't want to talk about it," Nick said tersely. He started sanding again. Out of the corner of his eye he could see Carter's Topsiders flex.

Then the heels hit the floor and Carter said, "Right. Well, suit yourself. You will anyway. See you when I get back."

Nick shut his eyes. "Yeah."

Carter rummaged in the closet for his jacket, slipped it on, then opened the door and stopped, looking back over his shoulder. "You sure you're all right?"

"I'm all right."

Carter still looked doubtful.

"I'm fine," Nick said more forcefully. "Go on. And," he added rashly, "bring her back here afterward. I'll buy a bottle of champagne. We can celebrate."

It was a stupid thing to say. Stupider even to do, Nick thought. But for all that he cursed his idiocy, it did make a perverse sort of sense.

It was called facing your worst possible nightmare. His grandfather had been a great believer in it.

Nick remembered well the afternoon he sat there in his grandfather's workshop telling him about Wally Tompkins, the hotshot from a rival high school who had struck him out four times—the last one with the bases loaded—when they had played that spring.

"He'll do it again," Nick remembered saying fatalistically. "He'll do it again."

His grandfather puffed on his pipe, considered the boy hunched on the stool next to him, then laid a hand on Nick's shoulder. "And if he does, so?" he said finally.

"Well..." Nick groped to reply. "I'll look like an idiot again."

"Are you an idiot?"

"No!"

"So what more?"

"I'll let down my team."

"There's only one way to help a team?"

"Well, no, but—"

"What more?"

The quizzing went on until Nick began to realize that even if he struck out, it wasn't the end of the world. He was capable, competent, worthy, only at times fallible.

So he had gone out there and faced Wally Tompkins. He'd struck out. He'd survived.

Next time up he'd hit a homer.

So tonight he'd face Carter and Diane in the afterglow of their engagement. He'd smile and offer them champagne. He'd survive.

But he knew he'd never ever get another at bat, let alone a homer.

HER PLANE ARRIVED at seven. At least that's when it was scheduled.

Nick imagined the whole scene: Carter waiting, scooping her into his arms, grinning like a fool, popping the question yet again, and being told yes—here Nick shut his eyes—then sweeping her into his car, and within the hour arriving back at his place where Nick, steeled, would be waiting with his duty bottle of champagne.

By nine o'clock Nick had revised the scenario to include a quiet candlelit dinner for two at The Sign of the Dove or some other posh Upper East Side place.

By eleven he had added a nightcap at the top of the World Trade Center.

By midnight he had tacked on dancing at the little Soho nightclub that he knew Carter was fond of.

By two he'd imagined them taking in the last set at the jazz club right around the corner.

By four he was frantic.

By six he admitted the truth: Carter and Diane were not coming back here, had no intention of coming back here.

They had undoubtedly gone from the airport to Diane's apartment (with or without any intermediate stops) and were at this very moment—his eyes shut again—consummating their engagement in Diane's wide, welcoming bed.

And that was a worse nightmare than he'd ever let himself imagine.

He drank the champagne by himself—the whole bottle of it—then went into the bathroom and was thoroughly and disgustingly sick.

THE DOOR OPENED shortly past noon. Nick was lying on Carter's sofa, his face buried in the cushions. Slowly, with the utmost care, he turned his head.

Carter's Topsiders stood still before him.

He drew a careful breath, clamping his teeth against the nausea that threatened. Then, just as carefully, he levered himself up and swung around sideways, dredging up a painful smile from somewhere, expecting happy faces to smile down on him.

Carter was alone.

It was easier this way, Nick told himself. Easier to face Carter first. Then Diane.

His eye caught the champagne bottle, which lay on its side under the coffee table. He noticed Carter looking at it, too. He gave a rueful shrug.

"I . . . decided not to wait," he said. "You didn't come, after all." He tried to make his words sound light and carefree, but his voice was rusty, as if he hadn't used it in years.

Carter didn't say anything. He looked, Nick decided, as if he'd had a hard night. His eyes were bloodshot, his shirt creased, his hair rumpled and his tie askew.

"But . . ." Nick said when he could form the words, "I suppose that's the way it goes." Then he made himself ask because, after all, Diane didn't have the corner on the social skills market, "Did you have a good time?"

Carter turned his head. He stared away out the window across Central Park and beyond. The words, when they came, fell tonelessly from his lips.

"She turned me down."

IT WAS CRAZY to hope.

It was worse not to know.

Nick was sure Diane's refusal to marry Carter would have nothing to do with him; he was sure he was making an idiot of himself by seeking her out and asking.

But he couldn't stay away.

He'd done his best by Carter. He'd squelched his natural inclination, which had been to shout hallelujahs from the rooftop, and made himself and Carter a pot of strong black coffee. When they'd drunk in silence, he made another.

It was over the second pot of coffee that he had ventured his first question. "Did she . . . say . . . why?"

"Probably." Carter stared moodily into the murky black liquid. His fingers knotted around the mug. His hair drooped across his forehead, looking as lifeless and unhappy as he did. He shoved it back, but when it fell forward again almost immediately, he ignored it.

"So...why?" Nick felt like a heel asking. He couldn't help himself.

Carter's dark eyes met his squarely. "It was long and complicated and sincere and every bit what you'd expect from Diane." He flexed his shoulders, then hunched them again. "The gist of it was, she doesn't love me."

Did she love *him?* The question filled Nick's throat as if he'd swallowed a stone.

He could still feel it now as he made his way up the front steps to Diane's brownstone. He made no immediate move to ring the bell, hoping someone would come out instead. He wasn't sure he wanted her to know he was coming.

If he was going to be rejected, too, he wanted it to be face-to-face.

But no one came out and no one went in. And after twenty minutes of shifting from one foot to the other, alternately cursing and praying, he rang the bell.

There was no response for quite some time. Then he heard a faint, "Who is it?"

"Nick."

"I don't—"

"Please! I just want to talk to you!"

"It isn't necessary. You don't—"

"I do! Please, Diane!"

He didn't know why he was bothering. He had his answer, didn't he? There was certainly no enthusiasm here. No joy. No expectation.

But at the moment his shoulders sagged and he was ready to turn around and go away, the buzzer sounded and Diane said flatly. "All right. Come up."

The door was shut against him when he got there. She wasn't making it easy for him, he thought grimly as he raised his hand to knock.

The door opened slowly and Diane stood before him, her hair pinned back, her expression drawn. She looked pale but composed, not loving in the least.

He licked his lips, tucked his hands into the pockets of his jeans, shifted from one foot to the other and regretted once again his decision to come.

In the top two of people Diane Bauer least wanted to see at that moment, Nick Granatelli was the only one higher on the list than the man whose proposal she had just turned down.

It wasn't fair, she thought. How dare he?

Had he come to tell her about his own bride-to-be? she wondered. Probably, she thought, tasting irony. They were such good friends.

"What do you want?"

"I . . . you . . ." Oh, hell, what was the point? He shoved a hand through his hair. His head ached abominably. "Cartersaysyouturnedhimdown."

Diane gave a jerky little nod as she stepped back to let him in. Then she pressed her lips together in a tight line. Her eyes were as hard as stones. "You're not here to do a John Alden for him, are you?"

Nick frowned. "Huh?"

"To talk me into marrying him?"

He shook his head and immediately regretted it. "No. No, I'm not."

"Then why are you here?"

"I just wondered . . . why. Why you're not going to marry him, I mean."

"What business is it of yours?"

He shrugged awkwardly. "I suppose it isn't, but . . ." He faltered, groping for words that would make it all right or at least get it over with. "I love you," he said.

He couldn't imagine why he'd said it.

He couldn't think of a worse thing to say. Yet he couldn't have retracted it if he'd tried.

Diane stared at him. Her mouth opened as if she might respond, then closed as if no response were possible.

"I'm sorry," he muttered. "I shouldn't have—I don't mean to—" He shook his head, defeated, dismayed.

Diane was now looking equally dismayed at him. Were those tears welling up in her eyes? They couldn't be, he thought at the same time she began blinking furiously and swiping a hand across her eyes.

"Damn you," she said, and her voice broke. "Oh, damn you, Nick Granatelli! Why in God's name would you come and tell me that? I could have survived without that!"

Nick frowned, confused. What the hell right did she have to talk about surviving? That was his problem!

"Why did you come?" she demanded angrily. "Did you want my blessing maybe?"

"Blessing?" Nick stared at her, baffled.

"On your wedding. You and Virginia Perpetti!"

"Ginny?" Nick croaked. "What about Ginny?"

"Don't give me that. You don't have to play dumb with me. I know."

Nick didn't. Nick felt as if he'd slipped out of his own reality into someone else's. "What in the hell are you talking about?"

"I just came back from St. Louis, remember?" Diane's voice was icy.

He nodded. "I remember. But—"

"Actually I just came back from a wedding. A wedding for which I was required to buy a new dress and a hat. A hat that I bought at the Mad Hatter." She gave Nick a significant look.

"You went to Frankie's?"

"I did."

"And she told you I was marrying Ginny Perpetti?" He couldn't believe that.

"Not Frankie. Your other sister. Sophia."

That he could believe. Didn't want to, but could.

Sophia was a chip off the Granatelli block. If his father said something was going to happen, it did. Sophia shared that same view of reality. But to think she was still hanging on to that ridiculous idea after all this time!

"No," he said.

Diane just looked at him.

Outside a siren wailed. Someone was pounding down the stairs. A door slammed. A horn honked. "No?" she repeated in a barely audible tone. It was still disbelieving, but not quite as forceful.

Nick shook his head slowly, adamantly. "No. I am not marrying Virginia Perpetti. No, I am not going back to run Granatelli's. No, I am not even in the restaurant business anymore. I quit at Lazlo's the day after Christmas."

His mouth was dry. His knees felt weak.

Her mouth was dry. Her knees felt weak. What was he saying? What did he mean? Why, she asked herself again, had he come?

He'd said he loved her. Yet he didn't look loving. His expression was unreadable and his blue eyes were clouded with an emotion she didn't understand. She waited, not knowing for what.

"Why," Nick asked her again, "did you turn Carter down?" There was a gentleness in the question this time, a hint of hope. Diane could have been imagining it; she didn't think she was. Her fingers knotted together.

"Why did you come?" she asked him.

"Because I love you," Nick answered, and Diane said the words along with him.

Their gazes met, locked. Their souls touched.

And Nick, shutting his eyes and holding on to the moment, bent his head. "Yes."

HE HAD LOVED her for years. But never like this.

Never with the fullness of heart and soul, mind and body that existed between them now. He had never before given her all of himself; he had never had all of her.

It was everything he could have wished for. The warm, welcoming bed he had envisioned her sharing with Carter, he knew she had only shared with him. The arms that drew him into her embrace had held no one else the way they held him.

And his own love of her was all the more wonderful for having been so long in its realization.

At first there were no words, only touches. At the last there were pounding hearts and sounds of love.

And in the aftermath, with nothing but their love settled between them, he dared to ask, "Will you marry me?"

And he held his breath until he saw her smile and he felt the word "Yes" whispered against his lips.

She snuggled against him, feeling both shattered and whole. The world as she had known it, in the space of a few hours, had spun like a kaleidoscope, arranging and rearranging itself in myriad patterns—promises. But none of them equaled the beauty of the one in which she found herself now.

She turned her head slightly and kissed Nick's bare chest. She felt his lips graze her forehead, felt his shoulder solid and warm beneath her head, then closed her eyes and drank in the pure, perfect happiness of it all.

"Sleepy?" Nick asked her, his voice tender.

She shook her head and opened her eyes. "No." She looked up at him, smiling. "I just keep closing my eyes and opening them again, daring you to vanish. Am I tempting fate?''

"I'm not going to vanish," Nick promised her. "You're stuck with me for life."

"Thank God."

"Amen," Nick agreed. "I thought you would marry Carter."

Diane pushed herself up on her elbows so she could look down into his dear face and thought how close she'd come to doing just that. "I nearly did," she told him.

Her mother's relationship with Matthew had almost convinced her it would make perfect sense. It was only when she realized how strong Carter's feelings were and how one-sided their love would be that she'd found the courage to say no.

Nick's expression grew grave. "He could give you a damn sight more than I can. He's got a successful business, a penthouse on Columbus Avenue, and a trust fund worth millions. Maybe you should reconsider."

Diane eyed him carefully, pondering his words. "Maybe I should," she said.

Nick's expression was startled. "You'd better not!" he muttered, grabbing her as her mouth swooped down to nip at his nose.

"You idiot!" she chided. "Do you really think millions matter to me, or penthouses?"

"No, but—"

"Carter is a wonderful person. He'll make some woman a great husband, but not me. When I thought you were marrying your Virginia—"

"She's not my Virginia," Nick protested. "She's *never* been my Virginia. We were engaged once, by default."

Diane laughed, amazed that she could even find such a thing funny. "As I was saying, when I thought you were marrying her, I considered marrying Carter. My mother, after all, had married Matthew and they had a wonderful marriage.''

"So why didn't you?'' Nick felt almost safe asking the question now.

"For Carter's sake.''

Nick scowled. "What's that mean?''

"I had known passion,'' Diane said simply. "I had known deep love, just as my mother had. So had Matthew briefly, years ago. His first wife died in childbirth when they'd been married only a year. But Carter—'' she shook her head "—as far as I know Carter only recently woke up to the fact that love exists. What we shared was not a deep, abiding, passionate love.''

Nick smiled his relief. He stroked her arm, her hip, basking in the light of love in her eyes.

"Someday the right woman will come along,'' Diane went on. "And I didn't want Carter to find her when he was married to me!''

Nick grinned. "Thoughtful of you.'' And damned lucky for him, he thought, aware of how close his escape had been.

"Careful of me,'' Diane said. "Marrying Carter wouldn't have worked for that reason, but mostly for another one.'' She leaned over and kissed him soundly. "I've never stopped loving you.''

Nick shook his head, believing now, grateful to God for Diane's wisdom, still bemoaning his own lack of it. "I walked away from you,'' he reminded her.

"I remember,'' she said dryly.

He winced. "I didn't want to. It was the hardest thing I ever did. But I couldn't drag you into the mess my life was about to become.''

"Noble Nick Granatelli.''

He flushed. "I try."

"You're very trying," she agreed. She kissed him again. Then again. "I must be making up for lost time," she mumbled.

Nick grinned. "Go right ahead."

So she did, and he helped her. And it was another hour before they began talking seriously about the problems that lay ahead.

"What will your sister say?" Diane asked him when once more they were lying snuggled together under the comforter.

"Sophia? She'll say congratulations, what else?" Nick replied firmly, then sighed. "She'll come around, really. Don't worry. She's not a bad sort, just a bit bossy. But if you know your own mind, she doesn't feel she has to make it up for you."

"I hope they like me."

"I like you," he said. "I love you." He rolled onto his side and looked at her. "More to the point, what about your mother? Your grandmother? I can't imagine that Gertrude Hoffmann will think I'm the catch of the year."

"She doesn't have to as long as I think you are."

"You're prejudiced."

"I am," she agreed. "My mother, I predict, will be ecstatic. She believes very deeply in true love. And my grandmother... well, let's just say she and your sister Sophia might find they have a lot in common."

Nick grinned. "Can't you just see it? Gertrude and the Granatellis?"

"Sounds like a geriatric rock group," Diane said.

"I'll bet it'll rock St. Louis to the ground." He groaned. "Imagine what they'll do with our wedding."

Diane smiled. "It will undoubtedly be the Wedding Of The Century."

"If they don't kill each other in the process."

"They'll behave," Diane assured him.

Nick lifted a skeptical brow. "Oh, why?"

Diane smiled. "Because if they don't we can always threaten to elope!"

St. Louis, Missouri, June 1991

IT WAS OVER.

The Wedding Of The Century had been accomplished, the champagne had been drunk, the toasts had been made, the dances had been danced, and the bride and groom had, at long last, made good their escape.

"Thank God," Nick said, falling on the hotel room bed, closing his eyes and undoing his tie even as he fell. "I never want to go through that again."

Diane, standing over him, looked quizzical. "Do you think you might have to?"

His eyes flicked open. He saw her smile and reached out a hand to drag her down on top of him.

"I'm never going to have to," he growled. "I told you that today. Vowed it, as a matter of fact, in front of God and most of the western civilized world."

"So you did," Diane said primly, though what she was doing, wiggling against his body like this, wasn't prim in the least.

"Stop that," Nick muttered. "Or at least let me get undressed first."

Diane sat up and folded her hands, still smiling, waiting expectantly. There was a warm wickedness in her gaze. "By all means, undress."

And Nick, burning under her gaze, began fumbling with his cuff links. "You're full of it, you know that?" he grumbled as she took over the job for him, undoing them with ease, then turning her attention to the studs on his shirtfront.

"Me?" She was innocence personified.

"You, oh, Deb Of The Universe. You've been tormenting me for the past week," he accused. "A touch here, a kiss there. And that's all!"

She grinned, unrepentant. "I suppose you wanted me to wrestle you to the ground in front of my mother and grandmother and your fifty thousand relatives?"

Nick grimaced, then shivered as she trailed her fingers down his chest, over his ribs, past his navel, then unbuckled his belt. "We haven't had a lot of time to ourselves, have we?"

Diane slid down the zipper of his black trousers. "Not a lot, no."

Her hands urged him up, and he stood and stepped out of them. Then, as she held out her arms to him, he wrapped her in his, pulling her close, reveling in the beat of her heart against his.

"But we do now," he whispered and thanked God for second chances, for first loves, and for a future in which he would experience the wonder of both. "We have a lifetime, my love, starting now."

Diane kissed his chin, his cheek, his ears, his lips. "Prove it."

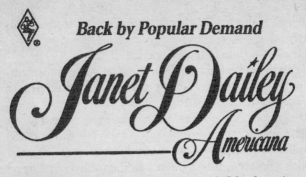

Back by Popular Demand

Janet Dailey

Americana

A romantic tour of America through fifty favorite
Harlequin Presents®, each set in a different state
researched by Janet and her husband, Bill. A journey
of a lifetime in one cherished collection.

In April, don't miss the first six states followed by two
new states each month!

Available wherever
Harlequin books are sold.

JD-A

Take 4 bestselling love stories FREE

Plus get a FREE surprise gift!

Everyone loves a spring wedding, and this April,
Harlequin cordially invites you to read the most
romantic wedding book of the year.

With This Ring

ONE WEDDING—FOUR LOVE STORIES
FROM OUR MOST DISTINGUISHED
HARLEQUIN AUTHORS:

BETHANY CAMPBELL
BARBARA DELINSKY
BOBBY HUTCHINSON
ANN McALLISTER

*The church is booked, the reception arranged and the
invitations mailed. All Diane Bauer and Nick Granatelli
have to do is walk down the aisle. Little do they realize that
the most cherished day of their lives will spark so many
romantic notions. . . .*

Available wherever Harlequin books are sold.   HWED-1AR